THE
PLAYER

*Friday night lights hide more
than they reveal…*

FELICE STEVENS

DEDICATION

To everyone struggling to be themselves. You are seen and loved.

ACKNOWLEDGMENTS

Thanks to my editor Keren Reed for everything you do. To Hope and Jess from Flat Earth Editing, thank you for going the extra mile and then some. Thank you to Dianne from Lyrical Lines for the super eagle eyes. And thank you to Reese for always blowing my mind with the most gorgeous covers and knowing what I want without me saying.

And always, thank you to the readers. Your support means everything.

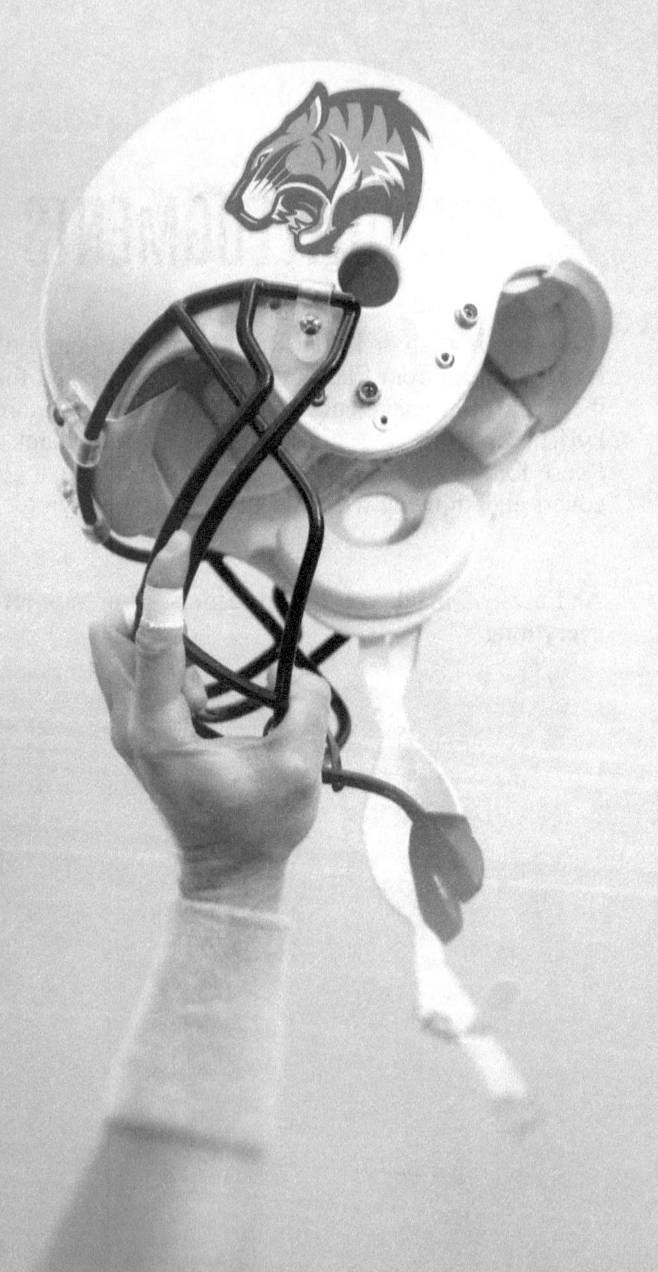

"There is no greater agony than bearing an untold story inside you."

\- MAYA ANGELOU

CHAPTER ONE

They say you can't go home again.

But here he stood, on the field of his former glory years, thinking of those Friday night lights and cheers so loud, if he stopped to listen, memories of them still whispered in the sluggish, late August air.

The crowd rose to their feet. The quarterback launched a perfect spiral to him, and he raced into the end zone with four seconds left on the clock and caught the winning touchdown.

"Keller! Keller!"

The ground shook, and the state championship was theirs. His teammates piled on top of him, then carried him on their shoulders.

At seventeen, he'd thought the world was his.

"Keller? That you?"

He spun around to see his old teammate, Bobby Contard, standing by the fence. God, he looked…old. Thinning blond hair and a paunch most likely from sitting in a recliner, downing too many beers in too short a time. The same wide, goofy smile.

"Hey, Bobby. Yeah, it's me."

"Son of a bitch. Keller Williams. It's really you."

They stood face-to-face, former teammates who hadn't seen each other since they'd left for college. Keller had been drafted to the NFL while Bobby had flunked out, returned home to their small Upstate New York town, and gone to work at Home Depot.

"How're you doing, Bobby? Been a minute."

"Longer than that, but yeah." A quick duck of his head. "Sorry about your arm. Sucks, man."

Devastation came in all forms. For Keller, it was a bad hit that had upended him as he'd been about to make a catch. It knocked the wind out of him and sent him crashing to the ground, his arm bent at a frightening, unnatural angle. He'd heard the *snap*, and before passing out from the pain, had known with overwhelming clarity that it was the last time he'd ever play football.

"Yeah. It's healed okay now, but man, I can tell the weather better than those people on TV." He forced a grin.

"Whatcha doing back here? Just passing through and come to see your old haunts?"

"I've been back other times. For my mom."

Just saying it brought the inevitable, knife-twisting pain in his gut.

Bobby scratched his head. "Oh, yeah. Sorry about that."

"At least they got the bastard who hit her." A drunk driver had taken the Main Street curve too fast and hit an icy patch, sending his car spinning out of control. It had smashed into a group of people in the parking lot of the Overlook Diner. Three wounded, one dead. His mother, Patricia Williams. She'd been out celebrating her sixtieth birthday early with her girlfriends. The next morning, she was to have gotten on a plane to come visit him for a fabulous weekend together in Vegas. Keller had made all the plans for them—spas, shows, and a spectacular dinner. Instead, he'd found himself making arrangements for her funeral.

"And to answer your question, no, I'm not passing through. I'm coming home."

"Home? To Overlook?" Bobby scrunched up his nose. "Why? Nothing's changed from when you left. It's still the same quiet little town. Nothing like Vegas, I'm sure."

Overlook was hardly the hot spot of Upstate New York. Situated midway between Cortland and Syracuse, there wasn't much going on, but it was for that precise reason that Keller was happy to return. Fourteen years in the NFL, he'd seen it all—and had enough.

"I was ready for a change. And I got a call from Coach Weaver."

Bobby's eyes grew wide with sudden understanding. "*You're* the new high school football coach they hired? We heard they'd gotten someone, but Coach Weaver wouldn't say who. Damn, Keller. That's awesome." He hesitated. "My son's on the team—quarterback. Holds the record for completions in a single season. We're hoping to get a scholarship to college." Pride shone from his round face.

"Guess it runs in the family, huh? You had some good moves back in the day." He grinned, and Bobby cackled. "I'm thinking you don't play much anymore?"

"You got that right." He rubbed his stomach. "Mary's too good a cook, and I'm too tired after standing on my feet all day. But I'm a great armchair quarterback. And my boy—Shane—he's good, Keller. Real good. I think he's got what it takes, and I ain't just saying that because he's my kid. Fact is, the whole team is solid. You've got some damn good prospects to work with."

"Is that what he wants? To go pro?" Keller could tell him it wasn't all about the cheering and the bright lights or the money. All of it was great, but the blood, sweat, and absolute domination the sport exerted over your life wasn't something to be taken lightly.

"He's thinking about it."

In his professional days, he'd worked with a lot of summer programs for kids and could always tell whether it was the parents' dream or the child's. He'd make sure it was Shane who wanted to be a professional football player and not Bobby reliving his failed dreams of stardom.

"Guess we'll see when school starts. I figured I'd swing past and see how the place looks nowadays, get an idea what I'm working with before I meet with the kids."

Bobby nodded, then checked his watch. "I'd better get going. Knowing Mary, she'll send out a search party." He bit his lip. "Would you like to come for dinner? She always makes plenty."

Touched by the invitation, Keller still declined. "Appreciate it, but I think springing a guest on your wife would forever put me in the doghouse." Seeing Bobby's face fall, he rushed on. "But how about we meet up next week? Is The Flame still around? They always had the best steaks in town. I'd love to take you all out for dinner."

"Yeah, it's still there, but we don't go. Kinda pricey."

"So let's do it. I'll make a reservation."

"Gee, Keller. You don't gotta do that."

"I know. Give me your number, and I'll let you know when."

Bobby nodded. "Okay. I'll tell Mary. Thanks. Thanks a lot." They shook hands. "Glad you're home, Keller. It'll be good having you back."

He hoped so.

Bobby drove away, and Keller walked the field a bit before returning to his car. His shoulder and arm throbbed from carrying things from his mother's house to Goodwill, and if he wanted to be able to turn the wheel, he needed to take something to ease the ache. Three years after the last surgery, the pain had lessened, but it would never completely vanish. He'd suffered a compound fracture of the humerus, torn muscles in his shoulder, and damage to ligaments and tendons, yet he was lucky. It had taken him sixteen months to recover from the various surgeries, but no amount of physical therapy would ever make him whole again. Now, at thirty-eight, he had to pivot and begin a new life.

He clutched the bottle of extra-strength ibuprofen and stared at it for a moment. Right after his surgeries, he'd taken the hard stuff, but when he'd begun to crave higher and higher doses, he cut himself off. Under no circumstances would he fall into that black pit. He'd seen it happen to way too many players. It was a promise he'd made to his mother when he'd been drafted: stay away from the drugs and the drinking; don't become a statistic.

He popped the pills. *Well, Mom, at least you never had to worry about me getting a girl pregnant.* His marriage—and quickie divorce—was so long ago, he'd almost forgotten it had ever existed. He'd thought he could maintain the facade, but an inability to get it up for Tiffany on a regular basis had proved his undoing. He'd found her sleeping with other men, giving him the out he needed, and he'd been happy to let her go.

He drove through the streets, remembering the sights of his former hometown—the hidden areas by the tracks where he'd had his first kiss from a guy. The woods where he'd lost his virginity to a girl, pretending she was a man. He passed the waterfalls where the team had celebrated their state championship by getting drunk on smuggled beer. He grinned, recalling how he'd thought he was so cool, sneaking into his house at three in the morning, only to find his mother wide-awake and waiting for him with a list of chores that would keep him grounded for the rest of the school year.

God, he wished he could hear her voice again. That night she'd sat him down and explained how she wouldn't let him run wild. How people told her he'd end up a no-goodnik because she was a single mother and didn't have the time to watch over him properly. He hadn't realized until then that his behavior had reflected on her as a person, and he'd vowed to never bring her shame.

I'm sorry, Mom. I'm going to make sure I do right by these kids, like you taught me.

He wiped the wetness from his face and continued to drive.

Before he realized it, he was twenty miles out of town and approaching the next one, and figured he could use a break and something to eat. He didn't have much at the house and wasn't in the mood to be home and alone.

Spying a main street, he drove past a shop selling homemade candy, a women's boutique clothing store, and various storefronts. All closed, as it was late, but a bistro caught his eye. A sign pointed him to the parking lot around the corner, and he drove in, his tires crunching on the gravel, and found a spot not far from the dumpsters. Not valet parking on the Vegas Strip like he'd been used to while on the roster for the Vegas Players, but this was his life now, and he knew it could be worse.

When he walked inside, it was crowded enough that he didn't think he'd find a seat at the bar, where he always liked to park himself, but luck was with him. A tall woman with long red hair and a full sleeve of tattoos was rising to her feet.

"Kept it warm for ya." She slung her purse over her shoulder as luminous dark eyes slid a lazy path up Keller's body. "Unless you'd rather I stay and see what else I can warm up."

Amused but not interested, Keller gave her a half smile. "Not tonight. But thanks for the very generous offer."

"Too bad." She shrugged and walked away.

Keller waited to catch the bartender's eye and ordered a bottle of Heineken, then faced the crowd. The music wasn't obnoxiously loud, and there were many people at the tables on dates. To his surprise, he spotted a gay couple in the corner, and surreptitiously watched their interactions. For some reason, his eyes smarted and burned. Damn, he was getting sentimental in his old age. Did he want that? He wasn't sure, but he knew he wanted the option to have someone in his life for more than a bump in the night.

Since his injury, he'd put his recovery first and had worked to get into shape again—or as close to where he could use his arm without pain. Sex had been the last thing on his mind. But now? So many years out of the spotlight, he had to wonder if it was finally his time. If he couldn't be healthy in body, at least he could try for his soul and heart. Because hiding all these years had taken a mental toll, and he was damn tired.

Beer bottle to his lips, he scanned the crowd. A man sat in the corner, looking out of place. He was dressed in a suit and tie, and from the way he kept checking both his watch and phone, Keller assumed he'd been waiting for a while—for his date? Keller drank his beer and ordered a burger, and as he ate, he kept an eye on the man.

He was sexy as hell, with messy black hair falling over his brow and full lips he kept nibbling at. Long legs stretched out from beneath the table, and Keller focused on the man's fingers playing along the stem of his wineglass, imagining them on his body.

Twenty minutes passed, and Keller finished his beer and food while the man grew more agitated. It was obvious the guy had been stood up. "Whoever let you down is a damn fool," he muttered.

The man stood, leaving half his glass untouched, and huffed out a sigh. He didn't leave, though, instead weaving his way through the crowd to the rear of the bar, where the restrooms were. Without thinking, Keller rose to his feet.

"Be right back."

The bartender shrugged. "Sure."

Inside the restroom, he found the man staring at the slightly askew mirror. His eyes widened when Keller stood next to him to wash his hands.

"Get stood up?"

The man wet his lips, and his brow furrowed. "Excuse me?"

Close up, he was even more arresting than from Keller's initial vantage point at the bar. Mistrustful, green-flecked blue eyes gazed at him. The harsh fluorescent light reflected off pale skin, as if he spent most of his time indoors, and prominent cheekbones stood out on his thin face, with the shadow of stubble darkening his jaw. Keller had never liked the jock type, preferring instead a long, lean body.

Rein it in. The dude is likely straight.

"I noticed you looking at your phone and your watch for a while. A sure sign that you're waiting for a date who didn't show."

A flush stained his cheeks, but the man remained silent and splashed some water on his face, then turned to go.

"I'm sorry if I offended you." Keller had no clue why it mattered, but he didn't want this man to be upset with him. Probably a throwback to his playing days. His coaches had taught him to keep all the fans happy, even if they booed him on the field.

The man shrugged. "Not sure why a stranger is talking to me in the bathroom about my failed date, that's all."

"I'm Keller Williams. Now that you know my name, we're not strangers," he said, hoping no discussion would ensue about his past career and what he was doing now.

Instead, the man froze, his face paling even more. "Unreal," he muttered, shaking his head.

"Aren't you going to tell me your name?"

Those beautiful eyes dripped with scorn as the man pulled a paper towel from the holder and wiped his face. "I have to go." And without another word, he walked out, leaving Keller slack-jawed and alone in the ugly little bathroom.

"Damn. What the hell did I say?"

He returned to the bar and his beer. The man, he saw, sat at his small table, texting.

"Want another one?" the bartender asked.

"No. Just the check."

He handed over his credit card, and the bartender's jaw dropped. "Shit. You're Keller Williams?"

"Last time I checked, yeah."

"Damn, can I get your autograph? I have your jersey. I can't believe I didn't recognize you!"

More than happy to oblige, Keller was soon surrounded by a group of fans for whom he signed napkins, T-shirts, and anything else they thrust in his face. All the while, though, he kept an eye on the despondent man he'd spoken to in the bathroom, who was still sitting in the corner, his mouth drooping in a frown. Why he'd become so involved in a stranger's date, Keller hadn't a clue, but when the man rose to his feet and left the bistro, Keller did the same and tossed out a hundred to the bartender.

"Gotta go, folks. I'll be back again. I'm living in Overlook now."

Keller exited the restaurant, but there was no sign of the guy, so he headed to his car. The sultry air hit him like a wet slap, and mosquitos buzzed past his cheeks. Unseen crickets chirped incessantly from the thick hedges surrounding the parking lot. Not his glory days for sure, yet maybe there was the scent of possibility as well. He wondered what would've happened if he'd come to the bistro with a male date. Would there have been an outcry? People taking pictures on their phones to show everyone they'd seen Keller Williams with a man? *Oh my God, did you know he's gay?*

The two men eating there on a date had seemed to be feeling safe enough. It was an experience he'd never been able to enjoy.

A lingering stare, a subtle brush-up in a club. A hookup between two men so desperate for human contact and to be themselves, they'd take that risk for a moment of pleasure. Keller had lived that clandestine life so he could keep an unforgiving career that in the end had betrayed him, forcing him to walk away.

As he approached his parking spot, he spied a man sitting in a car, windows open, head down on the steering wheel. Fearing something was wrong, Keller stopped several feet away, unsure if he was intruding or if the man was ill. Just in case it was the latter, he called out, "Everything okay? Do you need me to call someone?"

Blue-green eyes met his, and with a start, Keller recognized the man he'd spoken to in the bar.

"Are you sick? Do you need me to get you some help?"

The engine roared to life and the wheels spit up gravel as the car took off, leaving Keller standing like a fool, wondering what the hell he'd done to deserve such a reaction from a complete stranger.

CHAPTER TWO

Niall Harper had always done the right thing.

Growing up, he'd listened to his parents. Helped with the chores around the house. Gotten good grades. Gone to college, married, and tried to be the best husband he could. Attended church and listened to the sermons, even if sometimes what was said had made him die inside.

In fact, living his life had Niall dying a little bit every day.

He'd met Angie freshman year at the college bookstore, and they'd become inseparable. Angie had been his best friend, his first and only lover. They'd married a year after graduation, and she'd gotten pregnant two months later. Niall received his master's in library science and a teaching certificate, and was hired at his alma mater, Overlook High School. Angie stayed home with baby David, but when he turned five, Angie went to law school, got a job in Syracuse, and they bought a house after Angie's second year bonus. He would pick up David from day care and make dinner for when Angie came home.

He'd been content.

Not happy, because he'd never been happy. But he loved his son with a fierceness he'd never known he possessed, and would do anything for him, including staying in a marriage that had hurt his heart and shriveled his soul.

Niall wanted his son to be everything he wasn't—strong and popular and friendly. Happy. He wanted David to never have to pretend to be someone he wasn't. And he got his wish—now David was fifteen and had a huge circle of friends. He was on the honor roll and played for the high school football team, the Overlook Tigers.

And if Niall had to live a lie, so be it. He'd make the best of it because that was what he'd always done. He'd do what was right for his family because that was what he'd been taught. To do the right thing.

And he had, until two years ago, when Angie had sat him down and upended his world.

"I love you, Niall, but I want a divorce."

"What? Why?"

Her smile was sad. "You know."

His heart pounded, alarm bells ringing. Mayday! Mayday!

"No. I don't. You're my best friend—"

"I don't want a best friend to make love to me. I want hot, passionate sex with a man who can't wait to rip my clothes off. We've never had that. Ever."

He hung his head. "I'm sorry I'm not as romantic as you want, but I can try."

She put a cool hand to his hot cheek, and he trembled. "You shouldn't have to."

"Is there someone else?"

"No. I've never cheated on you. But I know I'm not

who you want."

"Why would you say that?" He searched his mind for clues…but he'd never done anything to raise suspicion, not that he knew of. "Angie…I go to work, come home. I've never looked at another woman."

A single tear slid from her eye. "I know you haven't. But the other day, my laptop died, so I borrowed yours, and since mine is a newer model, I couldn't use your charger. I wasn't snooping, I swear." She hung her head, and her long dark hair fell over her face. "These websites popped up…ones where men ask questions about how to handle marriage to a woman when they're gay." She tucked the shining strands behind her ears and met his gaze straight on.

Wanting nothing more than to curl up and die, he pulled away from her. "I'm sorry. I didn't know what I was doing. I—"

"Niall, stop. It's okay. I'm not angry. I'm just sad for you, that you had to hide who you really are. To live a lie."

"I'm not lying when I say I love you."

"But…?" she urged, and he couldn't keep up the facade. Not anymore.

And yet, even after all the years they'd been married and a child together, he couldn't say it out loud. That would make it too real. Too final.

"But…" He tried to say more, couldn't, and tears welled up in his eyes.

"Oh, Niall." Angie put her arms around him, and he clung to her. Like she'd done for David when he was a colicky baby, she rocked and soothed him. "It's going to be okay. I promise. The worst part is over."

"I thought…I mean…I do love you. And David…I couldn't be more proud. He's my pride and joy. My everything."

"We can work this out with the minimum of legalities. No fuss."

He nodded. "Whatever you want. But what about David? Are you going to want sole custody?" A pang hit his heart at the thought of losing his son. "Are you moving out, or do I have to look for a new place?" His head spun.

For the first time, Angie seemed at a loss for words, and she covered her eyes for a moment before squaring her shoulders and meeting his gaze. "I got a job offer. In Chicago. I think, with David having lived here all his life and being in high school, it would be best if he stays with you." Her lips trembled. "I wouldn't want to upend his life completely."

Shocked, he stared at her, but he could hardly get upset when he'd hidden so much.

"Are-are you sure?"

"Yes." Angie had always been the strong one. "He can come to me for holidays and summer vacations. This offer is for partnership. I'll make enough that I won't need alimony. You can stay in the house, and I'll pay half the mortgage and taxes and contribute to his college fund and expenses. We'll tell him tonight."

Brisk and efficient, Angie had taken control, making David see that it was in his best interest to remain where he was. At first David was upset, but they had always been an extremely close family, and in the end, it had all worked out. Chicago wasn't that far, and for the past two years, David had spent his summers there and they'd switched off holidays.

It was all very adult, and people used them as an example of how parents should behave in divorce. He didn't even mind knowing Angie was dating, or listening to David tell him stories of her new boyfriend, Grant. Niall was happy she was living the life she wanted and deserved.

He wished he could say the same.

He'd joined a gay dating site and had finally screwed up the courage to meet someone for a drink. The man never even showed. Then he'd seen Keller Williams and had almost thrown up.

What the hell was he doing in town?

Niall replayed their conversation and congratulated himself that he'd kept his identity a secret. Not that he'd expect someone like Keller to remember they went to the same school and had taken a few classes together. Popular football players like Keller Williams didn't look at geeky librarians like Niall Harper.

And Niall intended to keep it that way. He finished his coffee and rinsed out the mug just as footsteps pounded on the stairs.

"Dad, can you drive me to school? It's the first day of practice, and I don't want to be late. We get to meet the new coach."

Love swelled in his chest as he gazed at David. His joy in life. If he couldn't find physical love, at least he knew the pure happiness of loving his son.

He dried his hands. "Sure. I was going to go in anyway and start setting up the library. We got a lot of new books in over the summer, plus computer software."

"Cool."

He grabbed his keys and wallet. "Let's go." He slung an arm around David's shoulders, grateful he wasn't yet at the stage where he pulled away from affection. They backed out of the driveway and began the eight-minute drive to school.

"Dad?" David stared out the side window.

"*Mmm*, what?" He turned onto the main road.

"How come you never date?"

His heart sank. Driving to school was not where he intended to come out to his son.

"I just haven't been ready, I guess. When the time comes, I'll let you know."

"I think Mom and her boyfriend are really serious."

"Oh?" His stomach cramped. "Why do you say that?"

David shrugged. "Just stuff he says. Like, when we get married, we'll need a bigger place, or, after we get married, we'll do this or that…but Mom never says anything."

She wouldn't, he suspected, until the two of them talked.

"Do you like Grant? I thought he was a nice guy." He'd only met Angie's boyfriend online, but he seemed pleasant, and he was crazy about Angie and did his best to be friendly to Niall. It was all very mature.

"Yeah, he's fine. I mean, he tries hard to do whatever I want when I visit, but he's not my dad."

"I'm sure your mother knows what to do. She's a very smart lady."

"Yeah." David chewed his lip. "How come you got divorced? I know you said you fell out of love, but you and Mom get along so good."

"Well," he corrected. "And we do, but sometimes people change. And your mother and I will always love each other, just not the way a husband and wife should."

"So…it was about sex."

Good thing he'd stopped at a light, or else he might've run into a tree.

"Uhhh…"

"Come on, Dad. I'm almost sixteen. We've had *that* talk. I know about sex."

His grip tightened on the wheel. The school was only two blocks away, but he had to know. "I know you do." He licked his lips. "Have you…"

"No, Dad, I haven't had sex yet."

Thank God. I'm so not ready for this.

"But I have kissed girls."

"Girls? Like multiple?" He frowned. "I don't want you to get a reputation as a player."

David turned red. "A player? That's so funny. I'm not. But at parties and stuff, you know how it is…"

No, he didn't. He hadn't ever been invited to parties in

high school. That was for the cool kids.

"Just don't let anyone push you into doing something you don't want. Plenty of time for that."

They reached the school, and he parked in the teachers' lot. David scrambled out.

"Okay, well, thanks for the ride. I can't wait until I get my permit."

Kissing girls and driving. Niall *really* wasn't ready for this.

"Text me when you're ready to leave."

"Don't know when that'll be with the new coach. Did you hear anything about who they hired? I can't believe Coach Weaver isn't going to be there anymore. He was the best."

"No idea. Sports and the head librarian usually don't mix." He shrugged. "But I'm curious to see who you'll be spending so much time with, so I'll probably walk over to the field and watch."

"Sure. Bye, Dad."

A group of boys tumbled out of a minivan, and the horn honked. It was Michael Hitchcock, the father of David's best friend, Chris, and one of Niall's closest friends. Michael and Dara lived a few houses down, and when Angie left, they became Niall's main source of support. They had him over to their house almost every week, and home-cooked meals showed up on the regular. Now that he'd learned his way around the kitchen, he'd been able to reciprocate. And of course, they were curious about the divorce, but he only told them that he and Angie "grew apart."

"Niall. What's up?"

He strolled over to talk to Michael through the open window. "Not much. Sad the summer's over."

"I bet you are. Looking forward to being a football dad again?"

"I don't mind. Everyone's anxious to see who the new

coach is. I still can't believe Weaver retired."

"Yeah. Man's a legend. And I can't believe you haven't heard anything." Michael eyed him with a grin. "Or are you holding out on a friend?"

"Not likely." His smile was wry. Michael should only know exactly how much Niall was holding out on him. "Librarians aren't exactly on their list of need-to-know. But we'll find out soon enough. I told David I'll go watch after I finish up what I have to do."

Michael nodded, then shifted into gear. "Okay. Gotta get to the hospital and deliver those babies. Text me the deets when you find out."

"I will," he promised and watched Michael drive off.

"Okay, let's get this show on the road," he muttered. "These books won't shelve themselves."

The first day returning after summer vacation was almost like starting over. You forgot that the door handle of the supply closet needed jiggling to open and that the lock on the second bathroom stall in the teachers' lounge didn't close all the way. He walked the silent halls, footsteps echoing. But it wasn't the kids he envisioned filling up the space with their noisy shouts and laughter. Instead, he saw himself at David's age—quiet and hoping not to draw the attention of the popular kids, who always needed an outlet for their energy.

Years ago, it wasn't called bullying. It was "Boys will be boys," and you were expected to put up with their shenanigans. All Niall remembered was getting his face shoved into the toilet, and he'd lost count of the times his clothes had been stolen or soaked with water when he'd shower after gym class. To this day, he still had nightmares about those incidents.

Seeing Keller Williams brought back all those ugly memories, and while Keller had never been present for any of his humiliations, Niall was certain he knew what his football friends had done to him. He and the quarterback, Bobby Contard, Niall's biggest tormentor, had been on the team together, after all.

And yet, none of that stopped Keller from featuring as the star in Niall's nighttime fantasies during his high school years. But who could blame him? Big and blond, with blazing blue eyes, Keller Williams was his wet dream come to life, and Niall had learned to do laundry specifically so his mother wouldn't have to deal with his sticky, stained sheets. Watching Keller was the only reason he'd sat through the football games in the bleachers under the Friday night lights.

Niall entered the library, his mind not on unboxing and shelving the books he'd ordered or on the software programs to be uploaded, but on the past Friday night. Over the years, Niall had followed Keller Williams's football career. He knew Keller had been married once and divorced less than a year after, and that the tabloids loved to show him partying it up in the off-season. Obviously, he'd kept his image as a big-time player. But after his injury and retirement from the sport, he'd dropped out of sight.

Why was he back in Overlook? When his mother died, Keller had returned only briefly, the press hounding his steps. From Dara, who was a real-estate agent, Niall knew he hadn't sold his mother's house and it remained empty.

"Maybe that's it. He's finally going to sell it and cut ties with Overlook for good. No other reason for him to be here in this little town."

But damn, he'd looked good. Better than good. He'd grown into his gorgeous face, and that rugged body hadn't run to fat after retirement. He'd never lost the power of that brilliant smile. His face burning, Niall recalled how merely talking to him and the proximity in the small bathroom had left him aching with need.

"Idiot. The man is straight. And a jock. He has no use for someone like you." He scrubbed his hands over his face.

The guy he was supposed to meet had never contacted him with an excuse, leaving him…slightly relieved, actually. He didn't really want to use a dating app. Despite everything, Niall was still enough of a romantic to want to meet someone spontaneously and be swept off his feet. He wanted to fall madly in love.

Several hours had passed, and with as much work done as he could manage for the day, Niall left the library and decided to check on the football practice. He was so proud of David—in his freshman year, he was named an Overlook Tiger "rising star," and held the record for rushing for an offensive running back.

Niall reached the field and saw the boys doing practice runs and sprints. From afar, he heard the coach yelling to them, "Let's go, let's go. Keep those knees up. That's it. Good going." It was too far away to see a face, but from his movements, Niall could tell he was a much younger man than Coach Weaver. He ran with the kids, shouting and keeping pace with them.

After the team had finished, the coach gathered them together in a line and talked to each player, giving them a fist bump before moving on to the next kid. Niall liked that. When David had expressed a desire to play football, Niall had needed to remind himself this wasn't his high school life and David wasn't him. Times had changed, and bullying was a topic discussed freely. And it proved to be the right decision, as David not only loved playing the game, but flourished in a team environment.

The coach slung an arm over David's shoulders and walked toward the gate with him. As they approached, a sense of unease rose in Niall, and his heart began to pound.

In the last twenty yards, David ran from the coach's side to meet him at the fence. "Dad, Coach wanted to meet you when I said you'd be here. He said that from what he's seen, he thinks we can take the state championship this year." David's eyes sparkled and a healthy flush covered his cheeks, but it wasn't his son Niall was staring at.

Keller Williams pulled off his Tigers cap, releasing all that golden hair. It caught the sunlight, creating a halo effect around him. But there was nothing angelic about the wicked smile that blazed across his face.

"Hello, again. Fancy meeting you here."

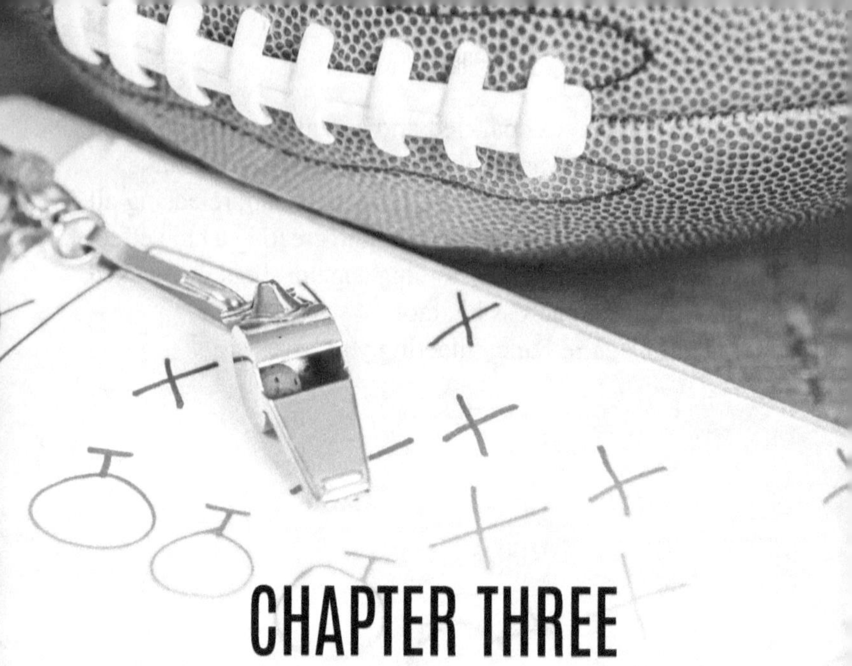

CHAPTER THREE

Well, now. Wasn't this an interesting turn of events?

The mystery man from the bar was the father of one of his players.

David's brow furrowed. "You know Coach Williams, Dad? How? You've never watched football on television. Only when I play."

For whatever reason, panic rose in the man's eyes, and Keller assumed it was related to the blind date. Was he cheating on his wife? There was definitely a story there. Before Keller could speak, David's father jumped in.

"I'm Niall Harper." To David, he said, "Your coach and I went to high school together here. But we didn't know each other. Not really."

Keller's jaw dropped. "We did?" Hard as he tried, he couldn't remember Niall at all. "Were we in some of the same classes? You weren't on the team."

Niall made a sound of disgust. "Hardly. I was one of the quiet ones. And I was a year under you, but we had a few electives together. Clearly, you never noticed me." Niall held out his hand to his son. "Give me your stuff, and I'll put it in the car while you shower and change, okay?"

In high school, Keller had kept his sexuality under tight wraps—twenty years earlier, knowing how casually the "queer" comments were tossed about, he never could've given the tiniest hint he was into men. He hadn't allowed himself to notice any of the guys in his classes.

But now? Keller set the ball cap on his head, moving the brim just so, which gave him a chance to assess Niall's tight, muscled body without being too obvious about it. Nice broad shoulders? Check. Flat abs? *Mmhmm.* Sexy, slightly long hair, and killer eyes. *Damn.* Who knew there'd be such eye candy among the dads?

Shut up, Keller. You're here to coach kids, not hook up. Besides, the guy is straight, and you're supposed to be, too. And for whatever reason, Niall was uptight near him.

David handed over his helmet, shooting him and his father a confused look. "O…kay. I won't take long."

Keller waited until David was well out of earshot. "I'm sorry I didn't remember you."

A snort escaped Niall. "I'm sure. I'm not here to make small talk. I have to go." He turned and strode away across the grass toward the teachers' parking lot. He opened his car door and tossed the helmet onto the back seat.

Not to be put off, Keller followed. "What if I don't want to?" He settled against the hood of the car and crossed his arms.

Niall slammed the door and whirled to face him, flushed and blue eyes shooting green sparks. "Listen, you can stand here all day and talk to the trees for all I care."

"Why're you so angry with me? Because I don't remember you from twenty years ago?" This over-the-top reaction was bizarre. "So what? We're almost forty years old. Who cares about high school anymore?"

"I don't care about high school, or you. I'm not angry. Anger implies feelings, and I have none when it comes to you. I just hope that as a coach you treat the kids on the team better than you and your friends did when you were players. Not everyone is a superstar and can get it right the first time. Coach Weaver was known for his encouragement and support. He never bullied or yelled at the kids."

"Bully?" Annoyed and surprised, Keller moved closer and pointed his finger. "You think I'm a bully? I saw you watched some of the practice. Did it look like I was yelling at them?"

"N-no," Niall admitted. "And I liked that you talked to each boy separately." His jaw hardened, a muscle ticking beneath the skin. "But that could be because you knew I was there."

Keller jabbed his finger at Niall. "Who the hell are you to say that? I don't do anything for show. I gave two hundred percent when I played pro, and I'm going to give that effort to the kids as their coach. I expect them to give me the same in return. And what are you doing here anyway? Are you one of those sideline fathers, second-guessing the coach's every play?"

Niall blinked. "Uh, no. I work here. I'm the school's head librarian, and occasionally I fill in and teach English lit if they need a sub."

"Oh." That was not what Keller had expected to hear. *Damn.* If they'd had someone who looked like Niall when he was in high school, he would've spent a hell of a lot more time in the library. "So I guess we're coworkers."

"Hardly," Niall scoffed, with a trace of lingering bitterness. "Librarians and the sports teams don't mix. Nothing's changed in that respect." He checked his watch. "I have to go." With that, Niall climbed into the car and slammed the door. It took several turns for the engine to turn over, and then he drove toward the general lot on the other side of the school.

"Jesus, what the hell crawled up his ass?" Admitting defeat, Keller retreated to the gym lockers, where he found the boys still in the showers or getting dressed. Keller knew how important bonding with your coach was, and he vowed to make that his priority. He waited until they were all present. David stayed as well.

"Hey, guys, I know I already said it on the field, but I think we've got the makings of a championship team. Let's make sure we keep up the energy every day like this, and nothing and no one can stop us, right?" He clapped to give them motivation.

"Right, Coach," they all yelled.

"Tigers, Tigers, hear us roar!" Keller kept up the chant and the locker room walls rang from their cheers. He raised his hands, and they quieted.

"Now, one thing I learned in the pros was that your team is your second family. And family always sticks up for each other. What hurts one of us hurts us all. So always be there for your teammates. But it doesn't stop there."

The kids shifted around, and Shane, the quarterback, called out, "What do you mean, Coach?"

"You're role models. Yeah, it's cool to be the jocks and popular because you're winning games, but don't let it get to your heads, 'cause you're going to meet the same people on the way up as you do on the way down. Use that popularity to be kind to others. If you see someone acting wrong, call them out. Let them know we don't tolerate that kind of crap."

"Yeah, we got the anti-bullying lectures," Shane drawled.

Keller eyed him. "Sounds like you don't put much stock into it."

Shane lifted a shoulder. "I mean, I'm not friends with

any of the geeks or library nerds. They stick together."

A couple of the kids snickered, and Keller frowned. He glared in their direction, and they hung their heads so as not to meet his eyes. He was going to make sure to quash that attitude real quick.

"Not liking the way that sounds, my man. The quarterback is the leader, and I expect you to set the example. I'm not telling you who to be friends with. I'm saying, I remember high school and how we thought we were untouchable because we were on the team. We were the players. I'm here to tell you, you're not. There's no 'three strikes and you're out' policy on my team, but I won't tolerate any derogatory language. If I find *anyone* here involved in *any* kind of misbehavior, you're out. I don't care what records you hold or who you think you are. Right now you're high school kids and nothing more. Take it from someone who had it all—it can be gone in the blink of an eye."

Several of the boys darted glances at his arm, and he nodded. "Yeah, that's right. My arm. You can ask me about my injury, but I'm sure you already know. I took a hit, and the damage was too great for the team to keep me on. Football, like all other sports, is a business first. They're out to make money off what you can do for them. I might've been king of the world one year, but if I can't produce, they're going to cut me. And that's exactly what happened. I retired, and I'm thankful every day for all the years I got to play, but"—he fixed them with a stern eye, especially Shane, who stood with arms crossed, like he couldn't be bothered—"I've seen plenty of kids right out of college, with great stats and drafted high with immense prospects, get injured early on and have nothing. Do well in school so you always have something to fall back on."

"Yeah, Coach Weaver told us that too," one of the tight ends piped up, and Keller grinned.

"I'm sure he did. He said the same thing to my team."

Keller gazed at their young faces, wondering if any of them questioned their sexuality like he had. "And another thing. I remember high school and being your age. I thought it was tough then, but you kids have it worse now in some respects. I know you all have stuff going on in your lives that you keep to yourselves, but if you feel like you need someone to talk to, I'm going to give you my personal cell number. I'll be your confidant and won't reveal anything you tell me. You don't even have to tell me your name when you call. Keep it anonymous. You can feel safe with me."

He recited the digits, and the kids scrambled to add it to their phones. A few kids stared at him, but when he nodded in their direction, they paled and ducked their heads.

God, he was so glad he wasn't a teenager.

"All right. See you here tomorrow, same time. Be prepared to work your butts off. I wanna see a championship banner flying on the flagpole by season's end. Am I right?"

"Yeah, Coach," they all yelled. "Tigers, Tigers, hear us roar!"

He left them, exited the gym, and got into his car. David got into his father's car, and Keller drove behind them out of the parking lot. They split off at the intersection of Main and Maple, Niall turning left, toward the big houses belonging to the doctors and lawyers who lived on that side of town, where there was more land and sweeping views of the waterfalls. Keller lived on the right, in the smaller, older homes lining the streets, each with a patch of grass in the front for a yard. In high school, it used to be his job to come home straight after his last class or after practice and do his homework, then whatever chores his mother had waiting. Much as he'd wanted to hang out with his friends, he'd known he was the man of the house and that his mother depended on him. He'd been allowed to go to the victory parties after the games, but that was the extent of his hanging out.

"Education is the only thing no one can take away from you," his mother used to say. *"That and your dignity. If you have pride in yourself, you're doing the right thing."*

Words he tried to live by, but sometimes it was hard, knowing he'd pretended most of his life to be something he wasn't.

He drove to his mother's house—his house now, he had to correct himself—and after parking in the narrow driveway, picked up his mail and paper from the cute little birdhouse mailbox she'd had installed at the bottom of the steps.

Leaving his dusty sneakers by the front door, Keller opened the advertisements and tossed the circulars, looking but not really seeing the papers in front of him. Was it odd to come home to this small town and tiny, run-down house after living the outrageous lifestyle he'd had in Vegas? Hell, yeah. He'd had a penthouse in the sky, overlooking the glittering lights of the Strip, with anything and anyone he wanted at his fingertips. Life in excess. His mother's death had woken him up, catching him in the nick of time, before he slid into an abyss from which few returned without damage. He wasn't kidding when he said everything could change in the blink of an eye. The phone call from a deputy informing him of his mother's death had destroyed him. His biggest cheerleader and the person who loved him unconditionally was gone forever.

His phone rang, and he smiled at the screen before answering. "Elijah, you bastard, how the hell are you?"

"How you doing, Country?" The booming voice of Elijah Randolph, best friend, former teammate, and now ESPN commentator, filled his ear, and Keller put the phone on speaker.

"You can stop calling me that any day now."

"Ha-ha, but it's fun. How do you like living in the boonies? Shot yourself an opossum for dinner?" Elijah cackled.

"Oh, shut up. We have DoorDash here just like you do in the city."

"But I bet your sushi isn't like Nobu or Morimoto."

Keller laughed along with him. "You'd win that bet, but we've got some damn fine chicken wings."

"Deirdre won't let me eat them anymore," Elijah grumbled, and Keller's lips twitched. "She doesn't want me gaining weight now that I'm not playing."

Elijah was a six-foot-seven teddy bear of a man who dressed in handmade suits to fit his bulk. As a teammate he'd been an asset, fearsome on the field, and holding more quarterback sacks than any rookie his first year. Keller had been one of his groomsmen when Elijah married his high school sweetheart, Deirdre, and Elijah was the only player who knew Keller was gay.

"Good for her." Keller snickered. "Bet those babies of yours are keeping you on the run, huh?"

"You bet. Kennedy thinks two-year-old Marli is annoying. It's hard to explain to a four-year-old that her little sister just wants to be her twin. They have me wrapped around their fingers."

His phone beeped, and he smiled at the picture of Deirdre and the two little girls, dressed alike, down to the pink bows at the ends of their braids.

"Man, how'd your ugly mug manage to get not only the prettiest woman in the world, but have the two most gorgeous little girls?"

"I don't question it. I just thank my mama every day for whipping my butt into shape."

"*Mmhmm*. I know Ms. Roberta didn't play." Elijah's mother had raised four boys—the oldest was a professor at Vanderbilt, one was a doctor in Memphis, and the other was a lawyer in Atlanta. Elijah was the baby of the family.

"All joking aside, how're you doing? Is it hard being in your mom's house? I know after my momma died, it took a while before I could step foot inside her place."

"It is and it isn't, if that makes sense. Yeah, I can afford a way better place in the nicer part of town, but if this house was good enough for her, I'm okay with it."

"I know you wanted your mom to move to a newer, bigger house, closer to you."

"Yeah, but she was like your mother. No wonder they were best friends." It still hurt to think of her in the past tense. "All her memories were here, especially of my dad. I might not remember him, but she did, and that's what matters."

His father had died when Keller was two years old—shot in a failed robbery of the sporting goods store where he worked. His favorite picture of his father was one of him holding him close, Keller wearing a tiny Buffalo Bills onesie. He wished he could remember him. All he had were the stories his mother told him. How his father had talked about taking him to his first football game and watching Keller play in the Peewee league.

"You met your team yet? I gotta tell you, I might be a little jealous of you getting to be on the field and involved with the game again. Sitting up in the booth in a suit, talking, ain't really my thing." He sighed. "I miss it."

"I met them today, and not gonna lie, yeah, it's pretty fucking awesome. These kids are so damn good—couple of little hiccups, but I'm not concerned. We've got a chance for the state championship, and I'm going to do my best to get us there."

"Sounds awesome, man. I might have to come up and visit." Elijah sounded like he meant it, and Keller jumped on his words.

"Do it, yeah. You have time before the pro season starts. The kids would go nuts to meet you, and I'd love your take."

"*Hmm*," Elijah mused, and Keller could see him stroking his goatee. "Maybe I will. Got some training-season shit to do, but I'll touch base when I have a better idea of my schedule. Does it feel weird—being at your old stomping grounds? High school kids…they can't be easy."

"It's okay. Being back here makes me feel like none of the mistakes I made in the past matter. Almost like I can start fresh." Niall Harper's angry words had made an impression on him, though, and Keller wanted to know why a virtual stranger disliked him so damn much.

Elijah chuckled. "Now you're sounding like all that New Age shit."

"You don't think people can get a do-over?" Keller was curious.

"Life is tough. It doesn't give do-overs. And why the hell do you need one anyway?"

Keller laughed. "I dunno. Your wife doesn't think so. Last time I talked to Deirdre, she told me I was perfect."

"Only in the sense that she doesn't understand why you don't have a man. I mean, I can see you're a good-looking dude. You have a job, money in the bank…and your jokes aren't all that bad."

"Ha-ha."

But Elijah wasn't giving up. "It's been a while," he said quietly.

He blinked, his laughter fading. It had been. A long while, in fact. Keller couldn't remember the last time he'd had sex, but certainly not in the past eight months, since he'd gotten the first inquiry from Overlook High about the coaching job and then moved home to start a new life.

"I guess it hasn't been important. And I can't imagine the small town where I grew up is the place for me to come out in all my glory. They might not want a gay man coaching their kids. You know people."

Elijah snorted. "Yeah. They suck."

"Don't knock it till you tried it. Know what I mean?"

Elijah howled. "Aw, man, whatja have to say that for?"

Keller fell onto the sofa, laughing again. "Go kiss your

wife. I'll talk to you soon."

"Later."

The conversation over, Keller wiped his eyes and put his feet up. He'd made light of it, but the fact was, the loneliness was ugly. Once he was let go from the Vegas Players, his personal assistant left with excuses, and he found a new agent when his old one stopped taking his calls. He had a few endorsements but nothing new on the horizon, as new stars took the spotlight. He'd spent his life in a team environment, and now, cut off from almost everyone he knew and the familiar world of lights and cameras, Keller wasn't sure he knew how to separate the player he'd become from the person he really was.

His phone rang, but this time he didn't recognize the number.

"Hello?"

"Keller, it's Dan Brockman. How was the first day?"

Brockman was the principal of Overlook High and a former algebra teacher—back in Keller's high school days.

"It went well. Put the kids through their paces. They're looking real good. You weren't kidding when you said they had a shot at the championship."

"Good, good. I'm calling to make sure you don't forget about administration day. Just because you're the football coach doesn't mean you get to skip out on that fun event. Everyone attends."

"I remember. It's Monday, right?"

"Correct. I'll see you at nine thirty a.m."

He winced. *Damn*. Back to school hours, and on a Monday of all days. "See you then."

Crap. He'd also forgotten the dinner plans he'd made with Bobby Contard and his wife, so he picked up his phone, made a reservation at The Flame, put the alert on his calendar so he wouldn't forget again, and texted Bobby the details. That accomplished, he switched on the television and scrolled through his phone, looking for someplace that delivered.

His finger stopped on the screen when it rang with an unfamiliar number.

"Hello?"

"Is this Coach Keller?"

"Yes, who's this?"

"I'm one of the players. You said we could call you."

He sure as hell did, but hadn't expected it to be so soon. "Of course. Do you want to tell me your name?"

"Not really."

He smiled. "All right. Is everything okay? Are you hurt or in trouble?"

"No. It's just…I don't know if I'm doing the right thing."

"What thing? Do you want to tell me?"

"I like guys. And I haven't told anyone. Over the summer we all hung out, and one night I was with my friend, and we drank some beer and did some stuff. Now every time he sees me, he doesn't wanna talk to me. He doesn't even want to be my friend."

Keller breathed out slowly. "He got scared."

"Yeah. He kept saying he can't be gay, that his father will kill him, but that didn't stop us from…you know…"

"It's okay. You don't have to tell me the personal stuff. My suggestion is to leave him be and let him work it out in his head. Either he'll come to realize who he is, or not. But pushing him isn't going to help either of you. Tell me how you're feeling about everything?"

"Okay, I guess."

"Do you feel safe at school?"

"I think so."

"Remember, there's no bullying allowed. I meant what I said. It's a safe space, no matter what your sexuality is."

"That's cool. I've been thinking of coming out, and now that you're there, I feel safer."

His heart pounded. "Thank you. I'm glad."

"I gotta go. Night, Coach. Thanks."

"Good night."

God, I hope I helped him.

When his phone calendar beeped with the notification that Monday morning he had an appointment at the high school, Niall Harper's scowling face popped into his mind.

"Everyone attends, huh?" A grin kicked up his lips. "Guess I'll be seeing you again, Niall. Whether you like it or not."

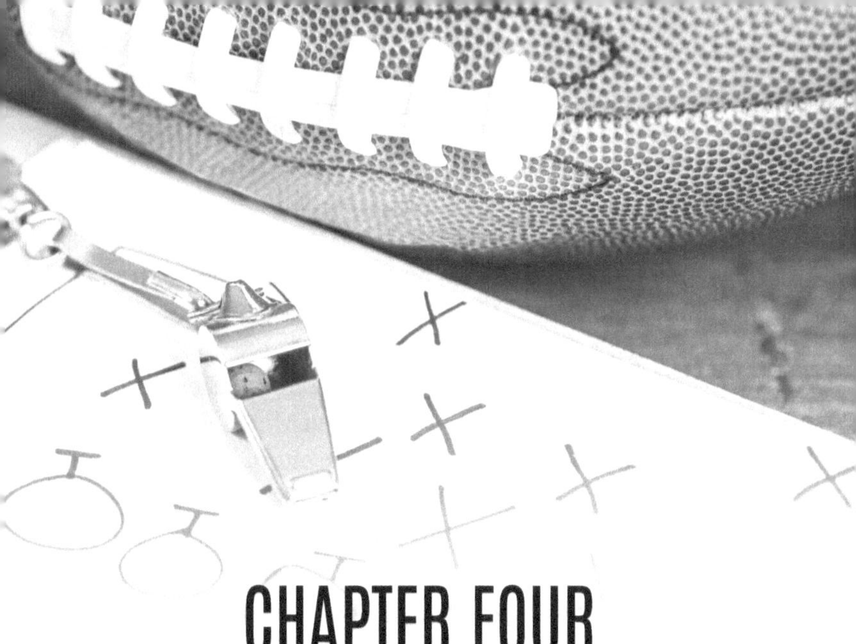

CHAPTER FOUR

With a smile, Niall held out his glass, and Michael poured his wine. "Thanks. I can use it after spending the whole day shelving books."

It was a balmy, end-of-summer evening, and he was having dinner at Michael and Dara's. It was the talk of Overlook that Keller Williams had come home and was coaching the high school football team, and everyone had an opinion. Niall kept his to himself.

"I'll bet. So tell me about the coach. I couldn't believe it when you told me. Who would've thought a former NFL player would ever want to coach a high school team?"

"Yeah."

His less than enthusiastic response didn't go unnoticed, and Michael raised a sandy brow. "What's wrong?"

Shit. He wasn't about to let twenty-year-old insecurities bleed into his life.

"Nothing. David thinks he's the bomb, and I watched them practice for a while and liked what I saw. Seems he's into teamwork and encouragement, and that makes for a winning season."

That sounded good to his ears, but Michael peered at him more closely. "Did you know him when he went to school here?"

Michael and Dara weren't native to the area. They'd moved from the city to Overlook when Michael had gotten "an offer he couldn't refuse," as he put it, to be head of ob-gyn at Overlook Hospital, and Dara got her real estate license. Niall had spent many summer weekends in their lush backyard, where Michael barbecued and they drank wine on the deck. The sparkling pool, once filled with the neighborhood kids, sat empty that evening, as Chris and David were out at a party down the road.

"We were in school at the same time, but I was a year younger and we didn't really know each other. He was the big man on campus, as you can imagine, and I was the library kid." With a casual lift of his shoulder, Niall hoped that would be the end of the conversation.

"Oh. Well, that was years ago," Dara said brightly.

Niall laughed. "I'm still the library nerd, and he's still the football player, so nothing's changed in that regard. He doesn't remember me, which I'm perfectly fine with." But he could admit to some curiosity about Keller. "I heard he's living in his old house? I'd have thought he'd buy in this area of town."

Dara nodded. "He is. Frank, the head of our office, went to deliver him a welcome basket like we do for all the people who move in, and Keller told him he liked the familiarity of it. It must've been hard on him to lose his mother so suddenly. I can understand not wanting to lose the memories. It hasn't been that long."

"No. Only a few years, from what I remember."

"Anyway, enough about Keller Williams." Dara eyed him, and Niall braced himself. He knew what was coming. "I met someone I think you'd like."

Yep. He was right. "Oh?" He sipped his wine and caught Michael's eye.

Michael shrugged. "I got nothing."

"Oh, stop. Marcie would be perfect for Niall. She's sweet, nice, and has been divorced about four years. No children, and she owns the new antique store two doors down from my office. We were in line for salads at the deli and got to talking."

"About me? How do I come up when you're deciding between ranch or honey Dijon dressing?"

"Very funny. I don't remember, but I did tell her that you're a wonderful man, and she's open to meeting for coffee." She blinked. "Whenever you want."

"Did you tell her I'd be calling her?" He frowned. "I prefer to set up my own dates, much as I know you love to try."

"I hate thinking of you sitting in that big house every night by yourself. Angie's got a boyfriend, and it's time you started living your life again."

"Dara, enough, come on. Give Niall a break," Michael interjected. "Let the man do what he wants, when he wants. I'm sure he has his reasons why he's not interested in dating."

You have no idea.

"It's okay, Dara, I'm not angry. Sure. I'll call her up. Coffee is no big deal. You know I appreciate it, but my focus is on David. These next few years are all I'll have with him until he goes away to college. There will be plenty of time then for me to date."

"I only want you to be happy." Dara tucked her hair behind her ears. "Who knows? Maybe you'll hit it off."

Marcie was as nice as Dara had said. They sat in Spill the Beans, the coffee place on the corner of Main and Walnut, and Niall was enjoying himself. They shared a love of mysteries, musical theater, antiques, and gardening. She was attractive and looked somewhat similar to Angie with her long dark hair and deep-brown eyes. Her figure was athletic, which made sense, since she was explaining how she ran five miles every morning before she got ready for work.

"It clears my head from the sleep fuzzies." Her eyes sparkled at him. "Do you run?"

Yeah, he wanted to say. *Away from my problems and who I am.*

He managed a smile. "I could probably do a mile, but then you'd have to pick me up off the ground."

"I am CPR certified." Her smile broadened. "If you ever feel like joining me, there's always room on the path for two."

God, he felt bad leading her on. She was *so* nice and he could try to make an effort to at least be a friend. "Maybe I will. I can use all the help I can get."

"You look fine to me."

Was he wrong to be there with her? His guilt grew as they finished their coffees and he noticed the clock on the wall. Seven p.m. Dinnertime. He had no place to be, as David was at Chris's for a barbecue—no doubt inspired by Dara's hope that he and Marcie would hit it off—and he wouldn't be home early.

"Would you like to have dinner?" Marcie asked.

He blinked. "Now? Oh, yeah, of course now, it's dinnertime." Why was he babbling?

"If you have other plans, that's okay. I was enjoying the

evening and thought you might want to continue it a little longer. I'd love to have a new friend in town. It's hard not knowing anyone here. My husband and I were supposed to start this business together, but he decided he'd rather date twenty-five-year-olds, so here I am, on my own. Dara was kind to take pity on me."

Why the hell not? Marcie was sweet and fun to be with.

"Dara and Michael are very good friends of mine. As you said, it's nice to have friends."

Marcie checked her watch. "How about The Flame? It's good for steak and seafood. I'm sure we can get in, and we're both dressed for it."

She wore a long skirt and a sleeveless linen top that showed off her toned arms. "You look perfect." It was over his budget, but he could splurge this one time.

Since they didn't have a reservation, when they arrived at The Flame they were asked to wait at the bar. She ordered a Pinot Noir and he a Chardonnay. Marcie excused herself to use the restroom, so Niall sat and stared into his glass, still feeling guilty that he was leading her on to believe there was a possibility of something more between them.

"We keep meeting over you sitting alone at bars."

Niall jumped and met Keller's laughing blue eyes. His fingers tightened around the stem. "My date is here. She's in the restroom."

"I'll keep you company until she returns." He swung himself onto the barstool—a tight fit, given his muscular thighs, which now pressed against Niall's, making his heart pound. "I'm waiting for Bobby Contard and his wife."

What a weak fool you are, still fantasizing about a man who didn't even remember your name. Nothing's changed. He's still friends with that awful man.

He shifted away and shrugged. "Suit yourself."

"You're divorced?"

"Yeah, for a few years now."

"And David lives with you, not your ex? Or does she live nearby?"

"No, Angie lives in Chicago. She got an offer for a partnership at a law firm, and we decided it was better for David to live here with me so as not to upend his life."

"Sounds like a very amicable divorce. Unusual."

"Was yours different?" Niall blurted, and the light in Keller's eyes dimmed. "Sorry, didn't mean to pry."

"I mean, you did, but it's okay." Keller's grin seemed forced. "I can't be the only nosy one. Yeah, it was all neat and clean. I barely remember it or her."

"How can you forget someone you were married to?"

Keller's blue eyes bore into his. "It was a mistake that should've never happened. I didn't love her."

"Why did you do it, then?"

When the hell had he gotten so bold?

Apparently, Keller wondered as well, because his brows flew up and he crossed those big, muscular arms. "Not that I owe you an explanation, but…haven't you ever done something you knew was wrong but because it was expected, you did it anyway?"

That remark hit too close to home, and spotting Marcie walking toward him, he slid off the barstool. "I have to go." He picked up her glass and his, and without waiting for Keller to respond, walked away.

"Let's check if our table is ready," Niall said, intercepting Marcie, whose eyes grew wide.

"Oh, wow. That's Keller Williams, isn't it? I read in the local paper that he'd come home to coach the football team."

"Yeah."

"Do you know him?"

"No," Niall answered firmly. "I don't know him at all."

Monday morning, armed with a giant-sized iced coffee, Niall walked into the high school. Dan Brockman greeted him.

"Morning, Niall." He handed him a packet. "Here are the materials you'll need for the day."

Niall glanced at the papers—sexual harassment, anti-bullying, active-shooter drill. "Gets bigger every year."

"Amazing how we managed to survive without any of it."

Recalling the taunts and teasing and how after escaping school, he'd go home and wish he could disappear forever, Niall frowned. "Some didn't. And if it helps even one person, it's well worth the effort."

Dan nodded. "You're in room 6B."

He waited by the elevators, greeting the teachers and other department heads he hadn't seen all summer. Inside the room, he sat at a two-person desk and opened the training packet. Starting with the self-guided tests with multiple-choice questions, he began reading the first scenario. He'd just finished the first page when someone sat next to him.

"Good morning." Keller's deep voice sent a thrill down to his toes, and Niall began to sweat.

"Hello."

"How did your date go last night?"

"Shh. I'm trying to do these tests." He glared at Keller, who lazed in his seat, looking way too good for a Monday morning. A blue Overlook Tigers T-shirt stretched across his broad chest, and muscles bulged from his biceps, showcased by the short sleeves. Dark-blond scruff dusted his jaw, and golden waves peeked out from underneath the Tigers' cap.

Keller said, "I bet you always were the perfect student."

The slightly mocking tone woke Niall up from his lusty fantasy. "Yeah, I was," he snapped. "And I bet you weren't. I'm surprised you even bothered to show up today."

Keller flushed. "What's that supposed to mean?"

"People like you always expect things to be handed to them because they're popular—like it was for all of you players in high school."

"People like me? What do you know about me?"

"Enough," Niall stated.

"Well, sorry, Mr. Perfect Student, but you don't know what you're talking about." Keller's demeanor turned glacial, his eyes hardening to blue chips of ice.

"I don't? Are you going to deny that the football players used to get special treatment? That you and your friends got away with shit no one else would have simply because of who you were?"

Acknowledgment dawned in Keller's eyes. "So it *is* about high school. I'm sorry I didn't recognize you, Niall. Frankly, I wouldn't recognize myself, looking back on those years now. I'd like to put it behind us, if you can."

Shocked at his insightful comment, Niall's harsh words died on his lips. "I have to start these exercises. Excuse me." This wasn't the Keller Williams he'd imagined. This man was sympathetic and understanding.

Embarrassed and angry—more with himself than Keller—that he'd let the situation spiral, Niall picked up his packet of papers and walked to the opposite side of the room, to a seat next to Marty Daniels, the chemistry teacher. "Mind if I sit here?"

"Not at all."

He parked himself, and Marty shifted in his seat. "He's gorgeous."

In the middle of reading the problem, Niall stopped and turned to look at Marty. "What?"

Marty whispered, "I said he's gorgeous. Keller Williams. Even if I were straight, I probably would have noticed."

Marty and he had rarely spoken, and Niall was surprised he was so open about his sexuality. "I didn't…I mean, I never…"

Saving his sorry ass, Marty waved off his stammering. "Don't worry about it. My friends say I gossip too much." His brown eyes twinkled. "I have your son this year."

"Yeah, I hope the sciences come to him naturally. They weren't my thing."

"I'm sure he'll be fine. As long as he comes to class and pays attention. Coach Weaver made sure the kids showed up. I hope Keller Williams plays by the same rules."

In spite of himself, Niall peered over the bent heads of everyone else in the classroom, and found a stone-faced glare directed his way.

"Damn, how'd you piss him off?"

Niall shrugged and returned to his tests.

After ninety minutes they got a break, and Niall breathed a little easier when Keller left the room. Marty turned talkative once again.

"You know, in a couple of circles I'm in, we play a game called Gay or Not Gay. Keller Williams comes up often, and ninety percent of the time, people say it's a yes."

Shock radiated through Niall. "Th-that's crazy. Why would anyone think that?"

Marty shifted closer, his voice so low that only the two of them could hear. "There were rumors about him when he lived in Vegas."

Niall shrugged. "I don't know. When someone's a celebrity, they tend to be fodder for the gossip mill. I don't think it's right to speculate and play games with people's sexuality."

"You seem very passionate about that." Marty grew thoughtful.

Realizing he was revealing more than intended, Niall quickly answered, "I just feel it's not right. That's all," then pointed at the clock on the wall. "It's time to start. Don't want to get stuck here all day. We'll both be here until five."

"Can't have that. I've got a hot date." Marty winked. "I've been seeing this guy, and he's been traveling for a month. I don't intend to let him out of bed."

Niall blushed. "All right, well, better get to it."

Marty cocked his head. "Am I embarrassing you? I've been told I can be a lot for some people."

Niall's smile was faint. "No worries." But he was glad when Marty bent his head to his packet and resumed reading.

The afternoon flew by without further incident. He worked on his tests, but he couldn't help noticing that Keller kept to himself—he went to lunch alone and was one of the first out of the classroom. Feeling guilty as hell, Niall thought of following him to apologize but decided to leave it alone. School was starting soon, and the only contact he'd need to have with Keller Williams afterward would be through a fence on the football field.

CHAPTER FIVE

The phone woke him, the loud ring blasting through his dreams. Keller grabbed for it and rolled over in bed, squinting at the glowing dial of the old clock radio on the nightstand.

"Four in the morning? Seriously?" He swiped at the screen. "Hello?"

The sound of breathing filled his ear, and Keller was about to hang up when he heard, "H-hello? Is this Coach Williams?"

An alarm blared in his sleep-fuzzy head. "Yeah. Who is this?"

"I don't know who else to talk to." The voice was muffled, and Keller rubbed his face and sat up, fully awake now, his senses tingling.

"Hey, it's okay. I'm here. What's wrong?"

More silence and the sounds of shuffling. "I just want

to be like everyone else."

"What do you mean?" Keller pushed the hair out of his face, wishing he hadn't had that third beer before bed.

"I think I like guys."

Releasing a *whoosh* of air from his lungs, Keller hoped he knew the right thing to say. "There's nothing wrong with that. Some men like men, some like women, and some like both."

"But everyone thinks I'm into girls. My dad...he wouldn't...I can't tell him or my mom."

"Hey," Keller soothed. "It's okay. You don't have to come out and say anything until you're comfortable." Was this the friend of the kid who'd called the other day? Maybe this wasn't such a good idea. God knew, he was not prepared for this.

Don't let me fuck this up.

"You can talk to me about it."

"I started having sex with this girl because she wanted to, but...I don't know."

"You don't have to."

"Then I kissed this guy." The voice dropped to an almost unintelligible whisper. "I ran away because it felt too good and he wanted to do other stuff. I didn't know what to do."

Keller knew exactly what this kid was going through: the torment he'd put himself through trying to fit in with everyone else, the sneaking around and worrying he'd get caught.

"I just wanted to know. But now I'm scared because I liked it."

At those words, Keller's heart broke. "You can talk to me. I'll never judge you."

"I can't," he cut Keller off, frantic. "Someone's coming. I gotta go."

And just like that, the call ended and Keller was left hanging. He tried closing his eyes, but sleep eluded him.

After half an hour of punching the pillow and rolling from side to side, Keller gave up, and he showered and went downstairs. Filled with nervous energy, he grabbed his car keys and left the house.

Twenty minutes of aimless driving through town and Keller ended up at the high school. He parked and walked the field, eyes streaming tears. How could he help someone when he couldn't help himself? He returned to his car but didn't start the engine. Hands on the wheel, he tightened his grip. He wouldn't fail. If he lost hours of sleep because some kid trusted him to hold a secret, he'd gladly yawn his way through the day.

Back at home, he worked on the team's playbook as he ate breakfast, while at the same time wondering which of the boys had called him. Practice was at one o'clock that afternoon, and his full coaching crew would be there. Maybe by then he'd know what to say.

"Looking good today, guys. Shane—practice the shotgun. Think of throwing that football like threading a needle through the coverage. Offense—spread out over the field and let Shane know where you are. Tackles—sweep the field clear for Shane to find a receiver. Hit 'em at the knees. It's all about anticipation. Learn to read your opponents. Defense—cover all the running backs, step by step. Find the holes in the line and get to the quarterback. Do you understand?"

"Yes, Coach," they all chorused.

"Let's do this. First game is a week from Friday. We are Tigers!"

"Hear us roar!" Their voices rose in the air.

In the locker room, he called his coaching team over. "Kids are looking good."

Leon Dupree, the assistant offensive coach, nodded. "Yeah. You stepped right in, and it's been seamless. They listen to you, and that's half the battle with teenage boys."

Leon had been with Coach Weaver for as long as Keller could remember—had been there when Keller had played for the team—and now he'd welcomed Keller with a handshake and the reassurance that he had no desire for the head position. *"My wife would kill me,"* he'd deadpanned with a twinkle in his eye.

As they spoke, Leon went down the roster, making notes about each player's performance during the practice.

"How're the boys?" Keller asked. "Anyone having any problems at school, with classes and such?"

"Boys are all good kids. No real issues to speak of."

"Any parents give you grief during the season?"

Hank Charles, his defensive coach, grimaced. "We got our share. Shane's father, Bobby Contard, thinks he's already in the pros, and a couple of others—mothers and fathers both—act like they know better than we do what plays oughta be called. Bobby Contard was a loudmouth when he was here, if you remember. Hope he's not going to turn Shane into one. Last year the kids were good, but they need a little push to get them to great. Lots of egos."

"Hmm." He could see it. Bobby had pushed him hard during dinner about the direction of the team. He seemed to think *he* was the quarterback again, not his son. Keller scratched his chin. "What about David Harper?"

Leon looked puzzled. "What about him? Kid's no problem."

"Looks like a good player," Keller said, "he'll be strong for a sophomore. How were his stats last year?"

"Real good, and he's handled his parents' split pretty well."

"Oh?" All ears, Keller didn't want to look as if he were fishing for info, though in reality, he wanted to know more.

"Yeah. Lots of times it really screws a kid up. But not David. Darndest thing is that the mother and father are still real close from what I've heard."

"Good. Just checking to make sure he's okay. Looks like his father keeps a close eye on him."

"He does, but he's not one of them in-your-face parents. Harper's quiet but supports his kid."

"Glad to hear. Sometimes the parents' problems rub off on their kids."

"You don't have to worry about David. Kid knows how to take the ball and run with it." Hank gestured with his hands.

"How about socially? Any of the kids having any problems at home, or with their peers?" Curious faces met his, and he hastened to explain. "With all the admin testing we just went through, I want to make sure we're in front of any potential issues. I know how high school kids are—lots of questions and hormones raging."

"Yeah. You had some real beauts on your team back then. I was surprised that David's father wanted him to play football, considering." Leon chewed on the end of a toothpick.

"Considering what?"

Leon's brows drew together. "You really don't remember?" Keller shook his head, wanting to hear more. "Your buddy Contard and a few others on the team made his life miserable."

Dread swirled in the pit of his stomach. "We're talking about Niall Harper?"

"Yeah." Leon nodded. "The librarian. He was always a quiet kid, and Contard was a punk. Loved to pick on the kids who weren't into sports."

Keller had been so caught up in his own world of hiding

and pretending, he'd never noticed, but now it all made sense. Niall's chilly reception and resentment toward him correlated directly with what he'd been put through. A generation might've passed since those days, but old hurts died hard. Or lived on.

"I never knew," he whispered to himself, and Leon nodded.

"Didn't think so. Never remember you in any of the shenanigans, but I also couldn't understand how you and Bobby Contard were friends. He had a mouth bigger than his brain, and he still does." Leon raised his brows, an inquiring look on his face.

"Bobby and I were on-the-field friends but never close. I didn't have time to hang out with the team. I had to go home and help my mom."

Leon and Hank both grew somber, and Leon squeezed his shoulder. "Don't think I said it since you came home, but I'm sorry about what happened."

Hank's hangdog expression deepened. "Yeah, I'm sorry too, Keller. I remember her from when she'd cheer you on at your games. I knew your dad too. Terrible thing what happened."

"Thanks." A bit sick to his stomach, Keller managed to feign a smile. "I'll go work on those plays, and we'll talk tomorrow."

He left the locker room and wandered about the field, the conversation with his coaching staff and the early morning phone call still in the forefront of his mind. Coming to a decision, he marched into the high school and headed for the library. A couple of students were sitting at computer desks as Keller passed by on his way to the head librarian's office. He knocked and waited but didn't hear anyone. He knocked again, and when no one answered, he opened the door and peeked inside.

The office was small and cluttered with boxes on all

sides, as well as next to the desk. A computer monitor sat on top, next to a phone and several photographs. Keller entered and looked around. Framed prints hung on the wall, and a few plants sat on the windowsill, their green leaves reaching for the sunlight.

Feeling no shame at snooping, Keller walked behind the desk and picked up a picture of David and Niall, taken after a game. Niall gazed at David with such pride, it made Keller's heart ache for his own father. He set down the picture, then spied another, this one taken at Christmastime, in front of a glittering tree. A tall, dark-haired woman—*must be the ex-wife*—stood beside Niall, who was holding baby David in his arms. She was pretty and intense-looking, her focus on Niall, but his was on David. It seemed to be early in their marriage, and they should've been at their happiest, with a new baby and celebrating the holidays. Instead, she radiated tension and Niall looked blank and ill at ease.

"What the hell are you doing in here?"

Startled, he dropped the photo and found a furious Niall standing in the doorway. "Oh, hey, hi." He put on his most charming smile, hoping to reassure Niall, and hastily rearranged the photographs. "I knocked, but you didn't answer, so—"

"So you thought you'd just come in and snoop around my office? Who the hell does that?"

"No. That's not what happened." Keller stepped away from behind the desk.

Niall's laughter rang out. "Could've fooled me." He strode inside and closed the door. "Were you not in here when I wasn't? Looking at my personal pictures, touching who knows what else? What do you want?"

"Your ex is a very pretty lady."

Niall made a face. "Angie's more than her good looks. She's smart and a good mother."

This wasn't going well. At all.

"I'm sure. Listen, can we go somewhere and talk?"

For the first time, Niall was speechless, staring at him like he'd sprouted an extra head on his shoulders. "You've got to be kidding."

"No, why would I be?"

"Be-because," Niall sputtered. "What do I have to talk about with *you*?"

The distaste in his voice was evident, and Keller struggled to remain civil.

"I think some things might've happened in the past that—"

"*Might have?*"

"Niall. I'd like to start fresh. Isn't that possible? I don't like this animosity you have toward me. Can't we move past it?"

"I'm fine as is." Niall leaned over the desk. "Would you mind leaving?"

Keller met Niall's angry gaze, coming almost nose to nose with him. Niall grew pale and his big eyes widened, his breath coming in short, soft pants.

"Yes. I would." Niall's mouth tempted, lush and filled with the promise of slick, wet heat. A tug of excitement curled low in his belly, and Keller had a crazy idea to press his lips to Niall's and see what happened. "I would mind," he whispered. "Very much. Please let me take you out for coffee."

"I don't want coffee."

"What about tea? Lemonade? A milkshake?" Niall's lips twitched, and Keller inwardly cheered that he was making headway.

"Are you always like this?" Niall murmured, and his eyelids fluttered half-shut. A pulse ticked at the base of this throat. Keller's heart pounded as the ache inside him grew to an almost painful, full-body throb. Was Niall into men? Into him?

"Like what?" He grinned, hoping Niall would lighten up and play along.

"Pushy. Demanding." Apparently, Niall wasn't about to tease or flirt with him. No more smiles forthcoming, Niall remained as unrelenting as a rock.

"Only when I want something bad enough. And I don't think those are bad qualities in a coach, football player… or a friend. Do you?"

"What?" Niall's eyes widened, and a frightened, almost frantic expression settled over his now flushed face. "No. I—please leave. I have work to do."

"Niall—"

"Stop. Just get out. I have nothing to say to you." Retreating to the far corner of his office, Niall crossed his arms and waited.

"Fine, but I *will* talk to you one day. There are things I need to say, and you're going to listen to me."

Niall's jaw thrust out, his eyes grew steely, but he remained silent.

Recognizing defeat, Keller left Niall's office and the library. He sat in his car, debating what to do, then decided that nothing was a good plan for the moment and drove home. Plenty of time to figure out Niall Harper. He had more important things on his mind, like which kids on his team needed his help, and what he could possibly do for them.

CHAPTER SIX

Was he going to try this again?

Freshly showered and dressed, Niall paced the living room, alternating between fear and the desire for human contact. A single, no-show date shouldn't prevent him from trying another. *I can't let one failure stop me. There's always going to be a first time. It's just a matter of when.*

David burst through the back door, holding a football, and Niall froze. "I thought you were staying at Chris's this weekend?"

His son stood wide-eyed and scanned him, taking in his slacks and button-down—a far cry from the jeans and T-shirt he usually wore on the weekends. "Dad?" His voice rose high. "Are you going out?"

"Ahhh, yeah. But are you home? I can cancel." He reached for his phone on the table.

"You got a date?" David dropped the ball, almost dancing

with excitement. "No way. I just came to pick up my gear. Chris's dad is gonna take us to the park. We're meeting up with some of the team to practice the drills Coach taught us." He leaned against the counter. "So who're you going out with? Is this a real date?" A smile burst over David's face. "About time."

Niall huffed out a short laugh. "Yeah? You've been waiting?"

To his surprise, David grew serious. "Yes. You should be dating. Mom has Grant, and I want you to have fun too. I hate that you sit at home by yourself every night."

It was one thing for David to want him to date. It was another to tell him he was meeting a man for drinks. *That* was a discussion for another day. Far into the future.

"Tonight you get your wish."

"Where'd you meet her? What does she look like?"

"Online and dark hair and brown eyes," he said, leaving out the fact that his date was six feet tall and weighed about two twenty. Niall slipped his phone into his jacket pocket and grabbed his car keys. "I'll talk to you tomorrow. Be good for Michael and Dara."

Rolling his eyes, David picked up his football. "Yeah, yeah. And you be good for your date, make sure you don't drink too much, and no funny business."

"Wise guy." Giving David a final wave, Niall left the house and prayed for his car to start. It took several tries for the engine to turn over, but eventually it caught and he drove away.

Lately he'd had problems with it stalling out, and he kept his fingers crossed, hoping he could put off that expense for another year. Angie was more than generous with her support, but that didn't extend to his personal vehicle, and a car payment was an added expense he didn't need. The house with its high property taxes—even if he only paid half—ate up a good chunk of his income, but he managed by being extremely frugal, never taking a vacation, and cooking almost every night. Still, his savings account was far from healthy, so he always jumped to take the substitute teaching jobs when they were offered.

He'd deliberately picked a place closer to Albany for his date, far enough away that he doubted anyone he knew would see him. It took him forty minutes to drive to the restaurant near Colonie, which gave him plenty of time to calm his pounding heart.

"It's just drinks. One glass of wine, and that's it."

Tim, his date for the evening, was a history professor at SUNY Albany. He was forty, and over their chats, he'd told Niall he'd come out about ten years earlier. His family wasn't accepting, but he'd made his peace with their absence from his life.

Niall entered the restaurant and immediately spotted Tim at a table by the window—and from Tim's smile, he recognized Niall as well. He stood.

"I see my dinner companion," Niall told the hostess and approached Tim. He looked a little older than his online picture, but his smile was easy and his eyes sparkled with warm golden lights.

"Niall? Hi, I'm Tim."

"Hi, nice to meet you."

"Thanks for driving all the way out here."

They sat facing each other. "Not a problem. As I said, I prefer to meet farther from home, since I'm just starting to date."

Their server approached, and they each ordered a glass of wine and decided on a charcuterie board to share. Tim took a piece of cheese.

"Tell me about living in the same town you grew up in."

Niall sipped his wine. "Well, Overlook is about forty minutes from here. I guess you'd call it out in the sticks compared to this area, but we think of it as bucolic. There's plenty of land where the kids can play, we all pretty much know each other, and it's a slower pace of life. We almost stayed in the Albany area when Angie and I married—we both went to SUNY Albany—and then she went to law school here as well but decided it was better to raise our son in Overlook."

"She gave up custody to you? Unusual for a woman." He brushed cheese crumbs off his lips and sipped his wine.

Niall bristled slightly at Tim's tone. "Angie and I made the decision that it was in David's best interest to stay where he was. He's very involved with the football team, and changing schools at the high school level and having him start in a new place without any friends would've been more harmful. They have a very good relationship."

"And you work at the same high school where you went to school? That must feel odd, walking through those halls. I couldn't imagine it."

"That's right, you said your father was in the army. So you moved around a lot?"

"Yes. Every few years. I can't even count the places I've lived, so staying in one place is odd to me. Now that I have tenure, I've settled down but still have the wanderlust."

Niall plucked a few grapes and ate them slowly as the silence grew between them. "It's good to travel, but I enjoy staying at home as well. There's something to be said for comfort and familiar surroundings."

"Where's your favorite place? I love Italy, but I've been thinking of going to Croatia and maybe Morocco." Tim's smile gleamed in the candlelight. "It's very romantic, I hear."

"I haven't been anywhere, really. It's almost impossible now with David's football schedule. And when he was younger, Angie couldn't get much time off, since she was working so hard to become partner at her law firm, and we had the house to take care of." For some reason, Niall felt almost apologetic. "We went to Barbados for our honeymoon, but that's about it."

Tim's brows rose high. "I see. Well, that can change. I love to travel. I go to Europe every summer. This year it was two weeks in Amsterdam, then another two in Prague."

"Sounds lovely."

"You wouldn't need a big house anymore either, once he goes to college. You could sell it and get an apartment."

Niall hadn't thought that far ahead, but he loved his house. It sounded like Tim was ready to change Niall's life to fit his. "I could, but I haven't thought about it. You have a place near campus?"

Tim finished his wine. "I do." He signaled the server, who came right over. "Another glass, please. Would you like one?"

He'd barely touched his. "No, thanks. I'm sticking to one since I have a long drive home."

"Should we order dinner? I'd hate for you to leave hungry, and it will give us the chance to talk and get to know each other."

Not that Tim wasn't attractive, but Niall felt zero physical spark, which was a shame. Online they'd connected so easily, but in person, he felt awkward. But maybe Tim was right and they needed more time.

"Sure." He consulted the menu. "I'll have the grilled salmon and a salad."

"And I'll have the sirloin and spinach."

With his glass refreshed and dinner sorted, Tim became more talkative. "Is there anyone left at the high school whom you remember?"

The last thing Niall wanted was to think about Keller Williams, but he was the first to come to mind. "Yeah, a few teachers, coaches, and some of the students are now teachers or administrators themselves."

"Must be odd, seeing people after so many years. Have they changed much or mostly stayed the same?"

"A little of both. I was the quiet kid in high school—surprise, surprise." He grinned. "I had a few friends, but mostly kept to myself. I wasn't in the same group as the people who are there now."

"High school is probably the single worst time in a person's life—at least it was for me. It's when I realized I was gay, but being surrounded by the military all my life, I knew I had to keep it quiet." Tim bit into a cracker. "Once I went to college, I was free. When did you know?"

Niall had to be honest, though it aggravated him that once again Keller Williams played a part in his life. "Everyone went to the football games on Friday nights. Even me. We'd sit in the stands, and I'd watch the players and couldn't stop staring at them. The power in their legs and the muscles in their arms. It was like a delicious buffet of look-but-don't-touch." He laughed. "Needless to say, I spent many sleepless weekends. It was a struggle to pretend to be someone I wasn't."

Their food arrived, and it was decent but nothing special, and Tim continued his questions. "So you haven't come out to anyone? No one knows?"

"Only my ex. And she guessed. When she told me my desire for her wasn't on a par with what she needed, I still couldn't come out and say it. I'm a coward."

"No. That's not true. It's something we always fear—rejection for who we are."

Niall considered Tim's words. "Maybe you're right. Anyway, she asked for a divorce. I couldn't blame her, and the split was amicable. As a lawyer, Angie always made more than I did as a school librarian, and now as partner, she's very comfortable. She pays David's child support and half the mortgage until David moves out. We both contribute to his college fund and all his expenses. She's happy now, and I'm glad for her."

"That's good, but your needs are just as important.

Have you thought of telling your son? Kids these days are much more accepting than in our generation. You might be surprised at how he responds."

The thought of coming out to David gave him stomach cramps, but Tim was right. David had queer kids in his friends group, and from what he'd noticed, no one paid attention to the same-sex high school couples he'd seen in the halls or when he chaperoned at school dances. And yet…

"Maybe. I have to think about it."

"What's to think about? He's your son, and you say you have a very good relationship. Better to tell him now than wait. That's what could upset and hurt him. Being gay is not a dirty secret."

Niall dropped his gaze. "I know. I've always known who I was, but it was a different era when I grew up. Small town meant smaller minds. My parents and I never talked. I think the longest conversation we ever had was what I'd want for dinner. They never told me about sex. God, I couldn't imagine that discussion."

"Are they still alive?" Tim asked.

"No. They were older when they met and married, and it took a while for my mother to get pregnant. She was forty when I was born, my father forty-eight. He died from lung cancer two years after David was born—he was never without a cigarette in his hand. My mother had COPD and heart issues, most likely from all the secondhand smoke. She died five years ago."

"I'm sorry."

"Thanks, but I have to say it didn't make much of a difference in my life. Maybe that makes me a terrible person." He shrugged. "My parents didn't like Angie—she's Italian, and they weren't happy we got married in the Catholic church. We never saw them except at Christmastime, and even then it was more out of duty than anything. They were very closed-minded people with whom I had nothing in common. Angie and I made sure that David would be raised to love everyone."

"I'm sure it will be okay."

They finished their meal, and Niall declined coffee. Were all dates like this—almost like a job interview with question after question? He didn't need lust, but as he'd suspected earlier, this would be a first and last time for Tim and him.

The check came and Tim took it, but Niall insisted on paying half. Tim frowned all the way out to the parking lot. They stopped at his car first—Niall had parked several rows past his Mercedes.

"Thank you again for the meal. I had a nice time." If he left now, he could be home in time for the eleven o'clock news.

Tim's eyes gleamed in the lamplight. "We could continue it at my place if you'd like. I'm only a few minutes from here."

"I—"

"Shh. Don't say no. I find you very attractive, and your innocence is a turn-on."

He reached out to touch his face, but Niall took a step away. "I'm not ready. I'm sorry."

Tim's gaze turned intense, but he merely nodded. "A kiss good-bye at least?"

He had little desire to feel Tim's mouth on his, so he gave a quick press of his lips to Tim's cheek. "Good night."

Swiftly and without looking back, he walked away, hoping his car would cooperate. He really needed to get a newer one. He didn't want to think of another winter getting stuck. It took several starts, but when the engine roared to life, he sent up a quick prayer of thanks. The last thing he wanted was Tim hanging around with an offer of help.

On the drive home, he did feel proud. He'd done it. Gone on a date for the first time with a man, and the world still continued along without incident. Maybe Tim was right and it was time to tell David. It was silly to keep it a secret. He had nothing to be ashamed about.

On Sunday evening, he sat in the living room, reading the newspaper, when David came home. He toed off his sneakers by the front door.

"Hi, Dad. How'd your date go? I wanted to text you, but we got invited to a party at Jane Saville's place and—"

"It's okay. Put your things away and come sit with me."

"Okay." David's brow furrowed as if he sensed something was brewing, but he did as told. "I'm just gonna get a drink first."

Niall heard the refrigerator open and close. David reappeared with a glass of ice water, and Niall said, "I'm so glad you never got hooked on sodas. Your mother insisted you not be allowed, except for special occasions. Or pizza." He grinned.

"Yeah, Coach Weaver always says water is the best thing." David parked himself in the love seat catty-corner from Niall's recliner and flung his feet over the arm. "So?" He cocked his head. "What's up? Did you have a good time? What's she like? How did you meet her?"

Heart pounding, Niall met David's inquiring gaze. "It was okay." He licked his dry lips. "I met him on an app. I went out with a man, David."

"A…man?" David's eyes widened and he paled; then pink washed over his face. "A guy? Wait…what? You-you're gay? B-but how?" He blinked rapidly. "You were married. When…? I don't understand. Didn't you love Mom?"

He rushed to David's side to reassure him. "Yes, yes I loved her. I still do. Just not…the right way." David's face flamed while his burned. "When I was growing up, it wasn't like now, with all the freedom to be who you are and Pride marches. Love is love hadn't visited Overlook yet. I'd see stories on the news of people getting beaten up…or worse. I was afraid. So I did what I thought was right and what was expected. But it was never the real me—that person I hid inside. And because she's so damn smart, your mother figured it out."

"Did you cheat on her…with other men?" David whispered, his face bright red.

Horrified, Niall shook his head violently. "No. Never. Absolutely not. I swear."

"Okay," David responded in a small voice, reminding Niall that for all his football playing, learning to drive, and partying with girls, David was only a fifteen-year-old kid. Being a teenager was hard enough. David shouldn't have to deal with his father's fucked-up life.

"I don't understand, Dad. How…I mean, you had me, so are you bi or…" David ducked his head, and Niall hugged him tight.

"It's okay to ask. I'm not bi, but I managed. And yes, we had you, and you're the single best thing to happen to me. I wouldn't change anything about my life because it would mean not having you."

If he was hoping for a Hallmark ending to the conversation, with David hugging him back, he was mistaken.

"I think I'm gonna go up to my room. Study the playbook Coach gave us. Is that okay?"

"Yeah, yeah, of course. I can order the pizza later." Inwardly, Niall cringed at his fake cheeriness, but Sunday nights were always pizza and watching television with a big bowl of popcorn.

"Uh, I'm a little full. We had a late lunch. Chris's mom made tacos. But you order for yourself." David ran upstairs, and to Niall, it looked as though his son couldn't get away from him fast enough.

"Yeah, kiddo. Sure. I'll see you later."

Head in his hands, tears rolling down his cheeks, Niall wondered if anything would ever be the same again.

CHAPTER SEVEN

"Hello? Coach Keller?"

Keller rubbed his eyes. *Two a.m. Damn.* "Yeah. Who's this?" Like the other times, the caller had blocked their number.

"D-do I have to give you my name? You said we could call if we have anything we wanna talk about."

Keller sat up in bed. "Yeah, yeah, of course. You don't have to tell me. First of all, are you in any trouble? Are you okay?"

"Yeah…I mean…I guess. I'm just really confused about stuff."

Keller breathed a sigh of relief. "All right. What're you confused about?"

"Um…well, it's my father."

A jolt of fear hit Keller. "He isn't hurting you, is he? I know you said you're okay, but I want to make sure."

"No, I'm fine. It's nothing like that. My father would never hurt me."

A massive weight lifted off his chest. "Good. That's great."

"It's just…" The boy's voice dropped lower and grew more difficult to hear. "Tonight he told me something really personal, and I didn't know what to say. I felt so weird. And I avoided him all night. We always hang out on Sunday nights. It's our thing. B-but now I just…" He trailed off. "I didn't have anyone else to talk to."

Filled with nervous energy, Keller flipped his comforter over and climbed out of bed to pace the bedroom while he talked. "I'm here, and I'll listen to anything you want to say. No judgment."

A shuddering sigh rattled from the boy. "I don't know if I should even say anything. I'm sure he hasn't told anyone else."

"Is your father in trouble? Does he need help?"

"No, it's not anything illegal. But…what do you do when everything you thought you knew gets turned upside down?"

Keller stopped his back and forth and sat on the bed. "I suppose it depends on what it is. If it's not hurting him or you, he chose you to confide in because he trusts you."

"I think he's scared I might be upset or even angry with him."

"Are you?"

"No. I love my dad. He does everything for me since my mom left."

Keller froze. As far as he knew, the only boy on the team whose mother wasn't home day-to-day was David, Niall's son. He forced himself to remain still.

"Is your father sick?"

"No. He's okay."

Relief rushed through Keller.

"I don't think I should tell you. It's really personal.

But…can I call you again?"

"Anytime. And I'll never repeat anything you tell me."

"Thanks, Coach." The whisper caught on a yawn, and Keller couldn't help smiling. "I think I can sleep now. Maybe I'll talk to my dad in the morning."

"That's a good idea. Sleeping on something that bothers you will always give you a fresh perspective. It sounds like you and your father have a good relationship, and talking might help."

"Okay, yeah. Maybe." A more pronounced yawn. "Good night, Coach."

"Night." The screen turned off. Was it David? It might be, but Keller couldn't be certain.

Keller lay in bed, turning the conversation over in his mind. What could have freaked David out so bad that he'd needed to call? The only thing he could imagine was Niall telling David he was dating. Maybe David was more worried about a stepmother living in his house than about his mother dating someone, considering she lived far away.

Still, it didn't explain what David had said: *"What do you do when everything you thought you knew gets turned upside down?"*

Could it have something to do with the strange vibe he'd felt from Niall during their confrontation in his office? Arguing with Niall had been a huge turn-on, and Keller could've sworn Niall felt the same. That recognition of mutual lust in his eyes when they'd gone nose-to-nose… *Damn.* He'd wanted to feel Niall's soft lips against his. Suck them and lick into his mouth.

"Stop it, you horny jerk," he scolded in the darkness. "This kid is hurting, and the other two are questioning themselves, and all you can think about is your dick. Don't be an asshole."

He closed his eyes and woke to the phone ringing. A glance at his bedside clock told him it was 4:37 a.m. He grabbed for his phone but knocked it off the nightstand.

"Dammit." Chasing it in the shadowed room, hoping to get it before the caller hung up, proved futile, and he turned on the light. By the time he found it under the bed, it had stopped ringing, but he saw he had a voice mail.

"Coach, I called you last week." That same muffled voice. Keller hadn't forgotten it. He couldn't. *"My mother found these magazines I hid under my bed. Of guys. She said she wouldn't tell my dad, but what if she does? He hates gay people."*

"Fuck," Keller swore and pounded the table with his fist. Keeping secrets was a hell of a way to live, and no one knew it better than him.

"I'm scared, Coach. What am I gonna do?" Some sniffling, and then, *"I gotta go. I'll see you at practice."*

The call ended, and Keller played it over and over until he had every word memorized. From now on, he'd make sure to sleep with the damn phone so it didn't happen again. He got up, made coffee, and ate a banana, chewing without tasting. What kind of a role model was he to others when he'd been incapable of handling his own life?

Maybe a run would do him good. He wanted to steer clear of the high school and the outdoor track for the time being, and recalled the path around the lake. He laced up his sneakers, grabbed a water bottle, and left the house. Several cars were parked in the lot, and he hoped the trail wouldn't be too crowded. He'd come to the park to get lost in his head. With nothing but the sound of birds and his pounding feet, maybe he could figure out what to do about the phone calls he'd received.

He started out at a slow pace, getting his legs into gear. With the morning air still cool and the sun filtering in through the leaves on the trees, the weather was perfect.

He hit his stride after half a mile and passed several people. Ahead on the path, he spotted two people running side by side, keeping an even pace with each other. Drawing closer, Keller recognized Niall. His companion was the woman Niall had been on a date with when Keller had met him briefly at The Flame. She was very attractive, and seeing Niall laughing and running with her, doubt invaded his mind as to whether his middle-of-the-night mystery caller was David after all. Niall certainly looked like he was enjoying himself.

Even though they'd argued the last time they spoke, it would be rude not to say hello, so he slowed his steps as he approached them.

He couldn't help admiring Niall's long muscular legs in his thin running shorts. A sheen of sweat gilded his face and arms, and damp patches darkened the front of his blue shirt and under his arms. Imagining the musky, hot taste of Niall's skin, lust roared through Keller, sending him reeling, and he needed a moment to gather his thoughts so he didn't sound like a babbling fool.

"Good morning, Niall." As expected, when Niall turned and met his eyes, he frowned, but the woman stopped and ogled him.

"Oh, you're Keller Williams. I'm Marcie Brown. My ex used to be a big fan, and I watched you play too. Niall." She elbowed him. "We saw you at The Flame, but Niall said he didn't know you."

Keller put on his most winning grin. "Niall, are you keeping me your little secret?" He held out his hand. "Nice to meet you." She shook it, letting her fingers linger against his palm as he drew away. Keller hoped she wasn't playing Niall.

"No, of course I wasn't," Niall grumbled. "I mean, we're not friends. He coaches my son. That's all."

"I'd heard there was a fuss about the team, but since I don't have children, I didn't bother to pay attention. Maybe I should have." Her gaze was assessing and frankly a bit obvious, and Keller felt uncomfortable, especially if she and Niall were a couple. Niall seemed oblivious.

"Niall's son is a star running back. He's definitely going to help us in our run for the state championship." He addressed Niall, who focused on everything else around them but him. "Are you coming to the game Friday night?" From David, he knew Niall always came to support him, but Keller wanted to poke him.

"Of course. I go to all of them," Niall responded irritably.

Niall was like a cat you awakened out of a nap—all grouchy and growly, ready to scratch, but still cute enough to want to pet.

"Good. I'll see you then. Nice to meet you, Marcie." He jogged away and headed home.

Much as he would have liked to stay and dig deeper, he had a busy week ahead. All his effort and concentration had to be on the team and their first game. Funny how he'd never thought he'd coach a high school team, but he'd caught the passion, and now that was the driving force in his life.

It was second and goal at the nine-yard line. Less than a minute remained in the fourth quarter, and they were a field goal behind. Keller had called a time-out—the team's last—and had his offense in a huddle.

"Okay. We're gonna run diamond formation. Shane— you're in shotgun. David, Freddy, and Brenden—you fan out like we practiced. Rest of you—cover Shane's butt and let him make a throw. Got it?"

"Yes, Coach," they answered in unison.

"Who are we?" he shouted.

"We are Tigers! Hear us roar!" they yelled.

The crowd in the stands were on their feet, and Keller's ears rang from the noise. The cheerleaders were doing their thing, but all Keller could see was his kids. Heart pounding, and sweating under those unforgiving Friday-night lights, Keller paced the sidelines. He hadn't been this nervous since he'd stepped onto the field for the Super Bowl.

"White 80. White 80, hut, hut," Shane called out. The ball was snapped and he fell back, waiting. Then scrambling. Keller heard the yells, and Shane threw it to David, who ran into the end zone. He jumped high, and Keller's heart stopped as his hands fumbled for a moment. David grabbed the ball tight and clutched it to his chest, even as the tackle from the opposing team knocked him off his feet. David held on.

The referee lifted his arms, signaling a touchdown, and from the roar of the crowd, Keller would've thought an explosion detonated. His ears rang.

With twelve seconds on the clock, the special team slowly walked to the field to make the extra point. The kicker did so easily, and the buzzer sounded. The game was over, and they'd won. David had risen to his feet and was mobbed by his teammates, and Shane was getting pats and high fives.

"We did it, Coach." They all ran to him, and he nodded, his assistant coaches flanking him.

Leon murmured, "A win is a win, but…"

He nodded. "Yeah. I'm not happy. Let's go to the locker room, and we'll talk."

He could see the local news station filming and didn't want to have his post-game talk with the team put on blast. Once inside, he fixed the excited faces with a frown. They quieted when they saw he wasn't celebrating with them.

"Yes, we won. But it was messy. Too many missed opportunities. We're a better team, and we got lazy. Defensive tackles—you let too many runners slip past you.

Offense—you had trouble completing the plays. Shane—you had two interceptions—"

"That's 'cause David and Brenden were double-teamed."

"I don't want excuses. You're the quarterback. It's your job to pivot and find someone else to catch that ball or make the run yourself. That's what makes a good player great. Thinking ahead."

Shane's cheeks flamed. "Yes, Coach."

The room grew silent, and Keller saw the dejected slump of their shoulders.

Hank pointed to David. "You have to learn to be a little quicker at the snap to give yourself time to get down the field."

David cast his eyes to the floor. "I will, Coach."

Keller tempered his frustration with a smile. "I'm thrilled with the win, but I think—no, I *know*—we're a better team than they are, right?"

Some nodded, and others mumbled, "Yeah."

It wasn't his intention to thwart their enthusiasm. They had won, and every win should be celebrated. "I can't hear you…We're the best, and we're gonna kick butt next time. Am I right?"

"Yes, Coach," they shouted in unison.

"Okay. Get changed, and we'll meet up tomorrow morning at nine for practice."

Hank clapped his hands. "Defense—we've got some things to work on. Show up half an hour earlier."

From the kids' chatter, he'd heard they were all going to celebrate their win at Chris's house with pizza, and Keller couldn't help smiling. He left them to shower, noting the cheerleaders were hanging outside, waiting. Several of the girls blushed, and a few stared at him blatantly, thinking he would respond, but he merely nodded. Once outside the locker rooms, he was swarmed by the local television and radio stations for interviews.

"Keller, how did it feel to coach and not play ball?" Several microphones were shoved in his face.

"Well, they're totally different experiences. But I love teaching the kids what I know and seeing them on the field."

"Keller, are you upset that this was supposed to be an easy win and yet it wasn't?"

He frowned. "No win is easy. The other team has excellent players and coaches, and everyone has an equal chance when we step on the field. It takes lots of practice and hard work. These kids gave two hundred percent, and their opponents did the same. Thanks, everyone."

He pushed through the crowd, signed a few autographs, and made his way to the parking lot. Lucky for him, he had an assigned spot, but he still had to wait for all the others to leave. As he inched along, he caught sight of Niall standing beside his car, visibly upset and talking on his phone. Keller pulled in front of him, cut the engine, and exited his vehicle.

"What's wrong?"

Niall's grim face met his. "Nothing."

He rolled his eyes. "Of course. Obviously, it's nothing. That's why you're standing in a parking lot at ten at night instead of driving home."

Niall huffed out a grumpy sigh, and Keller bit back a smile. It was fun teasing him.

"It's been giving me trouble lately. I'm sure it'll start eventually. I tried Triple A, but they said it would be an hour's wait."

This gave Keller the perfect opening. "I'll hang out with you. I've got nowhere else to be."

A sour expression settled over Niall's face. "Really? Someone like you is alone on a Friday night?"

"What's that supposed to mean? Someone like me?"

Niall lifted a shoulder. "I mean, you're a celebrity. I'm sure you have a hundred people you could call to be with."

"Is that what you think?" Keller asked, the longing for

what he'd lost hitting him hard. Not the partying, but the camaraderie and knowledge that he'd had a place to go. His mom would've loved this, and several times during the game he imagined hearing her voice cheering him on. He wished he had someone there to confide in. Elijah had been that person for him, but he had his family life now, and Keller needed to find his own path. "I'm the new guy in town. I might've grown up here, but I don't know anyone anymore. I'm alone, so if you'd like, I can stay until the tow truck comes." He grinned. "After all, you'll need a ride home."

"I mean, you can, but I don't understand why. And I'm sure the tow company can get me home."

"Why are you making it so difficult?" Frustrated, Keller jammed his hands into the pockets of his sweats. "I'm trying to be nice, and you keep slamming the door in my face."

"Better than getting it shoved in a toilet, wouldn't you say?" Niall lashed out. "I don't need your pity because now you feel guilty for the way you ignored everything while your friends tortured me when we were in high school. Nothing can make up for the humiliation they put me through."

Stunned and shaken by Niall's words, Keller remained quiet. The pain Niall still carried had bled into his everyday life, and Keller couldn't blame him.

"I'm sorry."

"For what?" Niall's lips twisted in a grimace. "That it happened, that you never did anything to stop it, or that you're friends with these people?"

His gaze clashed with Niall's. "I'm not responsible for what someone did over twenty years ago. Was it right? Absolutely not. Did I do it? No."

"Do you know how it felt, running through the school with no clothes and only a towel because someone thought it was funny to steal my stuff when I took a shower? Have you ever had to put on soaking-wet clothes in the winter because you found everything you owned shoved in the toilet when you came in after gym to change?"

"No," he whispered, horrified at what Niall had gone through. He'd been oblivious, wrapped up in his own misery of being responsible for things at home, missing his father, and knowing he was gay and scared to death his teammates would find out. "I'm sorry. I didn't know what they were doing to you." Sure, he'd heard the guys laughing about pranks they played on the underclass students, but he'd barely paid attention to them. And though it was the truth, it sounded lame even to his ears. Keller wasn't sure he'd believe himself either.

And Niall wasn't moved. "How could you not? Any one of you on the team could've said something, and Bobby would've stopped, but you didn't."

"I had no idea they were bullying you. That's the truth. I was on the team, but they weren't my friends. Contrary to what you think you knew, I didn't hang out with them." Keller toed the gravel at his feet.

Niall snorted. "Are you kidding? You were one of the most popular guys in school, the golden boy. I'm not buying it."

There had been so much to lose if anyone had discovered Keller's secret. What if they'd followed him around and discovered he met up with other guys? Seventeen-year-old Keller's confidence was reserved for the football field. Everywhere else he was a mess. And that included being oblivious to all the bullying tactics of his teammates and their bragging at how they teased the underclassmen. He'd lived inside his head, with little room for anyone else.

"I know my words now don't make up for what happened then. I doubt anything I could say would. But I'm not the same person I was when I was seventeen, and thank God for that. I don't think any of us are. I'm here now, and I'd like to help you."

Niall's phone rang and he answered it, turning his back

to Keller. His shoulders slumped. "I see. All right. Thanks." He faced Keller with an aggravated expression. "They said because of an accident on the thruway, their trucks are tied up. They have no idea when someone can come, and I'm sure I'll need a tow." He bit his lip, and Keller's heart skipped a beat. "I guess if that offer for a ride home is still open…" He left it hanging.

"Yeah, of course. Come on." He waited for Niall to lock the car, and then Niall joined him in the front seat.

Niall laughed for the first time that night. "Why did I bother to do that? The car's a clunker and it's dead. Who's going to steal it?"

Keller chuckled. "Force of habit? I've had mine garaged for so long, I never bother to lock it." He started the engine and moved to join the thinning crowd. Traffic flowed quickly, and they were soon out of the parking lot and onto Main Street.

"I live on Bayberry Court. It's pretty close."

Keller stopped at the light. "You know, it's kind of a tradition for the winning team to celebrate."

Niall shot him a look. "They are. Pizza party at Chris's house."

"But I wasn't invited. How about joining me for a drink?"

"I don't think so."

"Why? Are you dating Marcie?"

Niall's brows flew up. "What? No. We're friends." A wry smile teased his lips. "She couldn't stop talking about meeting you. I'm sure you could call her up and she'd be happy to help you celebrate."

The light turned green, and Keller knew he only had a few minutes to change Niall's mind. "I'm not interested."

I want you.

It was true. He hadn't been able to stop thinking of Niall since their first meeting, even before he knew who he was.

The pricklier Niall acted, the more Keller wanted to be stung.

"She's very nice and runs her own business. And she's into sports, and as you saw for yourself, she's very fit."

"If she's so perfect, how come you're not dating her?" Keller shot out, curious to hear Niall's response. The early morning conversation with the anonymous player came to mind. *Was* it David he'd spoken to? Had Niall come out to his son? Why did he care?

Because…I want to know. I want to know…him.

"Just take me home, please." Apparently, Niall didn't feel the same, but Keller prided himself on being a persistent bastard and wasn't ready to give up.

"Niall, come on. We haven't gotten off on the right foot, and I'm not kidding when I say I'm alone here. It's hard being back in Overlook without my mother." Only to Elijah had he revealed the truth. His mother had been his rock, and her death had left a gaping hole in his heart.

The annoyance in Niall's eyes faded. "Oh…yeah…I'm sorry about that. She was a very nice lady. It's horrible what happened to her. But you live in her house. Isn't that harder? How come you didn't sell it?"

"Because I want to keep her close to me. Maybe sometime in the future I'll be able to, but not now." As much as it hurt to talk about his mother, Keller continued to drive toward the main part of town, hoping Niall would agree to come out with him. It would be worth it, to get to know this grouchy man. He drove into the parking lot behind Fruit of the Vine, the little bar and restaurant in the town center.

He cut the engine, and Niall folded his arms and shot him an aggravated look. "Funny, but this isn't my house."

"I took a chance."

His brows rose. "So, you kidnapped me."

"If you can call bringing you to have a drink with me kidnapping, but I prefer to think of it as doing what's best for both of us."

"Is that so?"

Having fun, now that he could see Niall playing along, Keller continued. "I mean, why should both of us sit at home alone when we could be enjoying ourselves?"

"Half of that statement might be true, but it's yet to be seen if I'll enjoy being with you."

Keller's heart bounced happily at Niall's teasing.

"Was that a joke at my expense?" He opened the door. "I'll take it. Come on. Let's have a celebratory meal and drink. My treat." Still uncertain, he held his breath until Niall fell into step with him.

"Dinner together? I see the treat for you, but like I said before, what's in it for me?"

Keller grinned. Who knew Niall would be so much fun?

CHAPTER EIGHT

What was wrong with him?

Niall chewed on a piece of crusty bread, pretending disinterest as Keller gave his order to the server. He wasn't supposed to be enjoying himself. He should have insisted that Keller take him home, but he couldn't say the words.

"Niall?" Keller's voice brought him around, and he blinked.

"I'm sorry?"

Amusement glimmered in Keller's eyes. "Your order?"

"Oh, uh, I'll have the grilled shrimp." *Dammit*. Why did he feel so fumbling and unsure?

"And?" Keller prompted. "Your drink?"

"A glass of Chardonnay." He picked up his water glass to take a sip and cool his heated cheeks.

Their server left, and Keller leaned in close. "I'm just a regular guy. No need to be overwhelmed by my presence."

Of course Keller would say something outrageous while he was drinking, and Niall choked, spewing liquid. "What the hell? What's that supposed to mean?"

Keller's grin broadened. "I think you just proved my point."

Hoping his fingers didn't tremble, Niall set the glass of water on the table. "You're saying things to pull a reaction from me. I'm not overwhelmed by you. I'm…annoyed I let you drag me out here."

Keller's smile dimmed. "Is it really so bad? I just didn't want to go home yet, but if you're that unhappy, I'll get our meals to go and we can leave. I'll drop you at home."

Now he felt like a complete shit. "N-no, it's fine. I'll manage."

He accepted his wine from the server and was about to take a sip when Keller held his up. "To new friendship and leaving the past behind? Where it belongs?"

He couldn't refuse without seeming ungrateful, so he tipped his glass. "Thank you for rescuing me."

Their salads came, and Keller dug in, chewing with gusto and waving his fork as he spoke. "David's a great kid and has real talent. Do you think he's going to want to go for a college scholarship?"

Talking about his son was safe ground, and Niall's tension eased. "I know he loves playing, but does he have what it takes to go pro? I don't know…I'm not sure that's the right life for him. Maybe I should've been concentrating on it more and aiming for it like your friend Bobby Contard, but I've had other stuff to deal with."

Annoyance sparked in Keller's eyes, and he set his fork on the table. "Okay. Can we stop with calling Bobby Contard *my friend*? Jesus. I haven't seen the guy since I left for college and came home, and you're making it sound like we're best buddies when the truth is, I don't even like the jerk." He gentled his tone. "Please give me a chance to show you I'm not like him. At all."

Niall flushed. "It's easy for you. You weren't on the receiving end of the bullying."

The taut lines in Keller's face softened. "I know that now. And I'm really sorry you went through it. But…" He huffed and ran a hand through his hair. "Trust me, I am *not* the person you knew in high school."

"I didn't know you at all," Niall shot back.

"Exactly." Keller smacked his hand on the table. "And yet you still dislike me." He thrust out his jaw. "I'm not going to hurt you."

Niall sensed something dangerous in Keller's gaze, and a thrill ran through him. "I know that. Okay, we can try. That's all I can promise."

Happy now, Keller bounced in his seat like a kid. "Great." He drank half his wine, and Niall, caught up in his brilliant smile, felt reckless as well and drained most of his. Their meals were served, and Keller kept him laughing with stories of his mishaps on and off the field and how his agent and personal assistant both managed to keep it all out of the press.

"Where are they now? Your agent and PA?"

The light in Keller's expressive face faded. "Gone. Once I got hurt and the endorsements dwindled to almost nothing, they both found excuses to leave. I've got a new agent now, mainly for endorsements." He shrugged. "I've gotten used to the fact that no one stays. No, actually, that's not true. Elijah's stuck by my side since we met our rookie season. Our moms became best friends too. They're both gone, way too soon." He toyed with his steak. "You and your ex are still friends, though? That's unusual."

"Yes. Angie and I are close."

"Even though she's seeing someone?" At his startled expression, Keller shrugged and crunched a french fry. "David's mentioned it."

Niall placed a smile on his lips. "Yes, I'm okay with it. She deserves to be happy."

"So the question is, if she's such a wonderful mother and wife, why did you get divorced?"

"We realized we were great friends but not in love." It was the line that always worked for people. Except Niall should've realized Keller Williams wasn't most people.

"Did you ever love her?" His food forgotten, Keller propped his chin in his hand and gave him a penetrating, blue-eyed stare.

"Why—why would you ask me that? She was my wife. Of course I loved her." He finished his wine.

"But not the way a husband should?" Keller murmured.

"What?" he asked, overcome by that same heart-stopping sensation he'd felt in his office when they'd argued. His breath came in short, raspy pants, but he couldn't look away.

"It didn't feel right, did it?" Keller leaned in close. "She wasn't who you wanted."

God, he *burned*. What the hell was happening? Keller's lips were mere inches from his, and Niall ached to feel the hot press of his mouth. He blinked, realizing they were in a public space and people he knew could see him. Terrified, he shifted his chair away from the table and hastily shoved a shrimp and some vegetables into his mouth.

"I don't know what you're talking about."

"It's okay." Keller nodded. "I understand."

"I wish I did," Niall muttered, and without tasting his food, finished his meal.

"Coffee and dessert?" Their server waited at the end of the table, and while Keller nodded, Niall frowned.

"I have to be getting home."

Keller acknowledged the man waiting patiently by the table. "Then it's up to me. I'll have a chocolate mousse, but you can wrap that up to go. And the check, please."

"Sure thing." The server hesitated. "Mr. Williams, would

you mind…I mean, could I get your autograph? I know you must get this all the time, but I watched you play for years."

"Of course, but you have to call me Keller. What's your name?"

"Kyle."

"Okay, Kyle, here you go." Niall watched as Keller made small talk with the young man and he signed a piece of paper. "How about a picture?"

Kyle beamed. "Really? I didn't want to ask and be annoying, but that would be so cool."

"It's never annoying to talk to a fan. Here." Keller handed Niall the phone. "Take a picture of us, please."

Surprised at Keller's easy interaction with his fan, Niall took several and handed the phone to Kyle.

"Thanks so much, Keller," Kyle gushed.

"You get it printed out, and I'll sign it too the next time I come by."

"Awesome. I'll have your dessert and the check in a minute." Kyle bounced away, and Niall saw him rush to the others and show off the pictures.

"That was very nice. You didn't have to do it."

Keller frowned. "Sure I did. He was a fan."

A simple yet perfect explanation from a man Niall was beginning to realize wasn't as one-dimensional as he'd initially thought.

Kyle brought the mousse in a bag and their check.

"You don't have to pay for me," Niall said, pulling out his wallet.

Ignoring him, Keller signed it and gave a large cash tip. "Ready to go?" He rose to his feet. "You can pay next time," he flung over his shoulder with a cocky wink.

"Next time?" Niall scrambled after him. "Says who?"

Keller ignored him and walked away but was surrounded by several diners who ran up to him asking for pictures and autographs. Niall hung back and watched as Keller engaged with each person, always with a smile and a kind word.

"Niall?" Keller stood by his side. This close up, Niall could see the lines fanning out from his eyes, several faint scars on his brow, and a jagged one on his chin that peeked through his golden-brown scruff. Football wasn't all glamour and glory, and Keller must've suffered playing the game. His fingertips tingled, itching to trace the lines. "You ready?"

Afraid he'd be called out for staring, Niall nodded and walked away without a word. He remained silent during the car ride home, and to his shock, Keller did as well, until he turned onto Bayberry Court.

"You'll have to tell me the number of your house."

"Twenty-four."

Keller drove into the driveway and turned off the engine. "Pretty area. Have you lived here long?" As it had at dinner, that blue-eyed gaze captured him, and Niall froze, electrified by their proximity. Was he getting signals from Keller? The guy was straight. It didn't make sense. But neither did the ache of longing beating through him. Niall had never wanted to kiss or be kissed more. He cleared his throat.

"Uh, since David was little. Angie got her promotion and a big raise, so we could afford the mortgage. My salary alone would never cover living in this part of town." He laughed nervously, completely confused by his physical response to Keller's innocuous questions. It had to be the wine. He must've drunk it too fast, and it had obviously gone to his head.

Keller's expression intensified. "You're a good father, Niall. I can tell you've given up a lot for David."

Fear rushed through him. "Thanks for dinner and the ride home. I appreciate it." Without giving Keller a chance to answer, Niall fled from the car and ran into the house. His heart pounded as he locked the door behind him and leaned against it.

"Jesus, what's wrong with me?" He rubbed his face and

went to the kitchen to get a cold glass of water. His phone buzzed, and afraid it was Keller, he ignored it, but that made no sense as Keller didn't have his number. When it stopped and started up again, he pulled it from his pocket and saw it was Angie. With a smile, he answered.

"Hey, how are you?"

"I'm good. I heard the team won and David caught the winning touchdown. I spoke with him earlier. He's so excited."

"Yep. He played a great game." He heard a voice in the background.

"Grant wants to know if it's true that Keller Williams is really their coach."

"Uh, yeah. He is."

"Have you spoken with him? What's he like?"

"He's fine."

Of course he should've known Angie would notice something was off. "You don't like him?"

He made a fist on top of the counter. *God, would this conversation never end?* "No. I said he's fine."

"But there's something. You sound funny," she pressed. "Ooh, wait. It said in the news that he returned home to his high school, and you're about the same age. Did you know him?"

"No," he responded firmly. "I didn't know him at all." Leaving his glass of water in the kitchen, he went into the living room, where he paced the shiny wooden floor. "Anyway, David's not home. He's at Chris's. They're having a victory party there."

"Yes, he told me earlier in the week that if they won, that's where they'd go. And next week it's your place."

"God help me," Niall muttered, and Angie snickered.

"Oh, don't worry. It'll be fine."

Niall debated whether to tell her, but decided she should know. "I told David I started dating again. And that I was dating men."

"Ohhh," she breathed. "How did that go?"

He dropped into the chair and stared at the muted swirls of color in the Turkish rug in front of the sofa. "I'm not sure, but not well…I think. He's barely spoken to me since."

A FaceTime message popped up, and Angie appeared on his screen. "This deserves a face-to-face conversation. I wish I could've been there when you told him."

"It wasn't planned. I let it slip that I had a date, and he assumed it was with a woman. And the man I'd gone out with made me believe I deserve to have it out in the open."

"You do, Niall. Being gay isn't something to be ashamed of. You shouldn't have to hide who you are."

"I'd hoped David would feel that way. But…you should've seen his face." His voice caught. "He couldn't wait to get away from me."

"I'm sure it was just the shock."

Her attempt to comfort him failed. He knew the truth.

"I always take him to school, and on game day we have a thing where I make him a big carb breakfast—pancakes and waffles and bacon. Today he didn't want any of it, said he and the other guys were meeting up for an early morning run to get the mood going."

"Maybe that's all it was. New year, new practices? Come on, David loves you. He'll come around."

"He didn't say anything to you when you spoke with him?"

"No, but he was with his friends, so he wouldn't."

His heart sank. "I don't know what I'll do if I lose him."

"Niall," she protested. "That's not going to happen. Give him a few days to let it sink in."

His phone pinged. "Wait. It's a text from David." He pulled it up to read.

Is it okay if I spend the weekend at Chris's? His dad will take us to practice.

Yes. See you on Sunday.

K.

Dejected, he rubbed his face and repeated the message to Angie. "He's avoiding me. I never should've said anything. It's too soon. I could've waited until he went to college."

"Stop it, Niall. You deserve to be happy. When he comes home on Sunday, talk to him."

"Yeah, sure. I will."

She glared at him. "You won't. You're the ultimate non-confrontationist. Please start thinking of yourself. David will be fine. It'll all work out."

"Thanks, Angie. I'll talk to you."

The screen went dark, and he pulled up David's message again and sent another return text.

Okay, but I hope we can talk?

Yeah, sure.

He had to believe it would be okay.

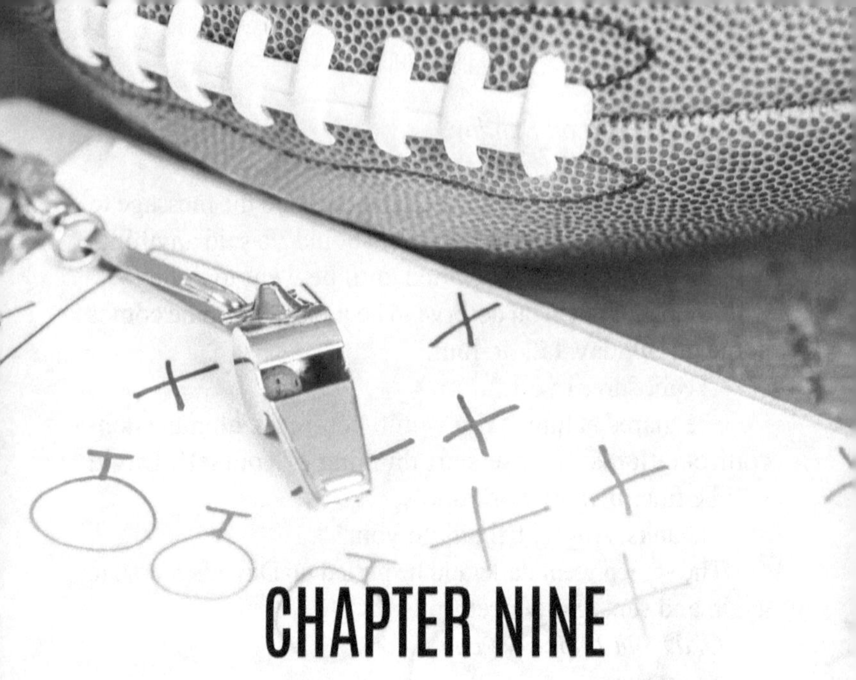

CHAPTER NINE

"Blue 80, Blue 80, hut, hut."

He'd started teaching the kids some of the NFL tricks of the trade, and calling out before the snap was one of the indications to get ready. They'd also begun learning his sideline hand signals.

From his vantage point, Keller watched the snap to the quarterback and nodded with satisfaction as Shane faded left, then ran right and hit Brenden downfield.

"Kid listened to you, Keller," Leon murmured. "He was getting puffed up in the head, thinking he was too good for coaching, but maybe you set him straight. It's hard for him living with a father like Contard who never shuts up about his high school glory days."

"I don't care what it was, but I'll take it. I didn't like having to dull their shine after the win, but I wanted to nip any kind of attitude early." He cupped his hands around his mouth. "Okay, that was good. Defense—practice your coverage." He pointed to Hank. "Get out there with them and make sure they follow the playbook."

After practice, the kids piled into the locker room. They sat on the benches, guzzling sports drinks, and he stood in front of them.

"All right, you were sharp out there. Shane—good passing. I like that you moved quicker out of the pocket. Eddie, Dalton, Chase, and Oliver"—he ticked off the guards and tackles—"nice protection, good blocking, keep it up." The boys' eyes lit up, and Keller figured that after giving them what for the previous night, they deserved the praise. "And Brenden, Van, Chris, and David—nice, sharp break at the snap. You made it downfield damn fast." He scanned the group. "I'm proud of all of you. And we're going to make sure we keep this up so Friday night we get another one in the win column. Am I right?"

"Yes, Coach," they all yelled.

"All right, hit the showers."

He drank his water and leaned against the lockers, chatting with Hank and Leon about some of his old plays, when he heard shouting. The three of them ran to the showers to see what was happening, and found Shane and Van standing naked and eye to eye, Shane holding Van's wrist in a hard grip.

"What's going on here?" Keller demanded. "Shane, let him go."

"Nothing's going on." Shane released Van and cast his eyes downward.

Keller stepped between them. "Listen. We don't fight. What did I say the first day? We're a family. We look out for each other. Look at me, Shane." He met the boy's gaze with a frown. "You got it?"

"Yeah, but—"

He folded his arms. "Yeah, but what? You gonna argue

with the coach? That's a surefire way to get benched for a game. Keep it up, and it'll be the whole season."

Shane paled, then laughed. "You can't—"

He put a finger up. "If I were you, I wouldn't tell me what I can or can't do, because you won't like my answer. Now go shower and get dressed." A muscle ticked in Shane's jaw, but he dropped his head and faced the row of lockers. A large bruise spread between his shoulder blades. Keller winced. "Wait a sec, hold up. How did you get that bruise on your back?"

Shane lifted a shoulder. "Me and my dad were practicing. I ran into a tree." He flexed. "It don't hurt, and it won't keep me from throwing."

"Make sure your mouth doesn't either. But you should have it looked at. Now go, all of you. Except Van."

Hank and Leon waited beside him.

Van had picked up a towel from the bench and wrapped it around his waist. His gaze remained fixed to the floor.

"Look at me, please. Have you had problems with Shane before?"

Van was one of the kids who wouldn't meet his eyes when he'd given the team his phone number.

"No," he replied softly and shrugged.

Van was a big kid, and surprisingly light on his feet, but he was also quiet. Keller was well aware that issues, concerns, and problems were often swept aside if the person was too intimidated to speak.

"Anything you feel like talking about?" Keller moved closer so they wouldn't be overheard. "You know you can tell me anything."

Van reddened, then lifted his chin. "I came out to my friends the other day. Some of the kids treat me differently. Not everyone, but like…me 'n Shane used to be friends. Now he's cut me dead." His voice trembled. "He's the one who's changed, not me."

Keller motioned with his hand. "Yeah? Changed how?"

Van blinked rapidly. "I dunno. Just, we used to hang out, and now he can't."

"Why not? Do you know?" Keller prompted, sensing something evasive in Van's words and body language.

Van shrugged. "No. He's just always with his dad. I gotta go, Coach. My mom picks me up, and she's got a babysitter at home for my little sister."

"Okay. Just know if you need to talk—about anything—you've got my number."

A brisk nod, and then Van hustled away to his locker. Keller sighed and dropped to the bench. There was more to Van's story than he was letting on, but he couldn't force the boy to speak.

One by one, the kids filed past him. Hank and Leon waited with him, and Keller pointed to his watch. "You guys go. I know you have families to get home to. I'll stay and make sure they all get out okay."

"I like how you handled that." Leon's approval meant a lot to him, as Keller knew he'd been with Coach Weaver for years. "George, for all his greatness on the field, really didn't have the best handle on the kids off it." Leon cracked a smile. "As you know."

Keller's grin was wry. "Yeah. And trust me, seventeen-year-old Keller Williams is kicking me in the ass all the damn time."

The three of them laughed.

"See you, Keller," Hank called out. "Good practice."

He cleaned up a bit and was about to leave when he heard a sound from the bathroom. Curious, he went to check, and saw Shane struggling to put on his shirt. The bruising he'd seen earlier wasn't confined to his shoulders—there was some along his ribs as well. Keller rushed to his side to help slide it over his head.

"Are you sure you're not in pain? Those look pretty

nasty. Maybe you should go to the hospital. Do you want me to call your parents?"

Shane's blond brows shot high. "N-no. I'm fine. It just hurts a little, I swear. I'll go home and take something for it." Shane's phone rang, and Shane barely had a chance to say hello before Keller heard Bobby yelling so loud, it was as if he'd put him on speaker.

"Where the fuck are you? I'm waiting out here. I gotta get to work."

Shane met Keller's eyes. "I'll be right out." He ended the call and shoved the phone into his pocket. "I gotta go, Coach."

"Sure, Shane," Keller responded gently.

Shane grabbed his backpack and ran.

Keller stood for a moment, then went to his car and drove to the sheriff's station. When the sergeant at the desk heard what he had to say, he ushered him into a room.

"You're saying you believe Bobby Contard is abusing his son?"

"I'm saying I think someone needs to check on what's going on in that house. The kid has massive bruising, and when I asked him, he said he fell into a tree. Maybe he did, but I also know his father is a hothead who believes in fists first. Please, just check it out," he appealed.

"Yeah, okay. We can send a couple of deputies over." The sergeant hesitated. "Would it be okay if I asked for your autograph?"

For the first time, he was annoyed at the request. This was too serious an issue to be thinking about anything else except Shane's well-being.

"Yeah. But you are going to send someone today, right?"

"Sure, sure."

He hoped they followed through, and that it was only him being overly cautious. In his car again, he sat and rested his head on the steering wheel.

"I miss you, Mom. You would've known the right thing to do." She'd always told him: *"Follow your gut about people. Your first instinct is usually correct."* Bobby Contard was a loudmouth who dwelled on the glory of his high school days and had never moved on. Was he taking his failure out on his son? Keller hoped he was wrong, but he couldn't ignore what he'd seen.

He drove away, needing to return to where he'd lost the most important part of himself, searching for answers.

"Keller, hi." Edna, the owner of the Overlook Diner, greeted him at the door. "I wasn't sure I'd see you back here."

He hadn't been too certain, either. Merely stepping out of his car in the parking lot and passing the spot where his mother died almost brought him to his knees. Knowing he'd missed her final moments was a knife-to-the-chest kind of pain that lived as a scar inside his heart. No matter how many years passed or how much laughter, he'd never be the person he was before the phone call telling him she was gone forever.

"I figured I'd try." Hands in his pockets, he shrugged. "Not sure I'll succeed, but…you know." His eyes burned.

"Yeah. I had a memorial bench put up for her. I don't know if you saw."

He hadn't. "I'll make sure to look for it when I leave."

"Did you want to eat here, or takeout? Or were you just stopping by?" A few people had lined up behind him.

"Seat them first. I haven't decided."

It should've been easier, but standing there, Keller found it difficult to take a breath. Spots circled in front of his eyes. *Was she at peace when it happened?* He wanted her final seconds to have been filled with joy. Why hadn't he insisted she come live in Vegas when he'd gotten hurt and retired? Maybe if he'd been more forceful, he could've worn her down, but he knew that was only wishful thinking.

"I belong here, and you have to find your own way."

"I'm sorry, Mom," he whispered and swayed.

A firm hand gripped his arm. "Keller? Are you all right?"

He gazed into concerned, ocean-blue eyes. "Niall? What're you doing here?"

A wry smile tipped up those generous lips. "Well, let me think. Usually people come to a diner to eat." The teasing light faded. "I'm certified in CPR. Are you okay? Do you need a doctor?"

"No," Keller murmured, hyperaware that Niall still held his arm and that he liked it. "I guess I'm a little overwhelmed being here, and I didn't have much to eat today. Practice ran a little late, as well."

"You should have something, then."

"Sit with me?"

Sudden awareness flared in Niall's eyes, and he released his arm. "I-I…" he stuttered, and took a step away.

"Please?" Keller bit his lip. "What if I faint and fall face-first into my coffee and drown? I'll need that CPR." He grinned, and Niall's cheeks turned pink under his scruff. Suddenly Keller felt better.

"You're killing me with the bad jokes," Niall grumbled.

"Maybe you're the one who needs CPR." When Niall remained silent, Keller fluttered his lashes. "I can tell you all about David's practice this morning," he wheedled.

"I guess I can stay for a little while," Niall conceded.

Mentioning David was the reason he'd won the prize of having Niall as his brunch companion. No matter how harshly Niall treated Keller, there was zero doubt in Keller's mind that he'd do anything for his son. Including eating brunch with his supposed enemy from high school. But

Keller was determined that once they left the diner, that would be in the past and he and Niall Harper would be friends.

Once at their table and the coffee poured, Niall stared at the speckled Formica tabletop before blurting out, "I want to thank you. For last night. I don't think I said it, but I do appreciate that you didn't leave me stranded at the football field. Seems the car needs a new alternator, and the gasket is shot—coolant has been leaking into the cylinders."

"Meaning?" He didn't know much about cars, but it didn't sound good.

Niall's frown overwhelmed his entire face. "Meaning I need a new car. Now. The repairs would be ridiculously expensive, and I don't feel like pouring money into a ten-year-old car." He brushed away the strands of hair hanging in his eyes. "I was going to pick up something quick here and head to the dealership to see if I can get a deal on last year's model or something. I've been putting it off long enough."

His dejection was painful to see. Keller had more money than he knew what to do with, and he could easily buy ten cars for Niall. He wished they were friends so he could make the offer, or at least loan him the money, but he knew that would put Niall's back up.

"I hope you can. They should have some bargains since the new cars are out and you don't want anything fancy, I'm sure."

That earned him a slight uptick of Niall's lips. "Not like what you're driving around, you mean?"

Keller had gotten himself talked into a Porsche Cayenne SUV—he liked its sleek lines, and the salesman had convinced him it would be good on the upstate roads.

"I don't know anything about cars," he admitted. "It looked nice, and hey," he shrugged. "It's a Porsche. I figured it would be fun to drive. But listen." An idea sprang to mind. "I'm not busy for the rest of the day. Why don't I tag along and keep you company?"

Niall opened his mouth, a protest welling up in those glittering eyes, and Keller held up a finger. "Come on. You want to take the bus to the lot? And if you don't find anything, have to take it home again or spend money on a cab? Use me. That's what friends are for."

Downcast, Niall focused his gaze on his coffee cup. "You're being very nice."

Keller laughed out loud. "I've been trying to tell you that. I *am* nice. I'm not the self-absorbed schmuck I was in high school." Keller lowered his voice. "Come on, Niall. Let's eat our waffles and bacon and get you a car."

Niall's dark brows flew up. "How did you know what I was going to order?"

Keller's grin threatened to take over his face. "I didn't. It's my favorite meal when I want to treat myself."

The waitress strolled over, pen to pad. "Ready, folks?"

Keller looked over to Niall, who despite his head shaking, was unsuccessful in hiding his grin. "Waffles and bacon, please, Marilyn. Extra crispy."

"Same for me, please."

"You got it. Would you mind if I asked for an autograph? My husband is a huge fan." She held out a piece of paper, and Keller took it along with her pen.

"Sure, what's his name?"

She blushed. "Just make it out to Marilyn."

Keller winked at her. "You got it."

Their meals came, and Keller decided to keep quiet and not push Niall, but it seemed Niall had a few questions of his own.

"What happened when you walked in? You really didn't look good, and I know it wasn't a ruse to get me to eat with you, because you had no idea I was even there."

"I was thinking about my mom."

Sympathy clouded Niall's eyes. "Oh. I'm sorry."

"It was her birthday. She was all I had. The only person who ever loved me. And in an instant…she was gone. I've been avoiding this place since I came home, but I wanted to prove I could do it."

"You can take your time. There's no need to rush it."

It hurt to breathe, but Keller forced himself to draw in air and gave Niall a wan, sickly smile. "Yeah? Maybe. I knew it would be painful. I just didn't know how much."

"And that's why you stay in her house?"

Keller's nod was short and sharp. "For her presence."

"And a little penance, maybe?"

Keller felt Niall's eyes on him. "I was a good son. I gave her everything."

"She probably wanted most what you couldn't give her. Time with you."

To his shame, a tear tracked down his cheek, and he brushed it away. "I called her all the time during the season and off-season, and I'd bring her to Vegas or take her on trips. I tried to get her to move there with me. I would've given her whatever she wanted. A house, car…anything."

Looking stricken, Niall leaned forward. "I'm so sorry. I didn't mean to make you feel bad. It sounds like you did everything you could for her." Niall tapped the table. "She loved you. And you loved her and did your best. That's all any of us can do."

Wanting desperately to change the topic of conversation, Keller asked, "Like you do with David? It can't be easy having a teenaged son to raise on your own, basically."

Niall's face drooped. "We're good."

"He's a nice kid and an excellent football player. I'm surprised you're so into him playing, considering your feelings about the football team."

"It was Angie's doing. She had him in cleats as a four-year-old. Her family was big into the game. They were all Orangemen."

"Ah. Good team. My alma mater. Is that what you'd like for him? He's big but fast. Light on his feet. I could see a scout going for him—maybe not top-tier schools, but definitely Division I."

"Like I've said before, we haven't decided yet. He's only fifteen. We have bigger issues to deal with."

His senses quickened. "Anything you want to talk about? I'm a good listener."

The tips of Niall's ears turned red. "David and I always work through everything. It'll be okay."

It would be, Keller decided, because he intended to keep his eye on the situation.

And Niall.

When they finished eating, Niall grabbed the check. "It's not the same as dinner, but I owe you one. It's the least I can do."

He crunched the last piece of bacon. "Damn, I should've gotten the eggs Benny."

"Oh brother," Niall muttered, lips twitching. "You never stop, do you?"

"I have no idea what you mean," Keller responded with a wide grin.

On the ride to the dealership, Niall grew increasingly nervous. "I hope they have something I can drive off the lot today. I can't be without a vehicle."

"I'm sure they will. Last time I passed by, they had tons of cars."

He pulled into Scarino's car dealership and parked. Niall opened the door. "Thanks for the ride, Keller. I appreciate it."

"I'm not leaving." At Niall's surprised face, he explained, "If they don't have a car, I can take you to another place."

Niall's cheeks grew pink. "Oh, uh, wow, that's really nice."

"I did mention my calendar is free. Use me."

Niall granted him his first full-blown smile. "Thanks,

Keller. I appreciate it."
   So do I, Niall.

CHAPTER TEN

"I can't believe how expensive a used car is." Frustrated beyond belief, Niall stared out the window of Keller's Porsche as they drove on the highway, paying little attention to the trees' beautiful early autumn colors. "It's been a long time since I had to think of buying one. I know Angie was going to look into one for David next year."

"She makes a lot of money, huh?" Keller asked, shooting him a quick glance.

Niall admired Keller's strong hands on the steering wheel. The sun caught the glint of golden hair on his forearm and also highlighted the thin lines of scars running from his elbow up under the sleeve of his T-shirt. Those injuries that had cut short a thriving career must've been devastating to a man like Keller who loved the game. Life hadn't gone as planned for him either. Realizing Keller waited for an answer, he pulled his gaze away.

"Uh, yeah. Mid-six figures, plus a big annual bonus. But she works her butt off."

"I don't doubt it. We have a few women coaches in the NFL, and they're great, but people concentrate on their gender more than the job they do. They're like bugs under microscopes. They have to work twice as hard to be taken as seriously."

"Angie loves it, and it gave us the chance to give David everything we didn't have growing up—the big house and peace of mind."

"Except for now."

"What do you mean?" His brows knitted.

"You're having a problem paying for a car," Keller said quietly. "The upkeep can't be easy."

Humiliation rushed through him. "I do the best I can. I make it work."

"I'm not saying you don't. I can tell you do everything you can for David."

"I do. And I will." He pointed. "There's the dealership."

Keller drove into the parking lot, and the moment they were out of the SUV, a salesperson joined them. No surprise there. Keller's car was more expensive than any available inventory, and the salesman must have been salivating at the thought of a trade-in.

"What can I do for you, gentlemen?"

Keller motioned to Niall. "He's the man. I'm just here for the ride."

"I'm Roy. What can I help you with?"

Niall glanced around. "I'm looking for a car—not more than five years old, and up to about forty thousand miles." Early that morning he'd worked out the finances and had a budget for what he could spend.

"Sure, sure. Lemme show you what I got."

He walked with Roy, aware of Keller trailing behind them. Of course, Roy showed him the high-end cars first.

"I got this gorgeous BMW X3 over here—"

"How much is it?"

"Only thirty-five thousand, five hundred dollars."

He winced. "I wasn't looking for a luxury vehicle. I was hoping not to spend more than fifteen to twenty thousand. Or two hundred and fifty dollars max a month for a lease, including taxes and extras."

"Not much inventory at that price." Roy's friendly demeanor vanished, and he stopped in his tracks. "We'd better look over there." He turned on his heel and led them to the far end of the lot. Niall checked out the stickers on the windshields. None of them were below twenty thousand, except for several older models that didn't look much better than the car he owned.

"This is so frustrating," he muttered, walking around the cars, peering into the interiors. "This one has almost ninety thousand miles."

Keller stuck his head inside the driver's side of another car. "And this one has fifty thousand. In a few years, you'll be in the same trouble as you are now."

Dejected, he leaned against the car door. "I know."

Eyes narrowed, Keller scanned the lot, and Niall wondered what was going on in that head of his because he had little doubt he was planning something. "Let me take a look. Maybe I'll find something," Keller said, and walked away.

He huffed out a laugh and called out after him. "What're you, a magician? You can't conjure a car out of thin air."

But Keller was already talking to Roy, and the two of them had their heads together. Once again, Roy was standing in front of the BMWs. Growing annoyed, Niall pushed off the car and approached them.

"I told you I can't afford this."

"Excuse us, Roy?" Keller patted the salesman on the shoulder. He waited until the salesman walked out of earshot.

"Look, Niall. I can get you any car you want on the lot for what you want to pay."

"What're you talking about?" Clearly, he was missing something. "You're not making sense."

Keller leaned against the trunk of the BMW, excitement brewing in those dancing blue eyes. "I made a little deal with Roy. I do a few commercials for his dealership for free, and he gives you a car at rock-bottom price."

He must be dreaming or hallucinating. "Wait, what?"

"Great, right?" Keller's grin was wide.

"Great? Great that I can't afford to pay for a car on my salary without someone else's help?"

"Don't think like that."

"Did you do this to humiliate me?" He strode away, but Keller ran after him.

"Wait, that wasn't what I meant. Niall, come on." Keller seemed sincerely distraught, and while it cooled his anger, the embarrassment remained.

"Maybe not, but it's how it looks to me. Like I can't take care of my family." Feeling the weight of the world on his shoulders, Niall sat on the bench in front of the dealership office. Keller sat beside him, his large frame disturbingly close.

"Can I ask you a question—and I hope you won't get mad at me…again?"

He shrugged. "Sure."

"Have you ever considered downsizing your house? It's beautiful, don't get me wrong, but it's pretty large for the two of you, and with David going to college in a few years, maybe it makes sense?"

His jaw hardened. "I won't do that to him. All his friends are in the neighborhood, and it was difficult enough for him to have Angie move far away. I know he says it's not a big thing, but they're close. I can't take away the home he's grown up in. Plus, we need the space for when his mother comes to visit."

"So you'll run yourself into the ground to keep up appearances?" Keller frowned.

Sensing judgment, he lashed out. "That's what you do for the people you love. Make sacrifices. You only have to think about yourself. I don't have that luxury."

He froze when Keller put a hand on his shoulder. "I'm sorry. You're right. I am selfish. I don't know about these things. I should've done that for my mom. Maybe she'd still be alive if I'd lived nearby." His hand slid away, and immediately Niall missed its warmth.

Guilt swelled inside him. "Shit. I didn't mean it like that. I'm sorry, Keller. You're not selfish. We do what we think is right at the time. Your home base was Vegas. You had to live out there—you couldn't fly across the country to play every time. I'm sure you had wonderful times with your mother."

"I tried. I did the best I could."

Before Niall could stop himself, he spoke from the heart. "We all carry the weight of memories that sometimes seem too heavy to bear. But when you share the burden with friends, it can help. Thank you for sharing with me."

"If I'm willing to do this to help you, what's it going to hurt—your pride?" A teasing smile lifted his lips. "I told you we'd become friends."

Niall chuckled. "You really are something else."

"So I've been told. Look, it's either this or we trade, and I'll give you my car and take one of these."

"You-you're being ridiculous," Niall choked out. Knowing the man, he'd probably do it too. Keller's gaze penetrated him to his very soul, the hidden part of who he was.

"Am I?" Keller murmured. "Don't tell me no. Please, Niall."

Their eyes locked.

Was he dreaming? He had to be because he wanted to tell Keller yes to everything. Including what he was imagining…

Maybe Keller was a witch and Niall had been placed in a trance because the next thing he knew, he was sitting in the office, Keller's powerful thigh pressed to his, and Niall was signing a lease for a ridiculously low price on a three-year-old BMW X6 SUV. He was promised the car's delivery by day's end.

"Keller," he began, once they were on the road again, but was cut off.

"Let me take you home."

"Okay." His throat was tight, and his heart pounded. Sweat dampened his shirt and ran down his back. There was no reason for him to be nervous, and yet he trembled. "I appreciate what you did. I just don't know why you're jumping through hoops for me."

"You don't?"

Keller turned onto his block and drove into his driveway. He cut the engine, and Niall opened his door. Without waiting for an invitation, Keller followed him up the steps, and Niall fumbled for the key before it slid into the lock and the door opened. The house was hushed and waiting, the air cool, shades drawn to keep out the harsh sunlight. He closed the door, and Keller stood right beside him.

"We've spent all day together, and you still don't get it, do you?"

"I don't understand."

"Maybe this will help," Keller said, then his lips came down over Niall's mouth and kissed the breath from his body. Niall clung to his shoulders, bones melting as Keller pulled him close. The hard dips of Keller's muscles molded to his, his erection huge and heavy on his belly, and Niall gasped. Keller took advantage and deepened their kiss, sucking his tongue, teasing and tasting.

"Keller," he moaned, shaking uncontrollably. "Keller."

Keller's large, rough hand gently cradled his face, and their kisses grew softer but no less searching. Niall couldn't fathom this was his reality, that Keller Williams was kissing him, but the waves of golden hair clutched between his fingers were silky to the touch, and the smell of sweat, heat, and man made him dizzy and reckless. Tentative at first, then growing bolder with unaccustomed desire, he touched his tongue to Keller's and sucked on it hungrily. Keller gave him the freedom to explore, all the while running his hands over Niall's trembling body.

His first kiss with a man, and like the dreams of his youth, it was with Keller Williams. Except this was no dream. It was reality, and he'd remember the taste of his tongue forever.

Keller's lips curved against his.

"I knew it."

"Knew what?" Niall whispered, afraid it was all a joke on Keller's part and he'd end up shattered on the floor.

"That you'd be perfect."

And Niall knew he'd be reliving this moment as the first time he'd ever felt alive.

"How…? I don't understand."

Keller's fingers ran across his cheekbones and traced his lips. "Understand what? How much I want you?"

"I didn't know." Niall hung his head and murmured, "That you're gay, I mean."

"We're alone." Keller nuzzled his neck. "You can say it out loud." He sighed. "My mother knew, and my best friend, Elijah. That's it. Now you. Three people. You are too?" At his nod, Keller kissed his cheek. "I'm assuming that's why you got divorced?"

"Angie found out. She said she didn't want a best friend who'd have to try harder to be passionate in bed."

Keller rested his cheek on Niall's temple. "If you'd been any more passionate, I would've ripped your clothes off right here."

Heat rushed to his cheeks. "I've never kissed a man before."

"Lucky me." That cocky grin he'd once hated, but now saw as teasing, tipped Keller's lips. "I never would have guessed," Keller breathed, and kissed his mouth. "But I do like being your first."

A door slammed, and David's voice rang out from the kitchen. "Dad? Where are you? What's Coach Keller's car doing in the driveway?"

They sprang apart, and Niall frantically tried to appear nonchalant. "We're in the living room."

Thank God the house didn't have an open-floor design, otherwise he and Keller would've been seen from the back door, and Niall was not ready to explain why Keller's tongue was down his throat. He placed his hands on his burning cheeks, hoping they'd cool off.

Don't worry, Keller mouthed to him, and Niall felt a rush of gratitude. He really had been wrong about Keller. In so many, many ways.

David walked in, brows knitted in confusion. "Hi, Dad. Coach? Is something wrong?"

"No, not at all." Keller was quick to reassure David.

"Are you home for the night?" Niall asked. The entire week, things had remained strained between them, and he'd been hoping to have some time together to try and talk things out.

"No." David could still barely meet his eyes, and Niall's heart shriveled a little. "We're going to the movies, and then Mallory Hart's having a party at her house. I needed to change and pick up some stuff. Chris lent me his bike. It's okay, right?"

"Yeah, it's okay."

They'd never had this awkwardness between them, and it broke his heart.

"Thanks."

"Have fun. But remember, tomorrow night you have to be home in time for dinner."

"I promise. But why is Coach here?"

Keller had remained quiet, and Niall looked to him, hoping his face didn't reveal his inner longing.

"Your father was having car trouble, and I helped him out."

"*Ugh*, Dad. When're you going to get a new one? One day it's just gonna conk out for good."

"Well, uh…I did. Thanks to Keller's generosity, I, uh…"

Coming to his rescue, Keller smoothly stepped in. "Turns out I knew the guy at the dealership, and he kind of owed me a favor, so I worked it out for your dad. The new car should be coming later today."

David's eyes brightened. "Awesome. What did you get?"

Niall chewed his lip. "A BMW X6."

"No way. That's so cool." Wide-eyed, David crowed with excitement. "Sweet. Can't wait to ride in it on Monday." He stopped and blinked, as if remembering the distance between them. "I'd better get going. I'll see you tomorrow night. See you Monday, Coach."

He took off, stomping up the stairs, returning less than five minutes later with a duffel bag. "I'm gonna shower at Chris's to save time. Bye." He left, and Niall didn't take a full breath until the door slammed.

"I can't believe this."

"What?" Keller folded his arms, and Niall wished they were holding him again but refrained.

"You know…you kissing me."

"From my recollection, it was a joint effort. You kissed me back."

Hot, then cold rushed through him. "I know, but it shouldn't have happened. You're my son's coach, and I'm the school librarian. And neither of us is out."

Keller's brows rose high. "And?" A wicked grin crossed his lips. "I bet we could have a lot of fun in the stacks."

"Don't be ridiculous. See? That's what I mean. It's wrong on so many levels."

"How so?" Keller made himself at home by sitting in the club chair. To keep his sanity—because now that he'd kissed Keller, he couldn't stop thinking about it, or him—Niall sat on the couch with the coffee table between them. He desperately needed to keep a grip on a reality he wished he could run from. Keller's soft lips, his hot, wet tongue…

Shit.

He wanted Keller's kisses again and that big, muscled body on top of his. He longed to know more. A shudder ran through him, imagining what being naked with Keller would be like. He rubbed his face.

"I can't believe you even have to ask. You're not out, so obviously you know the ramifications of being a gay teacher—plenty of people wouldn't be happy to know their son's football coach is gay. And me? I'm the school librarian, but what if they fire me? I need that income to live, plus I count on subbing English classes to make extra money to save for David's college fund."

"They can't do that. It's illegal."

Niall snorted so hard, he hurt his brain. "How can you be so naïve? They can do what they want under the guise of what's best for the students, or budget cuts, or…whatever. Plus, you have a one-year contract, I bet? With a morality clause?"

"There's nothing immoral about what we did." Keller frowned. "And actually, I have a four-year contract. Maybe you think I'm not smart, but I did graduate with a degree in business."

He hadn't known that, but his opinion remained the same. "I have to protect David as well."

"Protect him from what? Does he know?" Keller asked

more softly. "Things seemed strained between you."

Tears stung his eyes. "They are. I told him last Sunday I'd been on a date with a man. We've hardly spoken since. He couldn't wait to spend the weekend away."

"I'm sorry, Niall. But David's a levelheaded, smart kid. I'm sure it was just something out of the blue that shocked him. He'll come around. He has to."

"No, he doesn't. You know that. It's why you've kept quiet all these years. Because as much as everyone pretends to be so enlightened, they really aren't for the most part. It's okay to have gay friends, but when it's your own family, things look different."

Keller's jaw hardened. "What do you plan on doing?"

Niall remained silent. To his complete surprise, Keller rose from his seat, joined him on the couch, and took his face between the palms of his hands. "I'm asking because I want to keep exploring where this might take us. I like you, Niall. I'd like to see where it leads. I hope you want the same."

Keller leaned forward, and Niall's eyes slid closed, his heart pumping furiously.

A horn beeped outside, and they jumped, then laughed self-consciously. "That'll be the car," Niall said.

"Yeah." Keller gave him a quick kiss on the lips, leaving them tingling. "Let's check it out, make sure Roy did what he was supposed to."

Niall followed, wishing he had answers for Keller. The one thing he did know was that life shouldn't be this hard.

CHAPTER ELEVEN

It was almost one in the afternoon midweek, and Keller hadn't seen or heard from Niall since Saturday afternoon. He'd hoped Niall would ask him to spend the rest of the evening together so they could get to know each other better, but he'd been thanked for all his help in the driveway and told good night. Unwilling to press Niall, who was as nervous as a rookie stepping out on the field for his first game, Keller decided not to push him further, and retreated.

But now it was Wednesday, and he'd still not had the chance to talk to Niall about what happened. Because something was going on he didn't quite understand. He'd had more than his share of hookups and random sex, but Niall's innocence and sweetness triggered a different response. He'd joked about wanting to get him naked as fast as possible, but the truth was, he'd spent the days following that incredible kiss imagining the two of them snuggled together, watching movies on that comfy sofa. He wondered what breakfast would be like in that sun-filled kitchen, smiling across the table at each other. How it would feel to wake up next to Niall and slowly press his lips against the rapidly beating pulse at his throat. He enjoyed their banter and admired Niall's thoughtfulness and devotion to his son.

Unfortunately, Niall had made himself unavailable. Several times Keller had stopped by the library only to find him busy, either with students or with administrative work he was unable—or, more likely, unwilling—to put aside to talk to Keller.

To work off his frustration, he jogged around the track several times, then stretched. Instead of helping, it only made him wonder why Niall didn't want to talk to him. Breathing heavily, he stalked off the field and was about to enter the gym to shower when his phone rang. Elijah's face popped up on the screen. His heart happy, Keller took a seat in the stands.

"What's up?"

"How's it going? Haven't heard from you. Thought I would after your first win."

He scratched his head and sighed. "Yeah, sorry. I should've called."

Elijah cocked his head. "Uh-oh. What's wrong?"

"Nothing…exactly." It was tricky. He wanted to tell Elijah, but he couldn't because Niall wasn't out.

"*Mmhmm*. I've heard that before. Listen, I got a couple of free days and was thinking if you'd like—"

"Yes. When? I'll get the spare room ready."

Elijah snickered. "What's the matter, Country? Missing the bright lights of the big city?"

With the memory of Niall's kisses still fresh on his lips, Keller shook his head. "Nah, not at all. It'll just be good to see a friendly face."

Brow furrowed, Elijah peered at him. "You got

something you wanna tell me? Your kids looked good—I saw a YouTube video of the game."

"Yeah, they're a great bunch. I needed to ride their asses to keep them hungry, but you know how it goes—everyone tells you how great you are, you start to believe in your own hype and slack off just enough that an easy win becomes a fight. I think they know better now."

"Oooh, yeah. I remember that. Coach Slater busting our asses when we almost lost to the Jets. Man, that woulda been sad."

"Got that right. So when are you coming?"

"I have an interview on Thursday I gotta do, so how's Friday? I'll come up, catch your game, we'll hang out on Saturday, and I'll go home Sunday."

"Sounds like a plan."

"I'll text you when I'm close."

"All right." Already, knowing Elijah would be there lifted a weight off his chest. "See you."

He sat for a moment, then slid the phone into the pocket of his joggers and walked into the school. Classes were in session, so he made it through the halls with relatively few people stopping him for an autograph or wanting to talk about the game. He opened the door to the teachers' lounge and got himself a sports drink from the vending machine and a sleeve of peanut-butter crackers.

"Bet your coaches never let you eat like that when you were playing."

He peered over his shoulder to see a teacher sitting there, his face sly with laughter. It would be rude to take a seat at a different table, so Keller took the chair across from the man. He'd seen him in the halls but didn't remember his name.

"You'd win that bet. No junk food allowed. Carbs and protein only." He held out his hand. "Keller Williams."

They shook. "Oh, I know who you are. Marty Daniels, chemistry teacher. How're you settling in? Are you having culture shock?"

"A little," he admitted. "Both from returning here to live and to the high school that seemed so important at the time but now…not so much."

"Perception. We've all fallen prey to it. When I was in high school, my biggest fear was people discovering I'm gay. I grew up in a smaller town than Overlook and had to pretend every day." Marty's lips thinned. "You know how it goes. It's hard being someone you're not."

Keller crunched on a peanut-butter cracker. "Yeah. Must be." Marty was insinuating something, but Keller wasn't about to feed the beast. If he ever did come out, it would be on his terms. He took a swallow of his drink and thought of the early morning phone calls he'd received. "Do you have any kids who are experiencing anxiety or showing any signs of emotional distress?"

Marty steepled his fingers under his chin. "We all have kids like that." He swept a hand in front of him. "Look at what you've gotten yourself into. Posters on the wall instructing teachers to watch out for signs of sexual abuse, drugs, physical and emotional abuse…every week it's something else. Not to mention what to do in the case of an active shooter." He made a face. "Life is a mess these days."

"So why do it? With a chemistry degree, you could make more money for sure."

Marty stared at him. "That's rich coming from a pro football player who makes more as a coach than I do as a teacher. The kids, of course. I do it for them. I may not want any of my own, but that doesn't mean I don't love teaching them." His eyes twinkled. "And at the end of the day, I get to give them back to their parents. A win-win as I see it."

Keller's smile was faint. "But doesn't it take a lot out of you?"

"I get much more in return. Tell me something: do you remember your teachers?"

"Yeah, sure. Even my kindergarten teacher."

"And you're how old—thirty-seven, thirty-eight?"

"Thirty-eight, yes."

"How many other people do you remember from when you were five or six?"

Keller thought and made a face. "A couple, maybe."

"Bingo." Marty smacked the table. "Teachers make an amazing contribution to a child's life. Some might call it unforgettable. I'd like to think that when I'm gone, a small piece of me will remain, in the words I've used to explain a formula or thesis that sparked a child's imagination to become a scientist or a doctor. Or maybe it was when I stayed after school to provide a safe space to listen and give advice to someone questioning their sexuality. We're so much more than a simple class and homework assignment."

Keller's heart pounded. It hadn't been that way when he went to school, but he'd been more about figuring out how to hide his attraction to men. Because he knew if he'd come out, it would have been the end of the life he'd wanted before it had a chance to start.

"I never thought of it that way."

"You, especially, should. Maybe more than anyone. As a coach, you see these kids at their highest and lowest. They'll share their hopes and dreams with you, and more importantly, their fears. You have a chance to make an indelible impact on someone's life. Do you know how special that is?"

Keller's head spun. "I thought I was coming here to simply teach football and sportsmanship, but the more time I spend with them, the more I'm learning about myself."

Seeing a kid like Van, out and proud, humbled him.

"Every year it gets harder and harder to find people who want to give their soul to this job. It's not like when you played football and the money and accolades poured in for catching a ball. We're not raking it in, and no offense, but

I think what we do is a lot more important than throwing and catching a ball."

Unsurprised by Marty's in-your-face resentment, Keller wasn't about to get into an argument with him. He'd heard it and understood where it came from. "I'm no longer in the game, so I'm looking forward, rather than behind. I'd better get to the gym and prepare for practice. Nice talking to you."

The floodlights shone on the field, illuminating the game. "Hut, hut," Shane called out.

The ball snapped, and Keller paced the sidelines, watching his team move down the field. They were playing well and were ahead 10-3. It was second and four at the opponents' thirty-yard line. The running backs were in place, and they'd practiced this move all week. If it went as planned, Shane should be able to throw a touchdown.

Except he fumbled the next snap, losing four yards, and only Van's quick response of falling on the ball saved it from being a turnover. The groans from the stands echoed in the stadium, and he heard curses from the seats behind him.

"Fucking dumbass kid."

"What the hell is wrong with him? How could he fuck that up?"

God, he wanted to rip into the people sitting on their asses and playing armchair quarterback. They knew nothing about being on the line.

"Flag on the play. Unsportsmanlike conduct. Offense. Fifteen-yard penalty. Second and twenty-three."

Fucking hell. Shane had started pushing the defensive lineman who'd tackled him.

"Time out," Keller called, and the team rushed to him.

Shane bowed his head. "Sorry, Coach. I don't know what happened. I thought I had it."

"I don't *ever* want to see a fight on the field, or I will bench you faster than your next heartbeat. We don't lay hands on anyone. Got that?"

Shane nodded.

"Good. Now here's what we're gonna do." He outlined their strategy and kept their minds focused forward on the play to come rather than on what happened.

Someone yelled, "Don't fuck up this time, Shane. You don't wanna be a pussy."

This time, Keller did pay attention to the voice from the stands, whipping around to see Bobby Contard standing up in his seat, his fat face an ugly shade of red.

"Quiet down," Keller yelled and tipped his head to Elijah, who sat on the bench. Elijah rose to his full, intimidating six-foot-seven height and strolled over to stand in front of Bobby, who was still yelling obscenities at the kids. Security was up in the stands, so Elijah was on watch.

"I advise you to keep quiet, or the coach will have you tossed. By me."

Seeing him shut his face and sit, Keller smothered a grin and refocused on the team. "Are we ready? We got this, right?"

"Yes, Coach!"

"Good. Let's go out there and show them."

"We are Tigers! Hear us roar!"

To the cheers of the crowd, the team returned to the line of scrimmage. The ball was snapped, and this time, Shane made the throw to Chris, who caught it but was tackled before he could run anywhere.

"Third and twelve, let's do this."

They had to throw the ball, and everyone knew it. David, Brenden, and Chris were double-teamed, and it would have to be a precise throw, like that threading a needle he'd talked about. Shane received the snap, faded back a few steps, then scrambled to his right.

"He's open, dammit," Keller yelled from the sidelines. David was wide open, having ducked past the defensive tackles. Finally Shane spotted him and threw the ball. David made the catch, but unfortunately, the other team had also noticed David, and Keller's heart sank. To his shock, David threw the ball to the unprotected Chris, who ran it down the field for a touchdown. The crowd roared with approval.

"A flea flicker. Those kids pulled off a flea-flicker play, and I didn't even tell them. Son of a bitch." Keller cackled, and he, Hank, and Leon cheered, high-fived, and whooped it up along the sidelines. Elijah joined them.

"Man, that was beautiful. I forgot I was watching high school football. Damn, Keller. They are *good*."

Pride swelled in his chest. "They are."

Special teams ran in, the extra point was made, and the third quarter ended. With only a two-minute break, the kids ran to him, and he gave each one of them a fist bump.

"You kids are something else. That was incredible."

The excitement in their eyes and flushed faces greeted him.

David took off his helmet. "We saw it on television and practiced it over the weekend. We knew if we ever got stuck, we'd wanna try it. You told us to think on our feet."

"I'm all for innovation. Just, next time, share it with me. But that was impressive."

Elijah stood and clapped. "Kids, I'm gonna tell you, I haven't had so much fun at a game in years. Now I know why your coach is here. I'm just sorry I didn't get a chance for the job first."

The whistle blew, and on their high, they easily beat off a challenge from the opposition and went on to score three more touchdowns, blowing out the other team with a final score of 35-9.

The locker room that night was a different scene than the previous Friday. Keller stood with Elijah, Leon, and Hank, and couldn't stop heaping praise.

"What I was most impressed with was your ability to think on your feet. You saw an opportunity, and you all went for it. That shows not only excellent teamwork, but maturity. I couldn't be any prouder of all of you. Now go on to your party, and I'll see you Monday at practice, where you're going to show me how you worked out that play."

Laughing, the kids ran to their lockers, all except David, who came up to him and the other coaches. "If you wanna come to the after-party, Coach, it's at my house." He directed a shy smile at Elijah. "You can bring Mr. Randolph too. If you don't have other plans."

"Thank you, David. We'd love to come."

"Only if you promise to call me Elijah and not Mr. Randolph. Makes me feel old," Elijah joked.

Leon and Hank both declined, saying they had to get home to their wives.

"Stella would kill me if I left her at home for a pizza party, but you all have fun. Come on, Hank. It's my turn to drive home." Leon waved good-bye to them, and Hank followed.

"Okay, well, great. See you soon. You know the address, Coach. Oh, and thanks again for helping my dad with the car. It's so cool." He grinned and left to hit the showers.

Elijah watched as Keller cleaned up around the room, putting towels in the laundry bin and tossing bottles into the recycling.

"What did you do for his father?" Elijah asked when they were finally outdoors and walking to the car.

Keller dug the key fob out of his pocket. "Just helped him out. He needed a car, and I smoothed the way for him."

Elijah nudged him. "Look at that shit."

He craned his neck and saw Bobby Contard standing

nose-to-nose with Shane, finger in his face, yelling full force. Shane tried to pull away, and Bobby pushed him against the pickup. He continued to berate Shane and grabbed him by the arm.

"Dammit." He took a step forward, but Elijah put a hand on his arm. "Don't do it. That's his father."

"I don't give a shit. He has no right to lay a hand on that kid." Keller stomped up to the two of them. "Is there a problem?" He crossed his arms, and knew Elijah stood right behind him. Shane said nothing but hung his head and stared at the ground.

Bobby faced him. "I was telling Shane he's lucky you're keeping him because he's fucked up too much in these first two games. Kid needs to pull his head out of his ass and concentrate on what's important."

"Shane's a very good quarterback. Don't get on his back. And don't push him again, Bobby."

Red-faced, Bobby pointed at him. "Don't you be telling me how to raise my kid."

"Someone needs to watch what you're doing."

A nasty light burned in Bobby's eyes. "Some deputies showed up at my house, asking questions. You know anything about that?"

Keller wanted to put a finger in his face and tell him the truth, but he refrained, not wanting a full-blown fight to erupt.

Bobby continued to rant. "You better not have called them. You been hanging around with little pussy-boy, Niall Harper, I heard." Bobby sneered with contempt. "That wimp hasn't changed since high school. Not surprised a fox like his wife dumped him. She needs a real man to keep up with her."

"Shut up, Bobby." Growing hot, Keller took a step forward. "Real men don't need to hit their kids to make them listen, do they? Leave Shane alone. The only one who gets to tell him how to play on the field is me. Got it?"

"He's my kid, and he's gonna listen to what I tell him." He pointed to the truck. "Get in the car, Shane. Now."

Still silent, Shane began to make his way to the passenger side of the vehicle.

"Aren't you going to the after-party, Shane?" Keller asked.

"No, he ain't," Bobby answered for him. "He's going home and getting up early to practice throwing before I go to work."

Keller put a hand up. "Don't do that. He needs to rest the arm. Too much stress will damage it. Shane needs to ice it and use heat and stay off it until Monday. No throwing."

Surprising him, Bobby muttered, "Maybe you're right."

"Can I go to the party then, Dad? Please?" He looked nothing like the tough guy he pretended to be those first days.

"I ain't staying up late to come pick you up from there. It's across town."

"I'll bring Shane home, don't worry," Keller reassured Bobby.

"Please, Dad? I promise I'll work extra hard during our practice this week."

"Fine. Whatever."

"See you later, Shane." Keller gave him a wink, and Shane's tight expression relaxed.

Bobby got into the truck and drove away, and only then did he and Elijah return to his car. He left the parking lot for Niall's house.

"Whoo-whee, that is one angry mofo. What's wrong with him? Kid seems like a good player."

"Shane's good. He's going through something, but I can't figure out what. Yet. I'm hoping Bobby isn't laying hands on him at home." Keller explained about the bruising he'd seen and how he was the one who'd reported it to the police. "The sergeant was more interested in getting my autograph than the fact a child might be getting the crap beaten out of him. I'm glad they sent deputies, but knowing Bobby, he talked his way out of it."

"They only care when it's too late," Elijah said grimly.

"I won't let that happen. Hopefully he'll be able to have some fun at the party."

The lights were on, the party in full swing when Niall opened the door. He looked slightly harried. "Oh, hi. I wasn't sure you'd come."

"We wouldn't miss it. This is my best friend, Elijah. He's visiting for the weekend."

"The defensive tackle? Oh wow, yeah. David mentioned you were here and that he invited you."

"Nice to meet you. Your son has some great moves."

Niall's face lit up with pride. "Thanks. Come on in and grab some pizza before the ravaging hordes demolish it all."

They followed Niall, and Keller couldn't help but admire Niall's broad shoulders narrowing to his tight ass.

Elijah nudged him and whispered, "You can stop staring any minute now."

"Don't know what you're talking about," he muttered, and Elijah snickered.

"Man, my mama would wash your mouth out with soap for lying." His eyes widened. "Is that it? You and him…" He trailed off, and Keller put a finger to his mouth.

"Not here."

They entered the kitchen, where the half-glassed door opened to the deck and large grassy yard. There was a firepit where kids were toasting marshmallows, and an old swing set where he spied girls—presumably the cheerleaders—being pushed higher and higher, their laughter rising in the air.

"Nice place," Elijah remarked as they sat at the picnic table and ate their pizza.

"See me tomorrow when I have to clean up the wreckage." Niall's smile was wry and directed toward him. He couldn't help but grin.

"If you need help, I'm sure we can make ourselves available."

A group of boys ran over to them. "Could we get your autograph, Elijah, please?" Van asked.

"Do you mind throwing some balls?" Brenden pleaded. "That would be so cool."

"Go ahead," Keller told him. "I can't throw because of my arm, but they'll be happier with you anyway. I'm old news already."

"No way, Coach. Are you kidding?" Their voices rang out in protest.

"I'm just kidding."

Elijah got to his feet, but not before murmuring in his ear, "I see what you did there. Smooth move, my man. Go for it."

Keller waited until they were out of earshot. "I've been dying to get some alone time with you."

Niall turned pink. "Shh," he warned between clenched teeth. "What are you doing?"

"Trying to talk to you. When do you think we can see each other again?"

"I can't. Not this weekend. David's friends are staying over tonight."

"What about tomorrow night?" he pressed.

"Don't you have things to do with your friend? He seems very nice."

"Elijah's great. But he's leaving early on Sunday to get home to his wife and daughters. What about Sunday brunch?"

"I don't know…" Niall hedged, just as David ran over to him, breathless.

"Dad, Tommy Stone is having a party tomorrow night. It's a sleepover. Can I go? His mom is gonna take us to the laser-tag place."

"Wow. Sounds fun," Keller exclaimed, his grin as bright

as the flames dancing in the firepit. Niall shot him a look, but he was all innocence, even as he tried to think of how they'd make time to see each other.

"Okay. Just make sure you get home in time to do all your homework."

Like a typical teenager, David rolled his eyes. "I know, I know. I don't have much. I got a ninety-five on my chemistry quiz too."

"That's great. Okay, have fun."

David rejoined his friends, who were catching the footballs Elijah was throwing to them.

Keller grabbed a handful of chips from the bowl on the table. "So. About Saturday night?"

Somber-faced, Niall clasped his hands. "I don't know what you expect."

"Friendship first, and maybe more when we get to know each other better? Obviously, I've kept my sexuality under wraps, but now I'm not so sure I want to live that way any longer." He hesitated. "Are things better between you and David?"

Niall turned pensive. "In a way. We've avoided talking about it and stayed on safe topics like school and his games. I don't want to stir things up. Plus, I'm still not sure it's the right thing to do, with both of us working at the school."

"I'm all for taking it slow. We have twenty years to catch up on. Let's see where this takes us. Does that work for you?"

Before Niall could answer, a panting Elijah rejoined them, and grabbed a napkin to wipe the sweat from his face. "Damn, I thought I was in better shape. These kids got me working."

Keller cackled. "Must be DeeDee's home cooking. She does make the best food."

"Good thing you never said that in front of my mother."

Keller held up his hands. "No way. I'd give my soul for

Ms. Roberta's stuffing. *Mmm…*I can taste it now."

Niall stayed silent.

"David seems like he's very into the game. Is he gonna go for a scholarship?" Elijah poured some ice water from the pitcher.

"We don't know yet, but it's looking like it, I think."

"He's got a good shot, especially if the team wins the state championship."

"That's what we're going for," Keller added.

"Your wife's not here?" Elijah asked, and Keller tensed, knowing that Elijah had already heard from Bobby's earlier tirade that she'd left Niall.

"We're divorced but good friends. She flies in to catch at least one game during the season, but usually more."

"I see." Elijah finished his water, and they watched the kids tossing the football. Keller noticed David spending most of his time with Renee Dellacourt, one of the cheerleaders. He glanced around the yard. "Where's Shane?"

Niall peered into the darkness. "I don't know. He was here earlier."

They stood and walked the yard, finally finding him alone, sitting with his back to a tree, facing the fence. Keller approached him.

"You okay?"

Shane lifted a shoulder. "Yeah."

Keller sat beside him. "You know you can talk to me. I've told you that. Whatever you tell me stays between us."

Shane hung his head. "I'm fine. Just wishing I could be in college. Fast forward these next two years."

Oh, kiddo, don't rush your life.

Keller took a chance. "And away from your father? Does he…hurt you?"

Alarm flared in Shane's eyes. "I never said that."

"I know you didn't. I just have to ask because I saw him grab you in the parking lot. If he is—"

"It's okay. I'm good. He's just concerned about me getting a scholarship and doesn't want me messing up my chances."

"You haven't. I know a couple of college recruiters, and they're interested in seeing the team play. Keep it up, and I think as long as your schoolwork and behavior stays steady, you should be okay. Your father doesn't have to worry."

At least about that, he didn't, but Keller was going to make damn well sure there wasn't going to be a repeat of what he'd witnessed earlier in the parking lot.

"Thanks, Coach. I'm trying. I just…sometimes things are weird, you know?"

"Weird, how?"

Shane didn't look at him. "I dunno. Like…things are supposed to be a certain way, but they're not?" He snorted a laugh. "Like I said. Weird."

"No. Not weird. You're a kid, figuring things out. I didn't know anything when I was your age. And you know what? I'm still working on learning new things." He got to his feet. "Lighten up on yourself."

"Thanks, Coach." He jumped up.

"We'll be leaving in about an hour, so I'll come find you."

Shane nodded and ran toward the swing set, where a bunch of girls waved to him. Soon he had an arm around the head cheerleader, Marissa, who snuggled in close. Keller returned to the deck to sit by Elijah. Niall was nowhere to be seen.

"I know one thing," Elijah declared. "I sure am glad I'm not in high school anymore." He took another slice of pizza.

"You know it, brother."

A chance not taken was a chance regretted. Winning over Niall might be the toughest play he'd make all season, but he was ready.

CHAPTER TWELVE

Sunday evenings were always Niall's favorite. Pizza and movie night had been a tradition with them since David was a little boy, and while he knew it wasn't bound to last once David grew older, their close bond was a rock. His rock he could always count on.

Now, he wasn't so sure.

He hadn't taken Keller up on the two of them getting together Saturday night. There was still so much to work out in his head about what had happened between them, it was more important for him to be alone.

And with him and David still so shaky and cautious with each other, their relationship was his top priority. They'd barely had a chance to talk all week—David had been working on reports and studying for quizzes, and while Niall was pleased with how conscientious David was being, he was certain it was more avoidance than being studious. Now, another weekend had passed without them communicating.

Niall had spent his whole life putting himself second. He'd waited decades for his first kiss. Seeing Keller again could wait a few more days. And if Keller didn't understand, they weren't meant to be.

Niall checked his watch and saw it was nearing six o'clock. He hated being that parent, but he'd have to call if David didn't come home soon. On cue, the kitchen door opened, and relief surged through him at the sight of David's face.

"Hi, Dad." He dropped his backpack and duffel bag and sat at the table.

"Hi. How was the party last night?" He hoped he sounded casual. "Did you have fun?"

"Yeah, it was good." He fidgeted. "I'm sorry, Dad. I shouldn't have been like that when you told me you're gay." He brushed a hand over his eyes. "I'm really sorry. I didn't mean to make you feel bad," he whispered. "Please don't be mad at me."

More love than he'd ever felt filled his heart, and he rose from his chair to hug David, who clung to him as though he were still a child.

"I'm not. It's okay. I know. I know. It'll be all right." When they separated, he kissed David on the cheek before letting him go.

David sniffled and brushed his hair off his face. "Did you…did you see anyone last night? Like, go out on a date or anything?"

Or anything.

The thought of telling David he'd kissed Keller Williams, someone David liked and respected, his *coach*, made Niall's stomach cramp. He wasn't certain David could handle something like that. Hell, he wasn't even sure *he* understood what happened between them.

"No, I stayed home. Got some paperwork done, and of

course had to clean up after the party." He grinned. "That took all Saturday morning."

"Thanks, Dad, for everything. Everyone was talking about it. Coach Keller and Elijah Randolph at my house. So cool."

His excitement warmed Niall's heart. "I'm glad you had fun."

"Yeah. Coach is so amazing. Like…he talks to us and wants to hear what we're thinking. It's like he's more than a football coach."

He hadn't known Keller was so close to the kids, but it made sense. He'd proved to be a person concerned with those around him and willing to give his personal time without any thought of repayment. Keller must've gone through the same questions Niall had in high school, and while Niall had married and planned a life of loneliness, Keller had chosen to mask his pain by burying himself in football and one-night stands.

That kiss…

"Dad? You okay?"

He blinked and found David staring at him.

"Yeah, of course, kiddo. What did you do today? Hang out at Chris's?"

David turned red. "Uh, well, Renee and I went to the movies—her mom took us—then we hung out at the mall with Chris and Mallory. We had pizza."

"Are you and Renee dating?"

"I…yeah. Kind of. I guess. I like her."

"I'm okay with it as long as your schoolwork and football don't suffer. No late-night texting. And no bringing her over when I'm not here, or being in your room with the door closed when you're studying together."

"*Dad.*"

He chuckled. "Those are the rules. I'm sure you'll find plenty of time to be alone. But remember what your mom and I always said—respect women and listen to them. And always understand when they say no."

He nodded. "I know. Renee's really smart. She already knows she wants to be a lawyer like her mom, and she studies hard." A little self-conscious, he blushed. "She's a good writer and helps me with my English essays. And I help her with chemistry—we're in the same class."

How lucky was he to have this kind of relationship with his son? Niall knew to cherish every minute because one day David would be gone, and he'd be alone.

"I guess that means you're not interested in pizza, popcorn, and movie night?" He had an idea. "How about we go out? Have burgers at the diner."

"Awesome. I'm ready when you are."

"I'll get the car keys."

They sat in a booth, and David decided he wanted a chocolate shake as well. Marilyn brought it over and smiled. "Great game on Friday, David. I bet you kids take the championship. Especially with Keller Williams as your coach."

Before either of them could reply, he heard, "Why thank you, Marilyn. I appreciate your confidence," and Niall froze at the sound of Keller's teasing laughter.

"Hi, Coach." David waved to Keller. God, had anyone ever looked better in a pair of faded jeans? The blue Tigers hoodie made his bright eyes glow. Niall gulped his water. Jesus. He needed to calm down.

"Having dinner, you two? No Sunday pizza party tonight?"

David wrinkled his nose. "How did you know about that?"

Niall blinked rapidly, and decided he needed to speak. "I, uh, must've mentioned it at the party Friday night."

Satisfied with his answer, David sucked up some of his shake.

"Where's your friend?" Niall asked. "Did you leave him at home to pick up dinner?"

A bit of the light in Keller's vibrant face dimmed. "No. Elijah left this morning. I got sick of being in the house by myself, so I decided to come out and indulge in some fries. Sometimes you need a little crispy goodness to make yourself feel better."

"Dad?" David stared at him, brows raised.

Niall knew what David wanted him to do. He wanted it as well, but he'd have to keep his guard up.

"Want to join us? We just ordered our burgers."

Keller's face transformed from dejection to pleasure. "I'd love to. Are you sure?" But he was already sliding in to sit next to Niall. The two of them weren't small men, and Keller's legs were big and muscular. And of course, he was using their proximity to take advantage. Niall had nowhere to go—not that he wanted to. Keller was warm, and Niall wished they could stay in this crowded little booth forever. Keller placed the napkin in his lap, fingers brushing against Niall's thigh, and Niall had to stifle a sigh of pleasure.

Until he glanced over, saw the devilish smile on Keller's lips, and realized he was teasing him on purpose. David was busy scrolling on his phone and drinking his milkshake, giving him an opening.

"Stop that," he muttered.

"What?" Keller widened his eyes.

"Please?" He cut his gaze to David, and Keller's expression softened.

"Okay." Keller waved Marilyn over. "I'll have the cheeseburger and fries, extra pickles."

Niall wrinkled his nose. "Extra pickles?"

"What? I love pickles."

Their food came first, and he felt awkward eating, but Keller waved him on. "I'll manage." And did so by proceeding to eat the fries off his plate. Niall had never been with someone like Keller. He was so damn…happy. And being in his orbit made Niall happy as well. It had taken him this long to figure out what that dancing, fluttery feeling in his chest was. For the first time, he was himself.

"Do you mind?" His attempt to frown failed. He was having too much fun to pretend otherwise, and it looked like Keller felt the same.

"Not at all. They're delicious. Nice and crispy, exactly how I like them."

David chewed on his burger and ate his fries, then wiped the ketchup from his face. "Coach, I've been thinking…is it too late for me to consider a football scholarship to college? What would I have to do?"

Niall paused from taking a bite of his food. "What brought this up?"

David's cheeks turned pink. "Uh, well, I was talking to Renee, and she's planning to go to Syracuse 'cause that's where her mother went. They have a great team, so maybe I could get a scholarship there?"

Marilyn set Keller's plate in front of him, but Keller made no move to begin eating, his face becoming serious.

"My alma mater. I think you'd have a good shot if the team wins the next two years. I'll have scouts coming later in the season to observe you. Stay focused on school and getting good grades. Don't get into trouble, and get involved in community service, something you care about, not just for show. When the time comes to apply, if you're still interested in Syracuse, I'll put in a letter of recommendation for you."

"Awesome. Thanks, Coach." David happily tore into the rest of his food.

After they finished eating and the plates had been

cleared, Keller took out his phone. "I've been thinking it's important to have all the parents' phone numbers in case something happens on the field or if we're at an away game and you're not there."

While it made sense, Niall knew it was a way for Keller to get his phone number, and he was amused by his cunning.

"Sure. I think that's a good idea." He recited his number.

"I figured you would."

David excused himself to use the bathroom, and Niall waited until he was out of earshot. "That was pretty slick, Keller. I'm impressed."

"Guess you never watched me play, huh? I had some moves." He wiggled in the seat, and Niall laughed.

"You're too much."

Keller peered over his shoulder, rested his hand on Niall's thigh, and gave a squeeze. "You ain't seen nothing yet."

A shudder ran through him, and Keller's eyes burned with a fire he recognized from that one afternoon in his living room. "Not here. I can't."

"I understand." He dropped his voice. "But when can we see each other again?"

Another shiver and a fiery ache spiraled up from his belly. "I-I don't know. Stop by the library after classes are done. Around four? I'll wait for you in my office." He must be losing his mind to plan a rendezvous at the school.

Keller made a face. "Can't. Practice. It runs till five thirty or six. Every day. We have an away game next Friday night. Our first one, so I need to prepare them. I want to see you this week, though." He shifted away, and David came into view. "I'll think of something."

David returned. "I promised Renee we could FaceTime at nine. Can we go home soon?"

"Yeah, it's getting late to be out anyway. School tomorrow."

Keller slid out, and he followed. Before Niall could stop him, Keller had paid the bill for the three of them.

"Don't argue with me. You can pay next time."

David had already walked out of the diner, and they strolled slowly after him. The night air was beginning to pick up that crispness signaling summer's end. Niall watched David sit on a bench and text.

"I'm not sure I'm ready for a teenager in love."

"I'll keep an eye on him and let him know where his concentration needs to be if I see him become distracted."

"Thanks. I'll have to call Angie and tell her too. Let her deal with the fun." He chuckled. "I'd better go. It was nice to run into you unexpectedly."

Keller's gaze raked over him with a hungry intensity that took his breath away. "I'll text you later when I figure out how we can see each other. Because we will."

He strode away to his SUV, and Niall walked over to David.

"Ready?"

"Yep. All my homework's done, by the way."

"Good. I'm sure that has nothing to do with you wanting to FaceTime Renee, *hmm*?"

"*Dad.*" David rolled his eyes, and Niall laughed. The strain from the previous week had faded, and they were back to their old teasing ways. Nothing could've made him happier. They climbed into the car and drove off toward the Estates. On the way, they passed by Keller's house. The lights were on, and Niall pointed it out to David.

"There's Keller's house." He only knew because of the television coverage when Keller returned to town for his mother's funeral.

"How come you never mentioned you and Coach were friends when you went to high school here? I wish I could've seen him play in real time."

"We weren't friends. Fact is, I didn't even like him."

He turned down the road leading to their house.

"What? Why not?"

"It's a long story." Their driveway loomed before him, and he pulled in and turned off the engine. "It doesn't matter anymore." He left the car, and David hurried after him.

"No, tell me."

Inside the house, he flicked on the light and kicked off his sneakers. "Why? It was twenty years ago."

"I want to know. Tell me." David had inherited his mother's stubbornness.

"Don't you have a FaceTime to get to?" Not waiting for an answer, he walked into the kitchen, but David dogged his heels.

"Not for twenty minutes. C'mon, Dad. Why didn't you like Coach? He's so nice, and you get along now."

Yeah, we sure do. Our tongues, especially.

Letting out a long sigh, he grabbed a glass of water, more to give himself something to do with his hands. Why he was so nervous, he couldn't say.

"You can only imagine how popular Keller was at school—star football player, good-looking…he had it all going for him. I was the stereotypical nerd—I preferred books to people, wasn't athletic, and I didn't have many friends."

David sat in the chair at the kitchen island. "Did…did you always know you liked guys?" His cheeks reddened. "I'm only asking because when Van came out, he said he only started feeling it when he turned thirteen, so I—forget it. You don't have to answer."

"It's okay to ask me questions," Niall rushed to reassure him. "I love that we can talk like this and not have to hide. I guess I knew around the same time as Van. But I didn't do anything about it. My parents were way too uptight and conservative for me to ever think of telling them. It never crossed my mind to let them know."

"I'm sorry, Dad. So you and Coach weren't in the same friend circle?"

He choked out a laugh. "We weren't in the same universe." He set the glass on the counter and gripped it with his hands. "See, Keller's friends weren't very nice. And I'm using the term *nice* because the other words I could use to describe them are ones we've taught you not to use. Shane's father was the worst. They were bullies. And back then, the schools didn't do much to stop things, so we all put up with it."

Shocked didn't begin to describe David's face. "What? Did they hurt you?"

He shrugged. "Mostly emotionally, not really physically, except for the times they shoved my face in the toilet." It was humiliating but somehow cathartic at the same time to reveal it to David.

"Oh my God, Dad. I thought that was only in movies." He sat openmouthed. "What the hell? And Coach? He did it to you too? I can't believe it."

"No, Keller didn't participate, but I assumed— incorrectly, I now know because Keller and I talked it out—that he did know. And I hated all of them, the whole football team, whether they were the actual bullies or not. They were in that golden circle that never suffered any repercussions for what they did. So yeah, you could say I wanted nothing to do with Keller when I found out he was your new coach."

"I don't blame you. But..." David's brow wrinkled. "Now you're definitely friends, right? What happened?"

His lips twitched. "Keller is a very determined person. He insisted we discuss it. I let him know how I felt, and we agreed that twenty years is enough time and that we can put old hurts aside and try to be friends."

"I'm glad. The first day, Coach gave us a talk about how we have to be a family on the team and off, and make sure that if we see something bad happening to anyone, we step in to make it right. He told us that if he ever finds out we're involved in something like hazing or bullying, he'll kick us off the team. He even had all of us sign a good sportsmanship pledge."

Hearing that Keller had begun the healing process before the two of them had even spoken convinced Niall that Keller truly had changed and understood how harmful the past had been for kids like him. It cemented the warm feelings he'd struggled with, uncertain if Keller was serious about… whatever it was going on between them.

"I didn't know that. But I agree. We've always taught you to stand up for what's right and not follow the crowd simply because it's popular. I'm glad to hear he's holding you accountable."

"No one I know does that kind of stuff. We know it's wrong." David slid off his chair. "You don't have to worry about me."

"It's part of my job—librarian, substitute teacher, and official worrier," he joked.

David smirked. "Ha-ha. I gotta go." He hesitated. "I'm really sorry I freaked out about stuff. I love you, Dad. And I want you to meet someone and be happy."

His throat closed up. "Thank you," he whispered. He must've done something right in his life to deserve this wonderful child.

David ran upstairs. Still overwhelmed, Niall wandered into the living room and stared into the dark space of the fireplace. Soon it would be time for a cozy fire. Times like this, he wished he had someone to share the quiet.

His phone buzzed, and he pulled it from his back pocket. Keller's name popped up. Excitement swirled in his stomach.

"Hello?"

"Can you talk?"

Reflexively, he glanced up, and though he knew David

would be preoccupied with his FaceTime, he retreated to the kitchen.

"Yeah. How are you?"

"Not so good."

"Is something wrong?"

Keller's deep chuckle sent a delicious tingle through him. "Well…you're there, and I'm here, all alone."

"I, uh…yeah, I guess." His heart pounded. In his twenties, he'd been abysmal at flirting, and now at thirty-seven, he was discovering he hadn't changed much.

"I wish we could see each other soon."

"Me too," he admitted. No sense in denying it. Being with Keller had awakened a longing for physical touch he'd never expected.

"We'll figure something out. I'm not going to wait too much longer."

"Impatience isn't a good look," he teased.

"You know what *would* be good? You, next to me," Keller's low growl purred in his ear.

"I know." He sighed. "I'm sorry it's so hard to manage. I'd understand if—"

"If you're going to say what I think, you don't understand anything. I may have come across as a player because that's the image I allowed the public to see, but that's not who I am."

Footsteps pounded down the stairs, and alarmed, he whispered, "Hold on a sec."

David ran into the kitchen. "Dad, Renee invited me to come see her cheerleading competition on Wednesday. It's after practice, and her mom can drive me home. It's okay, right? She said I'll be home by nine."

He blinked. "Uh, yeah. As long as you get your homework done."

"I will. I promise. My classes end at one thirty that day, so I can do it before practice. Thanks. You're the best." He sped out and tore up the stairs.

When Niall put the phone to his ear, Keller was laughing.

"So my only question is: Wednesday night, my place or yours? What's it gonna be?"

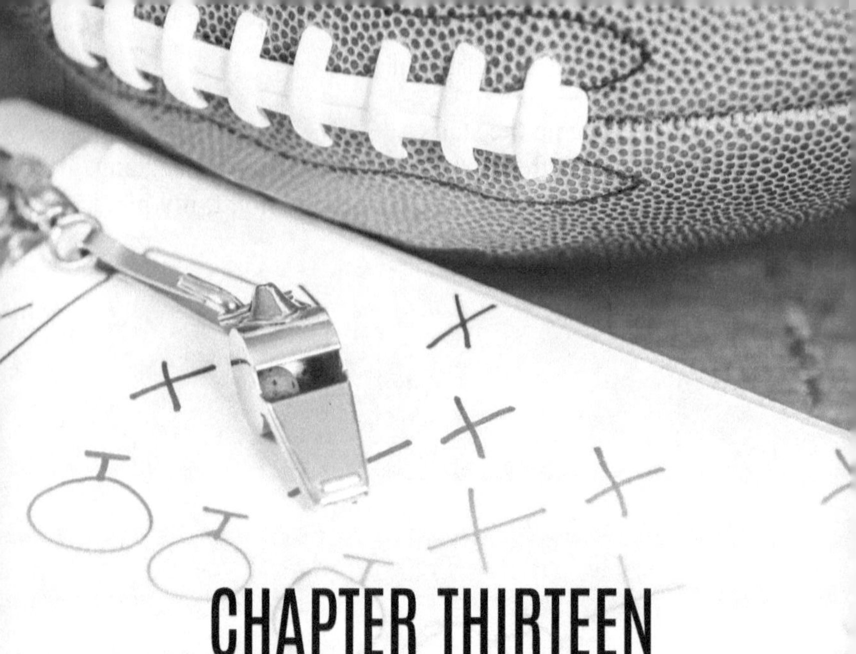

CHAPTER THIRTEEN

"Damn, get it together. He's just a guy."

Even Keller didn't believe his own words.

Just a guy.

In truth, Niall was simply that. A regular man with a regular job and the father of a teenager at that. The exact opposite of the slick men he'd been with over the years—groupies so into being with him, they'd signed NDAs and gone away happily with the autographs, jerseys, and other memorabilia he'd given them.

Not Niall. An innocent in his sexuality, someone who'd shared—no, *chosen* to give his first kiss to Keller. He touched his lips, recalling the hesitancy, then the growing passion when Niall's tongue licked at his. Had there ever been anything sexier? Not for him. Each time Keller thought of it, he grew hard with longing.

Would they take it further tonight than kisses? The

thought of Niall, naked in his bed, sent the blood rushing to his groin, making his dick ache, but he forced himself to think of something, anything, other than sex.

For the first time, he was enjoying a friendship with a man he was attracted to physically, but more importantly, on an emotional level. With zero experience in relationships, he didn't want to fuck this up. Keller cast a glance toward the ceiling, winced and made the call.

"God help me, I better not be making a mistake," he mumbled.

"What's up?" Elijah asked.

"I need advice."

"Yeah? Shoot."

"Uh, could Deirdre get on the phone too?"

"Deirdre? What…oh, *daaaamn*. I *knew* it." Elijah cackled. "When I got home I told her, 'Baby, Keller didn't say it to my face, but I think he's met a man.' "

"*What?*" Keller heard a shriek in the background. "Is that Keller? Give me that phone. Tell me everything." Deirdre's breathless voice had him shaking his head and laughing.

"Hi, how are you?" His attempt at nonchalance was short-lived.

"Don't even bother. Tell me everything about him. I thought Elijah was just fueling my wishful thinking."

He stretched out on the couch and stared at the fringe pillows. "I can't because he's not out yet, and it wouldn't be fair to him."

"Okay. I understand. So what do you want to know?"

Now that he had her on the phone, he felt foolish, but he needed someone else's opinion. "He's never been with a man before, and I don't want to push him. But we're seeing each other tonight, and I figured to let him set the pace. That's good, right?"

"Very good," she approved. "The main thing is that he should trust you. He's not one of your hit-it-and-quit-it guys.

Don't come on too strong. Physically, I mean."

He grew hot. "Um, yeah. He's very different from anyone I've ever been with."

"I like that. Just be yourself. There's no one better, and you deserve happiness. And I expect to be invited to the wedding," she stated.

"Oh God, Deirdre. Come on. It's our first official date. I've never had anyone over to my mom's house. Let me make it through that."

"I'm sorry, honey. How're you doing, living there? It can't be easy."

"She's everywhere I look. But I'd like to think—I'm hoping, at least—that she'd be happy I'm trying to move on."

"I know she would be. She wanted you to find someone. Whenever we'd sit together at the games or at the holidays, she'd tell me, 'I know this life won't be forever, and I want Keller to have someone to come home to, like Elijah does.'"

"I didn't know that."

"Uh-huh. She wouldn't tell you while you were playing because she thought it would distract you. But there's no doubt about it in my mind. I know she's up there, smiling down on you now. And loving every minute."

"Thanks, honey. That makes me feel better."

"Love you. I gotta go, Marli's calling for me. But you let me know how it goes. Here's Elijah."

"I will."

"Okay, listen. I think I know who it is, and if I'm right, he's a great guy. But you need to be careful when kids are involved. And you're the coach too."

He sighed. "I know, I know. I'll talk to you soon."

"Yes, you will. Bye."

A pulsating ache radiated along the length of his arm, and he cursed. The last thing he wanted was to take medication, but he knew from experience that if he didn't, it would only grow worse, to the point of freezing on him. He shook out two extra-strength NSAIDs, hoping they'd do the trick.

The doorbell rang, and his heart slammed. "You're an idiot," he scolded himself. "It's only Niall." But when he opened the door, he almost forgot how to breathe. Niall wore faded jeans and a black leather jacket. The white shirt underneath showed off the dark hair curling on his chest. Those glorious blue-green eyes glowed like the waters of the Caribbean. Strands of gleaming black hair fell over his brow, and Keller couldn't resist. He reached forward and brushed them away.

"Hi." He stepped aside. "Come on in."

Niall passed by, and Keller closed his eyes and took a breath. What the hell was wrong with him? He was acting like this was *his* first time with a man and not Niall's. He shut the door and contemplated Niall, who stood in front of him with a quizzical face.

"This is very homey." Niall gazed around him. "Your mother had good taste." He hung his jacket on the coatrack.

"Especially in sons." Keller winked, and Niall rolled his eyes.

"Seriously? You're going to start off with a bad joke?"

Keller was taller by almost three inches and had at least twenty pounds on him, but at the moment he felt as weak as a kitten.

"Should I do this instead?"

He cupped Niall's cheek and guided their lips together. The fire that had exploded between them the first time they'd kissed now leaped through his veins, and he struggled to keep his promise to go slow. The soft moans escaping Niall and the sweet rub of his tongue were fast becoming an addiction he willingly embraced. Breathing heavily, Keller released him.

Niall stood in front of him, eyes glittering, cheeks flushed, mouth red and swollen. The definition of temptation. Niall blinked, and his lips curved in a shy smile. "Yeah. That was better than any joke you've ever made."

What Keller wanted to say was, *What I'm feeling right now is no joke*, but he knew that would be too much, too soon, and he didn't want Niall to think he was pressuring him for sex.

"So what you're saying is, I shouldn't quit my day job to become a stand-up comic?" He grinned. "Let's sit. I figured we'd order some dinner and then…" He shrugged.

"And then?" Niall sat on the edge of the couch. "Keller, you know I've never been with a man. In fact, I've only ever been with Angie. I'm not…I don't know…" He hung his head. "I'm not sure what the hell I'm feeling or what I'm supposed to be doing, and—"

"Hey, hey. Slow down." He sat beside Niall, feeling his entire body trembling. A fine sheen of sweat gleamed on his face. "It's okay. I gotta admit I'm not sure either."

A broken laugh escaped Niall. "Are you kidding me? This isn't your first time. You—why are you shaking your head?"

"Sex with men before, yeah. But this? Dating? Being with a man I actually like, knowing that we aren't going to have sex? That's a first."

Wary, Niall shifted away. "Not have sex? What do you mean?"

"Is that what you thought would happen tonight?"

Red-faced again, Niall shrugged. "I…I don't know. I've only had one date with a man, and we had dinner and then he wanted to go back to his place."

Keller tensed. "On the first night?"

"Yeah. But I didn't feel a spark." Niall's gaze cut to him. "And now I know the difference."

The tightness in his chest eased. "I think what we have is more like a raging inferno than a spark. Even so, I figured you'd want to take it slow and get to know each other better. I don't want you to think I'm still that guy from high school."

"I think we're past that, don't you? I disliked you before even meeting you, and that wasn't fair." Niall studied the floor, his shoulders slumped as if he still carried that twenty-year-old weight. "But high school scarred me. Even now, I have trouble making friends because I feel less than. I always wonder if I'll end up humiliated somehow." Niall met his eyes. "I have hope now for the kids of today. David told me that you read them the riot act about allowing bullying to go on if they see anything. I'm glad you understand how damaging it can be."

Shame coursed through Keller. "I'm so damn sorry for what was done to you. I can't change the past, but let me try and rebuild some trust. Please? Besides…" He grinned. "It's a damn good thing you didn't look this good in high school 'cause I would've outed myself by needing to kiss you."

"Kiss me now."

Keller blinked. "What?"

Niall grabbed his face between his hands and planted one on his lips. Taken by surprise, Keller wasn't able to control his lust like he had for the prior kiss, and he pushed Niall beneath him on the couch, his mouth open, hot, and wet. This time there was no hesitation from Niall. He met Keller's seeking tongue with his own, and they battled, playing and teasing. An adrenaline high buzzed through him, and Keller moved from lips to jaw, nipping and sucking at the hot, rough skin.

"You're incredible," he panted. "First time I saw you in that bar, I thought you were so damn sexy."

"You did?" Niall breathed. "I was so mean to you."

"It didn't matter." Keller nuzzled into him, inhaling the warm scent of his skin. "You were so intriguing—who was this gorgeous man all by himself? I needed to know more. Teach me who you are." Niall's eyes glowed with an almost feral light, and Keller was captivated.

"I'm yours." Niall kissed him. He had no idea how

deeply those two words touched Keller. No one had ever wanted simply Keller Williams, the man off the playing field, and he was only just finding out who that was.

"Let's learn about each other. Together."

Niall arched into him, and Keller felt the thrust of a very large, hard erection. His fingers scraped along the front of Niall's jeans, and he watched his eyes grow hazy with lust.

"You like that?" Keller squeezed and kneaded the base of Niall's dick, still trapped behind layers of fabric. "You want me to keep touching you? We can stop anytime you want."

"Yes," he hissed, arching up into his hand. "Touch me. Please."

Gently, almost reverently, Keller popped the tab and slid the zipper down. The bulge of Niall's dick burst through the open space, the scent of his desire drowning Keller with its sweetness. "Look how perfect you are."

His face red, Niall licked his lips. "Friday nights after the games, I used to lie in bed and dream of you."

"It's me. And this is no dream."

Keller rubbed from tip to base, watching the fabric of Niall's briefs grow damper with each stroke. Soon Niall was humping against his hand. His eyes rolled back, his body bowed tight, and Keller yanked the waistband and caught the creamy release in his mouth, licking the sticky wetness from the red crown of Niall's throbbing cock. Niall lay twitching in the aftermath, breathing heavily. His own dick painfully stiff, Keller reached into his sweats, and with his gaze still firmly on Niall's disheveled, blissed-out state, came in his hand after only a few hard pulls on his dick. Eyes fluttering, he released himself and grabbed the box of tissues from the end table to wipe his hand. He glanced over at Niall and saw his cheeks wet, remorse shook him to the core.

"I'm sorry. I know I promised to take it slow, but—"

"No…you don't understand." Niall blew out a stream of air and wiped his cheeks. "I'm finally here."

"What do you mean?"

Eyes soft and with a glimmer of a smile on his lips, Niall sat up. "Since I was thirteen, I imagined what it would be like with a man, and now…it's overwhelming to be here. I'm me. Who I'm supposed to be."

He hadn't thought of it that way and it was difficult to catch his breath. "Thank *you*."

"For what?" Niall's dark brows pulled together.

"For trusting me. And giving me a part of you no one else has had. It's so incredibly humbling and special." He grinned. "And aren't you a surprise? Here I thought I was being all noble, and you attacked me."

Pink crept over his face, and his lips kicked up. "I know you said we should take it slow, but it's like the elephant in the room. I figured once we get it out of the way—"

"Whoa, whoa. *Out of the way?*" He gawked at Niall. "Sex is never something you should get out of the way. Let me ask you something. Was that how it used to be when you were married? A chore to finish?"

Niall's mouth drooped. "Yeah. I mean, it was hard," he whispered. "I tried to make her feel good, but I failed."

"That must've been difficult for both of you."

"I could pretend sometimes if I closed my eyes, imagining a man, but I know she wasn't satisfied with our sex life. Neither of us was happy."

"And now?"

"Now, after you…everything's different. It all makes sense." He ducked his head, and Keller's heart danced. Was anyone ever as sweet?

Unable to resist Niall's tempting mouth, Keller leaned in for a kiss. "Watching you come alive under me was beautiful."

"But I'm not sure about where to go from here. I don't know if I'm ready for more. Yet. It's overwhelming. Like I said, you're so much more experienced, and I know you're used to it being different. Plus, there's David."

"I know you have responsibilities." He was trying to be mature, though he wished they could have the freedom to see each other whenever they wanted.

"Something changed between me and David…I don't know what, but he came home this weekend and said he wanted me to be happy and that he was all right." Niall rubbed his face. "I'm not kidding myself that everything's going to be perfect. I'll have to face it again the first time I introduce him to a date." Groaning, he fell back on the couch. "Oh God, I can't imagine telling him about you and me. You're his coach, and you coming out is a whole lot different than me. I'm sorry I got you into this mess."

Niall was working himself into a state of panic, and Keller rushed to reassure him. "I don't see it as a mess. It's life, Niall. And when I look at myself, at the end of the day I'm almost forty and alone. Every night. There's only so much television I can watch or tinkering with the playbook I can force myself to do. Maybe that worked when I was younger, but it isn't where it's at now. Besides…" He grinned. "There's plenty we can do with each other now, until we take it to the next level." He kissed Niall's cheek. "I'm hungry. How about some sushi? I can order."

"Okay. Where's your bathroom?" Niall's smile was rueful. "I think I need to clean up a bit before we eat."

"First door on your right after the kitchen. What do you like to eat?"

"Anything. I'm easy."

"I'd say you're pretty hard, but I took care of that."

Niall groaned. "So bad."

Ridiculously happy, he placed an order for probably more food than they needed, but when it arrived, the two of them demolished every roll and piece of fish, leaving no leftovers.

Niall helped him clean up the containers and glanced

at his watch. "I hate to eat and run, but David's going to be home soon, and I need to be there." He slipped on his sneakers and took his jacket from the coatrack.

"I understand. Just one more thing…" He pulled Niall close and kissed him, plunging his tongue past Niall's open lips. Niall sucked his tongue feverishly, the intensity surprising him. There was so much more to discover about this man, and Keller itched to uncover his layers.

"That'll have to hold you until the weekend." Niall's expression became serious. "Thank you. I had a great time."

Keller answered by covering Niall's mouth with his, soaking in the sweetness of his lips. "See you Friday night at the game."

Then Niall was gone, taking all the light and life from the room. Keller wandered about, finally coming to rest in front of the small fireplace mantel where his mother had placed memorable pictures, chronicling their lives—her wedding, Keller's birth and the graduations, from kindergarten all the way through college. Pictures of him with his father that he studied almost every night. There were candid shots of him catching the winning touchdown in the Orange Bowl. He smiled at the picture of him and Elijah taken before his one and only time in the Super Bowl.

He picked up his parents' wedding picture, noticing he looked a lot like his father, wishing he had more memories of him to hang on to. "I'm sorry you had it so rough, Mom." With care, he returned it to its place, then brushed his fingers over his wet eyes. He went to take a shower.

The call came in at around one in the morning, which was unfortunate for him, since he'd only fallen asleep at midnight. Grumpy at being disturbed, he grabbed the phone, ready to bite the caller's head off. That quickly changed when he saw it was a blocked number.

"Hello?"

"Coach?" The voice was a whisper.

"Yeah, it's Coach Keller. Are you okay?" Always his first question. Keller dreaded the day he'd get a call from a kid in trouble. He could only hope he'd know the right thing to do.

"Yeah. I'm good. I…I called you a couple of weeks ago…about hearing something I wasn't sure how to handle."

His heart played a rapid beat. Was this David? It was so damn hard to tell.

"I remember. Did something happen?"

"Yeah…we talked it out, and, uh, I'm okay with it."

"I'm glad to hear that. Thanks for telling me."

"Yeah. I wanted you to know. I better get to sleep. Night."

Keller couldn't help smiling. "Good night." He ended the call. "David," he murmured.

There was little doubt in his mind after the conversation that it was David who'd called. The past weeks at the school had given him more insight into the teenaged mind than he had at that age, and Keller realized that despite what people thought, they liked structure and knowing what to expect. Niall coming out was a shock to David's steady, uncomplicated world, and he'd needed the time to work it out in his head. Keller had never doubted he would because David loved Niall and wanted his father to be happy.

But how would he react if he found out the two of them were involved? Keller had no clue about relationships in general; throw a teenage boy into the mix, and it became complicated. Add to it the fact that he was David's coach? That was a different kind of problem, one he wasn't yet ready to tackle. They were in a run for the championship, and that was his focus. Not his personal life.

Except, more than anything, he wanted to text Niall and say hi. But he set the phone on the nightstand and tried to fall asleep in his cold, empty bed.

"Keep it light and easy. Niall will understand."

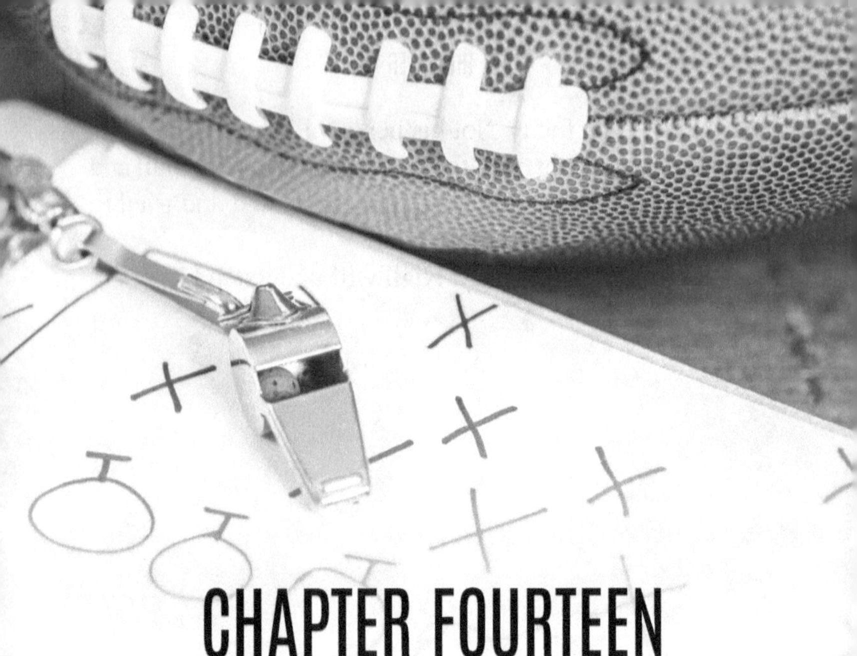

CHAPTER FOURTEEN

Had he done something wrong? Niall didn't understand why he hadn't heard from Keller since their night together. Staring into space instead of checking on library inventory, he jumped at the ringing phone, cursing at his interrupted fantasy.

"You're acting like a teenager—worse than David with his first crush."

But still…

The night he'd returned home from Keller's, he'd lain awake until after midnight. He'd run his hands over his body, touching where Keller had kissed him, unable to get comfortable. The bed had felt alien, and he'd imagined what it might be like to wake up and see Keller sleeping next to him. Every time he closed his eyes, he saw Keller's golden head between his thighs, his mouth on his cock as he climaxed, and he grew hard.

He had to stop thinking about sex during work hours. He wasn't a horny high school kid. Obviously, Keller was doing his job, and Niall needed to do his. He hefted the box of chemistry books that had come in and carried it from his office to the front desk, where the assistant librarian was helping a student.

"Thom, I'm going to get these books entered into the system and then get them to the chemistry department."

"Finally. I've been waiting for them." With a brisk stride, Marty Daniels approached him. "It's not easy to teach from handouts, and giving too many quizzes isn't my style."

Niall smiled at him. "Here they are. Ready for you once I check them off in the computer." He pulled up the inventory list and began the tedious process.

"Your son is doing very well in class. He's aced the two quizzes I did give."

Pride bloomed in his chest. "I'm happy to hear that, especially with all the emphasis on football. And now he's got a girlfriend, so I'm making sure he stays on top of his schoolwork."

"Better that than on top of her."

He winced but kept quiet, hoping Marty would shut up, but of course, wishes were merely dreams.

"They all do." Marty leaned against the counter. "But be honest with yourself. It's the age when those hormones start raging and all thoughts turn to sex. You remember how it was. I sure as hell do, only for me, I couldn't show it. Everything had to be a secret."

"It's better than it used to be." Niall continued to tick items off the list.

"For some. It all depends. In the city for sure it's more accepted than, say, up here. And if you're a teacher, especially of young kids, I wouldn't risk it." He lowered his voice. "By the way, remember what I told you about Keller Williams?"

On alert, Niall nodded, his fingers stilling on the keyboard. "Yeah."

"I have a friend who used to live in Vegas, and this guy he knows from one of the clubs said Keller hooked up with him. So it looks like I was right. He's definitely on the down-low."

Angry that Keller's private life was being discussed, Niall frowned. "I don't think it's right to speculate on someone's sexuality. It's not fair to him. Even if it's true, he must have his reasons for keeping quiet."

"Of course he does. He was a pro football player. But he's retired now."

"And a football coach. I'm sure there are plenty of narrow-minded people who'd object to a gay football coach, don't you think?" It hurt to know that Keller was the subject of scurrilous gossip. "Would you like someone talking about your sex life behind your back?"

Puzzled, Marty stared at him. "You're pretty worked up about this."

Fear trickled through him. "I just don't like poking into people's personal lives when it has nothing to do with me." He eyed Marty. "Frankly, I'm surprised you disagree."

Marty made a fist on top of the desk. "You know what bugs me more? The fact that I've been teaching at this school for almost fifteen years, and yet this guy waltzes in, and because he's a big name and a coach, he makes thirty grand more than me."

The envy in Marty's voice floored him. "You're joking. Keller's salary is why you think it's okay to spread stories about him?"

"It's not a rumor if it's true." Marty shrugged, and his nonchalance at the damage his yapping, jealous mouth could cause Keller angered Niall to no end.

Jaw tense, Niall tapped the keyboard, and with a final *click*, entered the last book. "All done."

"Can I take one of the carts? I'll return it."

"Yeah, sure." He turned away, anxious to see Marty gone.

"You okay, Niall? You look upset." Thom peered at him through wire-rimmed glasses. "Did Marty say something?"

Unwilling to get into it, Niall tried to brush him off. "I'm all right. Just, some people have no respect for boundaries."

"Marty?" Thom narrowed his eyes, looking annoyed. "He can be a jerk sometimes. Always talking or complaining about someone or something."

It was a bad trait he'd also noticed. Over the years, he'd chosen to ignore it, but coming into his own and embracing his sexuality meant he wasn't willing to accept unreasonable or ugly behavior anymore. Especially now that it concerned someone he was fast becoming attached to.

"Life is too short to be miserable."

"What a game, huh?" Michael slurped his soda as they watched the Overlook Tigers rout the Bellwood Wildcats by a score of 49-10. "The kids looked like they were on a mission."

"Yeah. They marched down the field every time they had possession." Niall scooped up some popcorn and crunched the last few handfuls. "They were awesome. Every play was executed with precision."

"And our two boys did great. Chris made two catches and rushed for almost fifty yards, and David made two or three catches?" Michael asked, scanning the field as the two-minute warning whistle was blown.

"Three," he responded proudly, watching the team on the sidelines. "And I think he rushed for thirty yards. He'll tell me."

All the boys were happy and excited except for one. Shane Contard. Earlier in the game, he'd gotten sacked, and when he left the field, his father had run through the stands toward the field, yelling and chastising him, calling Shane a loser and a wimp. Knowing Bobby Contard's ugly behavior, Niall could only imagine Shane's home life with a father like that, and felt sorry for him.

As always, Dara took pictures and showed them to him after. "Tell me which ones you want, and I'll send them to you. Coach Williams has really been great for the team. I don't recall the boys so focused, do you?"

"This one of him making the catch for their last touchdown, thanks." He handed the phone to Dara. "And yeah. Keller's been a huge asset."

"He's more than a gorgeous face. Although that doesn't hurt for us parents." Dara winked.

"Hey," Michael protested with a good-natured smile.

"Oh, you." She kissed his cheek. "A girl can dream, right?" She leaned over Michael to speak to Niall. "Sorry things didn't work out with Marcie. She's dating one of the guys in my office."

"I'm glad. She's very nice, but there was no spark."

"Okay, here we go." Michael set his empty cup on the ground. "Not that the ending is in doubt."

Bellwood's offense took the field at the forty-seven yard line, and with the win virtually assured, Niall could concentrate on the sidelines and Keller. He was in constant motion, and from his vantage point, Niall could see him talking into his headset to his defensive coach, whom he'd placed in the stands, likely so he could get a better handle on the opposing team's positioning. There was one moment, as the teams broke for halftime, when he thought Keller glanced his way, but it was over so quickly, Niall couldn't be certain. He hoped they'd have a chance to talk afterward.

The Bellwood crowd roared at the snap, and their quarterback scrambled, looking for a free player. The tackles came charging at him, and he threw the ball in what Niall knew was a Hail Mary pass to avoid being sacked. Those cheers turned to groans as the Overlook Tigers' defensive cornerback, Trevor Norwood, their leading pass interceptor, leaped high in the air and did it again. He ran it downfield for a touchdown. With the clock at less than ten seconds, the special teams took their time coming on the field for the extra point, and the game was over as the ball sailed through the goalposts.

"Did you see that?" Michael jumped to his feet as the contingent of Tigers fans in the stands went wild.

"Amazing. These kids are on their way to an undefeated season and possibly state championship if they keep playing like this."

"Our boys have their own personal fan club as well." Dara pointed. "Look."

Niall craned his neck and saw Chris with his arm around Mallory Hart, while Renee hugged David. "Yeah. Best friends dating best friends. It's sweet."

"Have you given David 'the talk' yet?" Michael asked. The stands began to empty, but they waited for the crowd to dissipate before leaving. "We reminded Chris of the responsibilities of dating."

"Yeah, I mentioned it to David, but I think I'd better be a little more specific. Things can get out of hand very quickly."

"We've always been open with Chris, but it's different when it's merely words versus reality," Dara mused. "I think it's a good time to start dating, as long as they respect boundaries."

"What have you set for Chris? Angie and I have talked about it, but mainly in schoolwork terms. Are you doing anything different?" As the custodial parent, he was the day-to-day person, and Niall welcomed whatever help he could get.

"We told him we know sex is exciting but that he's too young and there are long-reaching consequences—that he isn't prepared for—to taking that step. We told him we don't want him having sex yet." Her eyes glimmered. "I can only hope he listens, but it's hard to remember what your parents said when things are getting hot and heavy with your girlfriend. And of course, we talked about protection and STIs." She made a face. "All the fun stuff."

"I agree. We know teenagers don't listen, no matter how 'good' they are." He air-quoted. "I'm hoping to keep the lines of communication open with David. I wonder if Keller has spoken to them about it."

"You two have become pretty friendly. I heard you had dinner at the diner last week," Michael said.

The hair stood up on the back of his neck, and sweat broke out between his shoulder blades. "Uh, yeah. David and I went on Sunday for burgers, and Keller walked in. It would've been strange not to ask him to join us."

"He seems like a good guy. Down to earth. Did you know he gave the kids his personal cell in case they ever want to talk about anything?"

"No, I didn't. David never mentioned it. But I think Keller truly cares about the kids." He rose to his feet. "Looks like it's clearing out."

They left the stands for the parking lot and found their cars, which were next to each other. Michael ran a hand over the hood of the BMW.

"Nice wheels. Beats the clunker you were driving."

From Michael's questioning expression, Niall knew he was curious how he could afford such an expensive car, but he wasn't about to reveal the reality. It would lead to more questions he wasn't prepared to answer. Even though he and Michael were close, Niall still couldn't be sure how his friend would react to him coming out.

"It's great. And it was a great deal. The victory party's at Trevor's house tonight," he said, trying to change the topic. "Appropriate, considering he had that great interception." He kissed Dara's cheek good-bye. "I'll see you at next week's game."

"Absolutely."

They got into their Land Rover and drove off.

His phone buzzed with a text. *Can I see you later? Just finished up with the team.*

A smile Niall knew was dopey with happiness spread over his face, but he didn't care.

Where and when? Much as he wanted Keller, he knew it would seem odd for Keller's car to be in his driveway, but his vehicle wouldn't be any less conspicuous. The night he'd visited Keller he'd parked several blocks away, but that wasn't possible in the Estates, where street parking wasn't allowed.

Yours? Keller asked.

He thought fast.

Text me when you're here, and I'll open the garage for you.

See you in an hour. I have to go home first.

Ok.

Bellwood was about a twenty-minute drive away, which gave him ample time to shower and change. Niall stood in front of the bed, wondering if he and Keller would end up there, and rolled his eyes at his foolishness. "I'm not making out on the couch like a couple of horny teenagers." He stripped the sheets and put on new ones.

Would they go further than the other night? Was he ready? What did it mean for him and Keller if they did? Keller had never mentioned exclusivity or commitment. Did Keller want that? Did he?

"Now you really are acting like a teenager. Stop driving

yourself up the wall. You're both adults and almost forty. Sex is natural."

Nervous excitement swirled in his belly, and he decided a glass of wine would settle his racing brain. He took out a bottle of Chardonnay from the refrigerator and poured himself a healthy glass, which he downed in three gulps. He contemplated the rest and decided against it. "Don't want to be bombed when Keller gets here."

His phone buzzed.

I'm in the driveway.

Niall raced to the garage, and Keller pulled inside and cut the engine. Niall's heart slammed watching Keller exit the car.

"Hi. Great game. You took a shower, I see. Me too."

Keller's golden hair was damp and curled at his neck. He'd changed into a long-sleeved black shirt that stretched across his muscular chest and arms. Powerful thighs filled out the faded jeans, and Niall grew achy and hot at his approach. It must be the wine. It had to be. No other person had ever rendered him a babbling fool.

Keller's mouth settled over his, and Niall lost himself in the possessiveness of that kiss. Time ceased to move as he held on to that moment when Keller's arms came around him to pull him tighter.

"I wanted to be here sooner, but didn't want to come to you fresh off the field."

Niall buried his face in Keller's neck, drawing in deep, greedy breaths of his skin. The faint scent of soap and the stronger one of his cologne filled him to the point where he could stay like that forever and be happy.

"I wouldn't have minded."

Keller chuckled. "If I'm going to be hot and sweaty, it's because you'll make me that way."

Reluctantly, Niall released him. "Let's go inside. Do you want a drink? I didn't plan on you coming, so I only have wine. I don't know if you drink white or red, but…" He trailed off, sensing he was chattering. Keller kissed his cheek.

"I'm good with wine. Whatever you have."

Once they'd settled onto the couch with their glasses, Niall had to ask. "Why didn't you get in touch with me after Wednesday night? I thought we had a good time."

"A great time," Keller corrected, setting his glass on the table. "I didn't want you to think I was rushing or pushing you. Plus, I needed to concentrate on the game. But trust me, you were always on my mind."

Feeling foolish at his neediness, Niall took a big sip of his wine. "I'm being silly. Of course you have to think of the game."

"But the game is over." A dangerously wicked smile curved Keller's lips. "And now all I can think about is you." He plucked Niall's glass from his trembling fingers and placed it next to his.

"Yeah?" Niall asked, suddenly finding it hard to breathe.

"*Mmhmm.*" Keller shifted closer. "Specifically, you and me. Together. Me touching you." He placed a hand on Niall's cheek, mapping out the bones of his face and jaw with a surprisingly delicate touch. "You touching me."

Niall placed a hand over Keller's chest, and feeling the rapid thump under his fingers settled his nerves. "Your heart is beating so fast."

"That's what being near you does to me."

Niall ducked his head. "You don't have to say that to get me to want you. I'm nothing special. Just a regular guy." He hated that Marty's gossiping words popped into his mind, but he had to get it out there.

A fierce light burned in Keller's eyes. "Don't say that. That's not who you are."

"I'm glad you know who I am, because I sure as hell have no idea."

Keller brushed their lips together. "How about we explore who and what we both are, together? Because being with someone like you is a first for me too, and I'm kind of fumbling."

Keller nuzzled along his neck, and Niall's heart surged into overdrive. "You don't fumble." He gasped when Keller reached under his T-shirt to tease the tips of his aching nipples. "They used to say you had the golden touch."

"*Mmm,*" Keller hummed, releasing Niall for a moment and pulling off his own shirt to reveal that beautiful, sculpted chest. "I'm only interested in what you have to say. And touching you is more precious than gold."

Anxious to feel Keller's naked skin on his, Niall tugged his shirt off too and tossed it aside. "I say prove it."

Keller's eyes gleamed. Those strong arms caged him, and Keller dipped his head and licked a wet path along his torso, starting at his neck. Niall sighed, then hissed as Keller lightly bit his nipples. "Oh God, okay. Point made."

"I'm only just beginning." Keller's low chuckle against his stomach sent a shiver through him. "Cold?" he murmured, and Niall trembled, wondering...*hoping* to feel Keller's mouth on him again as Keller's lips and tongue continued their path.

"No, the opposite." He sighed. "I'm burning up." Keller placed a hand on the waistband of his sweats and waited. Niall nodded. "Please, I haven't stopped thinking about what it's going to be like."

Keller's eyes softened. "I want it to be good for you."

Taking the initiative, Niall grasped Keller around the neck and kissed him. "I'm thinking you're good for me. Let's go upstairs."

"Really?" Keller blinked. When he nodded, Keller took his hand, not releasing it until they were in his bedroom. "Whatever you want. Just tell me."

"You." Niall kissed him, wondering where all this courage was coming from, even though he trembled. "I want you."

They stripped off the rest of their clothes and lay naked beside each other. His gaze devoured Keller, from the rippled abs to the heavy erection and full balls nestled between his thighs.

"Touch me," Keller begged. "Please."

Knowing Keller was hard for him was a heady feeling, and Niall ran his fingers down the length of Keller's cock before gripping it. At Keller's sighs of pleasure, he grew bolder and rubbed tip to base, watching wide-eyed as Keller's hands grasped the sheets and he bucked his hips.

"Am I doing this right?" he whispered, but Keller didn't answer. He stiffened and groaned, his dick pulsing out a stream of come that ran over Niall's hand and fingers. His lips twitched. "I guess that's a yes."

Cracking one eye open, Keller motioned to him. "Get over here."

"Let me wipe up first." He crawled over to the nightstand and used some tissues, but Keller tackled him and pushed him to the mattress.

"You have the most beautiful ass."

"I do?" Shaking, he lay beneath Keller, falling into the liquid-blue fire of his eyes.

"Shh. We're not going there. Not yet. Tonight is all about exploring."

"O-okay," he mumbled, a little uncertain what that meant. His erection brushed against Keller's taut abs, and his breath caught.

Keller kissed him. "Let me take care of that for you." He nibbled from Niall's jaw to his belly button, and lust threatened to explode at the workings of Keller's tongue as it licked the tip of his erection.

"Keller, please, oh my God."

"Feels good, doesn't it?" Smiling lips kissed his throbbing length, and then Keller took the whole of him into the searing heat of his mouth. Keller began to suck, and Niall knew he wasn't going to last.

He slapped the bed, and despite his best efforts, he couldn't stop his hips from thrusting. Keller took it all in stride and increased the delicious friction of his tongue and lips, humming with pleasure, then reached down, fingers brushing the tense muscles of Niall's thighs before gliding along his balls. The little control Niall had clung to vanished.

"What the hell, Kellerrrr," he moaned, his skin too tight to contain the orgasm burning through him, and he burst into pieces, his cock jerking in Keller's warm mouth.

When he opened his eyes, Keller lay on his side, watching him. "Do you still believe sex is something you should get out of the way?"

Niall tried to gather his thoughts and his breath. "I'll step into the path of the Keller Williams express train any day to feel like this. I know you don't—"

"Please stop." His blue eyes narrowed with annoyance, Keller frowned. "Stop telling me what I do or don't know or feel."

"I'm sorry." Chastened, Niall turned his head. "I didn't mean to upset you."

"I'm not upset with you. I'm upset *for* you." Keller's fingers trailed over his naked hip.

Only moments earlier Keller had wrung the most intense orgasm from him, and Niall had thought he was finished for the night, but at Keller's touch, he grew half-hard again.

Keller said, "All these years…you have so much passion that's been locked inside you for too long. I hate that you've been denied."

Niall ran his hands over the expanse of Keller's chest,

loving that he was free to touch a man—this man. "So don't deny me."

Keller's eyes gleamed. "I've created a monster."

"*Rawr*," Niall growled, and kissed Keller.

CHAPTER FIFTEEN

They fell asleep with their arms around each other and woke up at one in the morning. Keller's stomach growled long and loud. He gave a sleepy Niall an apologetic smile.

"I guess the ham-and-cheese sandwich I grabbed at home wasn't enough. I'm starving. Do you have anything I can eat by any chance?"

Laughing, Niall swung his legs over the side of the bed and bent over to retrieve his clothes, and Keller couldn't help looking his fill. The man did have the most gorgeous ass.

"Do you have to ask? I live with a teenage boy, otherwise known as a human vacuum cleaner. Come on, let's raid the fridge."

"Great." He pulled on his underwear and sweats and followed Niall downstairs to the kitchen. As they passed through the living room, he heard his phone ringing.

Niall stopped. "Do you want to get that?"

"Yeah, I have to. It could be important."

Niall sat on the couch and watched as he answered. "This is Keller."

"Coach?" The muffled voice sounded fearful.

"Yes, are you okay? Are you hurt?"

"I'm fine, kind of. I just needed to ask you something."

"You can ask me anything."

He sat beside Niall.

"I was at a party tonight. And…" The voice choked up. "I-I kissed that guy again. I thought I could keep away, but…we did stuff."

"First thing I want to tell you is, please be safe. There's nothing wrong with kissing another boy. You're a kid and allowed to explore who you are, but be careful."

The laughter was bitter. "You say that, but my father… my father's gonna kill me if he finds out."

Niall continued to stare at him wide-eyed. Keller felt almost helpless.

"Has he gotten physical with you in the past?"

"He's just trying to make me a better player."

His hand gripped the phone.

"No, that's not the way it works. I'm your coach, and I don't put my hands on you, do I? Violence doesn't solve anything. Ever. Using your fists doesn't make you more of a man, understand?"

"Yeah."

"I hope so. I also hope you know that there's nothing wrong or bad if you are gay, or bisexual, or identify any other way. It's who you are. I stand by everyone on the team, and I'll always have your back."

"Thanks, Coach. I wish my dad were like that, but he's never gonna change."

"People can change if they want to. Sometimes people scream and shout because they're afraid, but that's no excuse."

"Maybe." The voice sounded doubtful, and Keller knew it would take more than words, but this was the best he could do, especially at one in the morning.

"Try and get some sleep. And you did nothing wrong by kissing a guy."

"Okay."

"Night."

The screen went dark, and hunger forgotten, he made no move to get up from the couch. Niall took the phone from his hands and held on to him.

"God, I feel so useless. I never know if I'm saying the wrong thing."

"I heard you gave your phone number to the kids, but I didn't think much of it. The way you handled that conversation was perfect."

Gratitude swelled in his heart, and he hugged Niall. "I'm so glad you were with me. I've had calls in the middle of the night, and it makes a difference to have someone by my side. Not just anyone. You."

Niall's smile was shy. "I'm glad I was with you too."

He liked having Niall with him, period. More than he'd imagined. He'd known Niall was a man who lived with his emotions tightly guarded, but he said what he felt from the heart, and that made Keller think. As a player, he'd always had a PA to handle the consequences of his words and actions. But now, with the stadium lights turned off and the microphones silent, all he had left was himself. For the first time, he was adrift. Alone. A player no longer. A high school football coach in a tiny town. Merely a man on the sidelines that no one knew.

Maybe it was time to let someone in.

He hugged Niall again, and rested their cheeks together. "You know what I really liked?"

"What?" Niall's breath tickled his ear.

"Waking up and having you next to me. I like seeing

you curled up on your side with your head on the pillow and feeling your feet on mine. I like smelling you on my skin." He licked Niall's cheek, and his heart pounded at Niall's sharp intake of breath. "And tasting you. I like you a lot."

"This is surreal. Like my fantasy come to life." His voice rumbled through Keller.

"Tell me your fantasy." He stroked Niall's back, enjoying the play of muscles under his hands. "Was it sexy?"

Niall shook with laughter in his arms. "Looking for an ego stroke?"

"Not my ego that needs stroking."

"Oh God, I should've known that would lead to a bad joke."

He set his hands on Niall's shoulders and met his inquiring gaze. "But there's nothing funny about the way you make me feel."

"I like you a lot too." Keller's stomach rumbled loudly, breaking the tension swirling between them. Niall rose. "Let's make you something to eat before you pass out."

He squeezed a handful of Niall's butt. "I could always nibble on cake."

After his sandwich was made, Niall took a bag of chips and sat across from him, a curious expression on his face. "Do you know who called you?"

He chewed and swallowed. "I have an idea, but it wouldn't be fair to speculate. And it doesn't matter."

"I know, of course not."

But Niall behaved as if he had something on his mind, and when the food was gone and the kitchen cleaned for the night, Keller held out his hand. "Let's sit for a minute."

"Uh, okay." Instant wariness popped into Niall's eyes.

"Why do you look so worried?" Keller asked as they returned to the couch.

Niall's shoulders hunched. "I guess things are going so well, I don't think it can last. I'm still trapped in the mindset of that kid running through the school, wearing only a towel."

Wincing at Niall's brutally honest words, Keller raked a hand through his hair. "I hate that you still feel like a victim. You're strong and capable. A single father to a teenage boy. I think you're great." He kissed Niall's mouth. "But at the table, you looked like you had something on your mind."

Niall's brow creased, then cleared. "Oh, yeah. During the game, after Shane was sacked, did you see Bobby Contard?"

He thought a second. "No. I was too busy to watch the stands." Unease wrapped around his chest. "Why? What did he do?"

Niall relayed the scene he'd witnessed, and Keller saw red.

"That bastard. I swear…" Needing to keep moving or else he might throw something, he jumped up and paced. "He's going to ruin that kid if he doesn't stop. I'm gonna have to talk to him. I can't have him abusing the kid while the game is going on. Or in general. I even went to the cops and told them I thought he hit Shane." He related what he'd seen—the extensive bruising—and Niall's eyes grew wide with horror.

"What did they do?"

He snorted. "Went to his house and asked him a few questions. I hope they took it seriously, but you never know."

"You did the right thing."

"I'm not so sure. Do *you* think Bobby is physically violent toward Shane?"

"Oh God, I hope not." Niall's expression was frank. "Look. Bobby Contard hasn't changed much from high school. Allowed to go unchecked, once a bully, always a bully. He's been on top of Shane since the boys were in Peewee league. And Shane puts up with it, you can tell, but this year…it seems like he's struggling. I mean, David and Shane aren't that close, so I don't know him well, but…"

It made sense. If, as he suspected, it was Shane calling him, he was dealing not only with questioning his sexuality, but also a father who had no trouble using his fists to make a point.

Thinking fast, Keller asked, "Any idea who his friends are?"

Niall's face screwed up in thought. "He and Van used to hang out together whenever they were at a party here, but other than that…sorry. I just didn't pay much attention." He yawned.

"Maybe the visit from the cops scared Bobby, but I doubt it. He's a time bomb." He checked his watch. "It's almost two in the morning."

Sleepy-eyed, Niall nodded. "You're staying here, right?"

Keller grinned. "I thought you'd never ask. I brought my bag but left it in the car."

"Well, go bring it in. You'll need your toothbrush. I don't like morning breath."

He blinked awake and glanced at his watch on the nightstand: 9:22. *Damn.* He usually woke at six, even on the weekends. Niall lay sleeping next to him, and he slipped out of bed, went to the bathroom, and brushed his teeth. He crept back under the covers and kissed Niall's ear, cheek, and jaw. By the time he reached his lips, Niall was smiling and gazing at him with sleepy, heavy-lidded eyes.

"*Mmm.* That's nice to wake up to."

"And I even brushed my teeth for you. But I don't mind a little morning breath, so…" He kissed Niall, pushing his tongue inside his warm mouth. Niall sucked his tongue with hungry abandon, and their cocks bumped and slid together.

He grasped them in his hand, and Niall's moans rose in the stillness of the bedroom. Hand slippery with precome, Keller increased the speed of his strokes, and he could pinpoint the exact second he knew Niall was ready to come. He used the wetness of his finger to tease around the rim of Niall's hole before sliding the tip past the tight opening.

"Oh fuck, oh fuck," Niall shouted and came, his face a mask of shock and pleasure. Watching Niall fall apart sent Keller over the edge, and his climax exploded through him like a firecracker. Sweat-covered and shaking, they clung to each other, and Keller couldn't resist taking a little nip of Niall's shoulder, then licking the reddened spot.

"I told you I wanted to taste you. Next time I'm going to show you something even better." He cupped Niall's ass and smoothed his hands over the perfect roundness.

"Better than this?" Niall shivered. "I can't even imagine. Nothing's ever been this perfect."

The trust in Niall's eyes almost did him in, but Keller was determined to go slow and steady, no matter how much he wanted to fuck Niall into the bed. He was dying to spread Niall wide and eat him out, listening to his screams of pleasure. He'd never wanted anyone as much as he wanted this man, but Niall still needed to work past his traumatic high school memories to ensure they'd stay firmly in the past.

"I think we need a shower and some breakfast." He bounced off the bed, leaving Niall lying in the tangled sheets. "What do you want to do today?"

Niall blinked. "Oh. I didn't know…" He turned red. "I wasn't sure you'd want to spend the day together," he said softly, and Keller's heart ached.

"I do, if you do." He sat on the edge of the bed. "I know we're keeping this quiet between us until we both decide it's right, but how about we get out of town and go apple-picking?"

Niall's face brightened. "That would be fun. We used

to take David before he got too big and didn't think it was fun to go with his parents anymore."

"Let's do it. Breakfast in or out?"

"I can make us bacon and eggs."

"Sounds good." He planted a soft kiss on Niall's lips. "Get that lazy ass out of bed. I'm hungry."

They showered and ate and decided to take Keller's car, in case David came home unexpectedly and saw it in the garage. The drive to the orchard took about forty-five minutes, and they picked a basket to split among themselves. They each crunched an apple, and at one point, hidden by a copse of trees, he pulled Niall close and kissed him, leaving them breathless.

"I couldn't resist. I love apples." He licked his lips and waggled his brows. Laughing, Niall nuzzled into his neck.

"You're silly. But cute." His tone serious, Niall put a hand on his shoulder. "Thank you for understanding I'm not ready to make us public just yet. I know you're aware of the ramifications. And it's not about you personally. Just…I've told David but no one else, and I'm not sure how to best go about it. It's been my secret for so long."

"I do understand. It's going to be tricky for me as well on several fronts." He set the basket of apples on the ground and leaned against the tree. "I'm certain I'll lose fans and some player friends. Probably the few endorsements I have left. But lately it's been harder to find a good reason to keep my sexuality a secret. I'm almost forty. Fuck it, I want to live my real life and be able to do the things every couple gets to do without being afraid. Here I am, coaching these kids and giving them advice about being true to themselves, when I'm the one hiding." He grimaced. "Am I a hypocrite?"

Niall put a hand to his cheek. "No. You're like the rest of our generation. Just trying to figure it out."

He slipped his arms around Niall's waist and pulled him close. "I have something figured out."

"Yeah? What?" Niall's breathless voice sent a powerful surge of lust through him.

"You and me. How much I want you. We're good together." He kissed Niall's neck.

"And you figured that out after one night?"

"Nope. I figured that out after that time in my house. I couldn't get to sleep because I wanted you in my bed with me. I didn't want you to leave. I like talking to you and hearing you laugh at my bad jokes."

Pink-faced and not only from the sun on his cheeks, Niall gave him a shy smile. "I felt the same. It took me forever to fall asleep, and the next morning I was exhausted."

If Niall only knew how that sweet innocence, coupled with the surprisingly hungry abandon he'd shown in bed, set his blood on fire. Instead of telling him, Keller couldn't resist the urge and took Niall's face in his hands and kissed him hard. The murmur of voices in the distance snapped him to the reality that although they were deep in the orchard, they could still be seen.

"We'd better go."

Inside the country store, Keller spied homemade apple and peach pies and took one of each.

"Two pies?" Brows raised, Niall folded his arms. "Isn't that a little excessive?"

"Sue me. I'm feeling a little extra right now. Wild and free." Maybe it was happiness. Something he'd lost since his mother died, and like an old friend he hadn't seen for years, it was hard to recognize, but he was ready to welcome the emotion back with open arms. "You do that to me," he murmured as he passed by Niall to place the pies on the counter to pay.

"Can I have your autograph, please?" The kid at the register gazed at Keller with adoring eyes. "I can't believe Keller Williams is here in our store. My dad's gonna freak out that he went fishing today and didn't work."

"And I bet you weren't happy you got stuck here." He'd seen people being discreet with their cameras, taking his picture and maybe wanting to share in his enjoyment of the day. "How about we take a picture and send it to him."

The kid's jaw dropped. "Oh my God, that would be so cool."

He handed Niall his phone. "Could you take our picture?" He turned to the kid. "What's your name?"

"Henry."

"Okay, Henry. Smile."

A small crowd had gathered, and after Niall took their picture, others felt emboldened to ask. It took close to half an hour before they could escape, and by the time they were on the highway toward home, the sky had darkened to twilight.

"You were more patient than I would've been," Niall remarked. "It's like that kid at the restaurant who asked for your autograph. How do you do it? You never stopped smiling."

"I know how lucky I am to have led the life I did. It gave me the chance to do what I loved, not to mention financial security beyond my wildest dreams. Interacting with the public is part of that life. My coaches always taught us to be grateful we had fans. A smile and a picture or an autograph is a small price to pay for the memories you leave them with. For me, it's just another day at the office, but for a kid like Henry, who might not be able to afford to go to the game and has only seen players on television…he'll remember this day."

Niall put a hand on his arm. "I know I've already told you, but I'm so sorry I misjudged you. What you said really resonates with me. I was a bookworm, and I know if I'd met any of the authors who'd helped me through my rough times, it would've meant the world to me."

Keller took a hand off the steering wheel and squeezed Niall's. "I wish things could've been different."

Niall returned the pressure, his smile filling his face. "They are now. Better late than never."

CHAPTER SIXTEEN

David called as they were walking into Keller's house. "Where are you, Dad?"

Instant fear shot through him. "I'm out. Are you home? Is everything okay?"

"Yeah. I just came to pick up some books. Chris's mom is dropping us at the movies, and then we're gonna have pizza and study."

"We? As in you and Renee and Chris and Mallory?"

"Yeah. Tomorrow we're gonna go to Van's. We have a history test next week, so we're gonna have a study sesh."

He couldn't help grinning. David's life was everything he could've wanted for his son.

"Okay. Enjoy your movie and study sesh." Across the room, Keller snickered.

"What did you do today? Where are you?"

"Uh, I went out with friends. Apple-picking. Now we're

going to have dinner. Maybe watch a movie."

"Dad, are you on a date?" David's voice dropped low.

"A date?" Panic rose in his throat, but then he decided to hell with it. He had to take the first step, and David had to learn this was his new normal. "Uh…yeah. I am. How do you feel about that?" Keller crossed the room and put his arms around him. Surprised he was shaking, peace flowed through him with Keller's body tight against his.

"I'm good with it. I don't like leaving you alone on the weekends, so I'm glad you've found someone to spend time with." He teased, "Just be careful. Don't go too far right away."

"David! Jesus." Niall choked, and Keller ran away to stuff his head in the couch cushions to muffle his laughter.

"Ha-ha. It had to be said, especially after all the lectures I'm getting lately from you and Mom about dating and sex."

A bead of sweat rolled down his cheek. "Don't worry about me. And make sure you listen to what we say."

"Trust me, I know," he groaned. "Renee is getting the same from her parents. I swear we're not. We talked about it, and we both agree we're not ready."

"I have to say, you kids are much more open about it than my generation."

"Well, Renee is really focused on school. It made me think more about what I want too. Football is great, and I love playing, but what happens if I get hurt like Coach? I need to have a plan. Mom agrees. She said this summer I can work at her office and see if I like it."

This was news to him. "Law school? I didn't know you were interested in law."

"I dunno. I guess I'll see. Anyway, I better get going. I'm taking my bike to Chris's. I'll call you later. Be good!"

"Very cute. Have a great time, and I'll see you tomorrow."

The screen went dark, but he remained gazing at the phone. "I'm not sure I'm ready for all this."

Recovered from his burst of hysterics, Keller patted the space next to him. "Come here."

He sat, and Keller wrapped his arms around him. "What I saw was open conversation, yet one with boundaries. I think that what you have with David is very special. The fact that you two can talk to each other like this is so helpful. Think about the boys who don't."

"Like Shane." He sighed. "I feel bad, knowing he has a father like that. I've seen Bobby over the years, and he still gives me dirty looks. Some people never grow, clinging to the glory days of their youth because they're stuck."

"And I walked away and never looked back until I got the call about coaching," Keller mused.

"How did that happen?" Curious to hear more about Keller's life, Niall shifted to face him. "Did you keep in touch with Coach Weaver?"

"Not really. I'd send him a Christmas card every year, but that was about it. I could've done more." Haunted blue eyes met his. "I was too busy living the life, and then after my mother died, I just didn't give a damn about anything. I turned to partying and just hanging out. She would've been so disappointed."

Past hurts were all too often accountable for the painful present, and Niall didn't enjoy seeing Keller upset. "Hey, it's okay. It's easy to beat ourselves up with the knowledge of hindsight. None of us are perfect. You're here now, and I can tell you're making a difference."

"You think so?"

"You are for me." The words had slipped out before he could stop them, but at the genuine pleasure shining from Keller's eyes, he was glad he'd said them.

"Do you really mean that?"

Niall nodded. "And not only for the sex, which from my very limited experience is incredible, but because you brought me out of my shell. You help me see myself more clearly."

"You'd already taken that step when I saw you in that bar the first time."

"True, but it's more than that. Knowing I have your friendship makes things easier. I feel like I can talk to you about almost anything, and you'd understand."

"You can. I feel the same way. And I might've been with other men, but I can't remember a thing about any of them." Keller shifted until they were nose-to-nose, a kiss apart. "Unlike you. You're unforgettable."

"You don't have to flatter me. I'm a quiet bookworm who's never been to a club and enjoys reading more than socializing. Not like your Vegas party boys."

Keller's lips twitched. "I don't believe in flattery because I've had too many people sucking up to me. I never say what I don't mean. You made an impression on me from that first day and I didn't even know who you were. And now that we've gotten closer, you're always on my mind." A puzzled expression crossed his face. "What do you mean, party boys?"

Niall's heart sank, but he owed Keller the truth about the rumors he'd heard. "I didn't want to say anything because I hate spreading gossip, but do you know Marty Daniels, the chemistry teacher?"

"Yeah, we've met." Keller's lips thinned. "He doesn't have the greatest opinion of me. Why? Did he say something?"

Debating how much to reveal, Niall knew his side was firmly by Keller's. "He said that someone he knew was friends with a man you hooked up with when you lived in Vegas. He called him a party boy."

Silent and slightly pale under his tan, Keller focused on the far wall of the living room, gazing out into nothing. "So much for NDAs. I guess the jig is up." The attempt to joke fell flat, and Keller sighed. "Look. I never said I was an altar boy. During the football season, I'd go months without sex, and I was fine with it because my focus was solely on the game and winning. But in the off-season…it got so damn lonely." He lifted his chin, and their eyes locked. "So yeah. I'd have guys up to my apartment. Different ones all the time. It was all supposed to be private, and every single one of them signed nondisclosures. I always knew I had to be careful. Or so I thought. But none of that matters now. If Marty Daniels knows, it won't be long before others do."

"I'm sorry." It seemed so inadequate, but he had no idea what else to say. "It's so wrong to gossip about someone's sexuality, and the fact that it's another gay man doing it… it's reprehensible," he stated.

"Thank you for defending me." Keller kissed his cheek. "You know, earlier I said I was tired of hiding. And I understand you need time to work out your own timetable— like you said, everyone's different. But maybe now's my time to step up and be me for once."

"You shouldn't be forced to come out because of the fear of rumors and innuendos. That makes me sick to my stomach."

"Are you thinking of me, or yourself?" There was no condemnation in Keller's eyes, only curiosity.

Startled by the question, Niall was about to deny it, but then took a moment to consider it. "Yeah, you're probably right. And I don't know why I'm holding back. The most important person in my life knows, and he still loves me. Nothing else really matters."

"And you have me." Keller's declaration brought him more pleasure than he'd thought possible. "You know that, don't you?"

"I—yeah. I guess I do."

Keller leaned in closer. "You guess? I see you need more convincing. Let me work on that."

Keller's warm mouth settled over his, the taste of his

tongue and lips a heady cocktail for the aching throbs of pleasure beating in his blood. He smelled delicious—warm skin, a hint of cinnamon and apple from the cider they'd drunk earlier, and something inexplicably Keller that turned Niall's bones to jelly. Hungry for more, he sucked at Keller's tongue as he tugged Keller's sweat shirt over his head, then yanked off his own.

"Don't bite it off," Keller joked, breathing fast, his eyes wide and glittering. "I need it for later." A quick press of his lips to Niall's, then Keller took his hand. "Come with me?"

"Okay."

Niall's heart pounded as they ascended the stairs to the second level. He knew he was going to walk into Keller's bedroom a virgin and come out having had sex with a man. But not any man. Keller was the sun rising to chase away the darkness. Someone he knew he could call if he needed to talk, or simply a hug. He'd brought joy to Niall's dull, gray life with his bad jokes, teasing laughter, and hot kisses. There wasn't anyone else he could imagine lying naked with.

Instead of getting on the bed, Keller kissed his neck and peeled off his athletic pants and briefs as he kneeled at his feet. Niall's cock swung free, and Keller held it in his large hand. Niall's breathing kicked into high gear, and he almost swooned when Keller licked a wet path from tip to groin. He buried his nose in Niall's wiry curls, and with their eyes pinned, Keller wet his fingers and trailed them between his legs to play in his cleft.

"Keller," he hissed. Swaying slightly, Niall grabbed hold of the bedpost to keep from falling. "What the hell are you doing to me?"

But Keller, busy kissing and licking Niall's sac, didn't answer. He palmed Niall's ass, brushed the pad of his thumb against Niall's hole and slid inside moving in and out.

"So gorgeous," Keller whispered, almost reverently, as he moved faster and harder. Deeper.

"Please, oh God, please. I…I…please don't stop touching me." His cock was close to bursting, and spots pinwheeled in front of his eyes. "I'm gonna come." Keller squeezed the base of his cock, and Niall's eyes flew open. "Wha-why did you stop me?"

That wicked grin creased Keller's cheeks, and his blue eyes danced as he undressed. "You'll see. Now get on the bed."

"But wait, what?" Niall protested, and Keller placed two fingers over his mouth.

"Shh," he murmured. He took Niall's hand and tugged.

They lay on the bed, him under Keller, and all the rough hair and heavy muscle pressed to his naked body put him in a state of bliss. He quivered, and Keller began to press gentle kisses from his lips to knees, laving every inch of skin with his tongue until he was a shaking, shivering mess. He barely registered Keller spreading his legs wide and separating the globes of his ass. Something hot and wet touched his hole, lapping and kissing. Gazing at Keller's blond head between his thighs, he alternated between wanting to die of embarrassment and exploding into flames.

Keller blew a cool stream of air into the cleft and pushed his tongue into his hole, sucking and licking. Niall's hips bucked, and he grabbed his stiff dick. He groaned and lost his grip on reality as Keller slipped two fingers past his rim and slid inside.

"Fuck—fuck me," he cried out, his come shooting from his dick and splattering over his hand and stomach. "Fuck me."

"I plan to." Keller rolled on a condom and slicked it up. "These are prelubricated, but because you've never done this, it'll make it easier if I use more lube." Keller loomed over him, a tender smile warming his eyes. "I want this to be perfect for you."

Niall reached up to touch Keller's face. "It will be

because it's you."

Keller nudged in only the tip and waited. "Breathe as I move. I'll go slow."

Pressure like he'd never known spread through him, and he wanted to tell Keller to stop. His head thrashed side to side, but somewhere along the way, the burning sensation of being split in two ceased, and pleasure took control. Keller slid in and out of him, and soon Niall was clawing at Keller's back, digging his heels into the bed to meet the push-pull of Keller's cock.

"Look at you. How much do you want my dick?" Keller growled as he drove harder. "Tell me."

"All. Everything. Fuck me," he moaned and grabbed his cock, which had thickened again to almost full readiness. "More, please," he gasped as his hand flew over his erection and that familiar fire spread through his veins. *Keller*, he mouthed silently and came, the trickle of sticky liquid slipping through his fingers.

Keller remained relentless, hips flexing, his heavy cock thrusting over and over until, with a harsh cry, he stiffened and came. Niall put his arms around Keller's sweaty shoulders and held him close, burying his face in Keller's damp curls, drowning in the scent of their lust. This was paradise, and he never wanted to leave.

"I hope I'm still alive," Keller said, his lips moving against his neck.

Bolder than he'd ever imagined himself to be, Niall smoothed his hands over Keller's ass, touching where he'd never been able to before. "Feels like it."

"*Mmm*. You like that? Touching me? You don't have to stop. I like it too."

Cheeks hot, he nodded and continued to map out the dips and planes of Keller's body. Muscles rippled beneath his fingertips. All so different from the softness of a woman. Niall rubbed his cheek to Keller's. "Touching you is a reality

I never expected. I didn't know *what* to expect, but it wasn't this."

Keller shifted and slipped out of him. He pulled off the condom, knotted it, and threw it away. Instead of getting back into bed, he perched at the edge. "I've never been with anyone for their first time. Did I hurt you?"

"A little in the beginning," he admitted, but seeing the worry rise in Keller's face, he rushed to reassure him. "But once you were, you know, inside me"—he dropped his voice to a whisper—"it was amazing. The most incredible thing. I was finally free." Saying those words out loud made him feel hot and turned-on all over again.

"You are the sweetest man. And I am one lucky son of a bitch." Keller held out his hand. "I'm sure you're sore. Let me take care of you."

Not wanting to seem different than Keller's other men, he attempted to make light of it. "I'm fine. Really. Don't make a big deal out of it." Did his ass hurt? Like fucking hell, but he'd endure it.

"Don't be ridiculous. It's a huge deal to me, and it's not even my first time. Now let's go shower."

"Has anyone ever told you how pushy you are?" Niall's attempt at sternness didn't even fool him, and his lips twitched.

"Yes."

Realizing he couldn't put it off, Niall slowly climbed out of bed, trying to conceal his grimaces and winces and failing miserably. Every muscle in his body ached, and he felt open and sore. Keller slipped an arm around his waist and held him gently.

"You *are* hurting. I knew it. Why are you keeping it from me?" he demanded. "I want to take care of you."

"I don't want that to be the only thing you remember about tonight."

"Impossible. I'll remember everything. What it was

like—so hot and tight, like velvet and silk squeezing me. You didn't want to let me go."

Niall wanted to say, *I don't*, but didn't have the courage. Too much, way too soon. "I'll never forget it."

"You made me feel like I was the only man in the world." Keller cupped his cheek, his lips sweet and warm on Niall's. "Now it's time for me to spoil you."

How could he tell Keller that as far as he was concerned, he was the only man in the world for him? Niall knew that making love to Keller had spoiled him for anyone else.

CHAPTER SEVENTEEN

The phone rang early Sunday morning, and Keller wanted to throw it against the wall. Niall lay sleeping, and Keller, seeing it was Elijah, grabbed it and ran downstairs so as not to disturb him.

"I hope you have a good reason for waking me up at unholy o'clock," he grumbled.

"Don't give me back-talk," Elijah snickered. "I've already been to church. Listen, we're going upstate today, not far from you, to do some apple-picking with the girls, and Deirdre wants to stop by and say hi."

"Yeah? Is that all she wants to say to me?" He smirked to himself. "I'm sure my phone call has nothing to do with this impromptu trip."

Elijah released a belly laugh. "Man, she's been asking me so many questions. *Have you heard from Keller? Who's the guy? Do you know him?* I figured I'd let her do the interrogation herself."

Keller chuckled. "When do you think you'll be here?"

"Probably four, four thirty."

"Sounds good. Stop by, and we can have some dinner."

"All right. See you then."

A sound on the stairs caught his attention, and Niall appeared. Keller tossed the phone aside. "Sorry. I didn't mean to wake you so early." He met Niall at the bottom of the steps and brushed the messy hair out of his eyes. "How are you feeling this morning?"

"Still sore," Niall admitted with a rueful smile. "But totally worth it."

Keller kissed him softly. "How about I make some coffee?"

"I'd like that. Who was on the phone?" Niall asked as they headed into the kitchen.

"Elijah. He and his family are going to stop by later this afternoon. We can all have dinner." He poured the water and measured the grinds. He still used his mother's old coffeemaker. She was never one for making a single cup at a time and loved having a full pot.

Niall's face drooped. "Sunday nights I always have dinner with David. Or try, at least."

Thinking fast, Keller took the milk out of the refrigerator. "That's okay. They're going to be here early—like four or so. I know you've met Elijah, but I'd like you to meet his wife, Deirdre."

Niall blinked. "Are we really doing this?"

The *beep* sounded that the coffee was done, and Keller poured them each a mug. "*This* meaning…what?"

Niall chewed on his lip, ignoring the steaming mug in front of him. "How are you going to introduce me to Deirdre?"

"Oh." It was so natural to be with Niall, Keller had almost forgotten.

"Yeah, oh. Despite what happened last night, I'm not ready to make the statement to the world yet."

"I understand." Keller sipped the hot coffee, thinking of how to work it out. "You can still meet them. We can stay here and talk. We don't have to go out."

Niall drank some coffee. "It's not that I don't want to meet her. Elijah seemed nice when he came to my house. I guess I get so caught up in being with you, I tend to forget about everything else that comes with it."

"Hey, it's all right. I like the way that sounds." Keller left his mug and took Niall by the shoulders, making eye contact. "But we'll work it out. Together. How about we get some breakfast and just spend the day together?" Anticipating Niall's response, he already had an answer. "We can go someplace out of town, and then you can decide what you want to do—go home or come back with me."

Niall's beautiful eyes were cloudy with doubt. "I'm sorry I'm making this so complicated."

"Stop worrying. It will all work out, I promise. Let's get dressed and go."

Niall made a face. "I have to wear the same clothes as yesterday. I'm not your size, so I can't borrow yours."

Keller grinned. "You'd look cute in my sweat shirt."

Niall rolled his eyes. "What is this, high school?"

Keller nudged his cheek with his nose. "Definitely not. The person I was with last night was all man. And it was fantastic."

"Yeah." Niall gazed up at him. "It was. I never knew it could be like that. There was always something missing with Angie, no matter how hard we tried. I didn't have to try at all with you. It was all natural and easy and…perfect."

Keller kissed him. "It was for me too."

They dressed and drove to a diner about an hour away, in a little town at the edge of a lake, and ordered waffles and bacon. In the middle of their meal, Niall's phone rang, and he looked at the screen and grimaced.

"Trouble?" Keller asked, crunching on a piece of bacon.

"No. It's Angie. I should answer it."

"Go ahead. It's fine with me." Truthfully, he was curious to hear what Niall would say, if anything, about the two of them. He didn't have long to wait.

"Hey, Ang. How're you?"

"I'm good." Her voice was loud enough for him to listen without the phone being on speaker. "So how's the dating life?"

Niall blinked. "I'm fine too."

Keller pressed his lips together, now making no attempt to conceal he was listening in.

"I'm sorry. How are you? Have you been dating different people? Is it difficult to meet people on an app? I kept waiting for you to call so we could talk about it but you never did." The hurt in her voice was evident. "I thought we were closer than that."

"We are, Ang. It's just…you know how it is when you first meet someone."

"Ohh, so there *is* someone special. Tell me."

Niall darted a glance at him, and he winked.

"I—uh, yeah. But we're keeping it on the down-low for now."

"Why? Are you still worried about what people might say?"

Niall shrugged. "Maybe a little. Plus, it's kind of complicated."

"Oh, please. Who cares what these busybodies think? What's complicated?" Her voice rose. "Don't tell me he's married?"

"No, of course not, Jesus, Angie. What the hell?" Clearly irritated, Niall's eyes narrowed. "I would never do that. *Anyway*…yes, I'm seeing someone, and David doesn't know about him yet, just that I'm dating."

"Why can't you tell me who it is?" Angie demanded. "I told you all about Grant when I first met him."

"Look, I'm at breakfast. Can we table this for another time? There's nothing wrong with what I'm doing. I just need to work things out in my head first. And so does he."

"He meaning your boyfriend?"

"He's not my boyfriend," Niall retorted.

Hold up. Keller didn't like the sound of that. They were sleeping together. Didn't that make them boyfriends? Wasn't that how it worked? He stuffed a piece of waffle into his mouth and chewed.

"Bye, Angie. I'll talk to you later." Niall, evidently having decided that the conversation was over, set the phone facedown on the table. "Sorry about that." He cut into his waffles. "She can be pretty intense when she wants to know something."

"I gathered." No longer hungry, Keller watched Niall eat for a minute. "Can I ask you a question?"

"Yeah, sure." Niall sipped his coffee.

"You were pretty quick to correct your ex when she called me your boyfriend."

"Oh, um, yeah, well, I figured…I mean…you know." Niall shrugged, his eyes everywhere but on Keller.

"No, I don't." He leaned in to speak softly. "Do you want to see other people? I know it was your first time, so I don't want to keep you from dating, if that's what you want."

God. Why was he being so nice? The thought of Niall kissing another man made him want to upchuck the breakfast he'd eaten.

"What? No, of course not," Niall sputtered. "Why the hell would I want that?"

The tension coiled in his belly eased. "So why didn't you want to say you have a boyfriend?"

Shouldn't he be happy Niall was taking it slow? Apparently not, because he was anxious to tell the world about the two of them. Which made no sense. Who was he? What was going on? Keller hadn't ever considered being someone's boyfriend, and yet now he wanted to hang a sign around Niall's neck that read: taken by Keller Williams. No touching. Even more strange? He wanted to wear a matching one.

"Because we haven't discussed it. I didn't want to presume, in case you had something different in mind."

"The only thing on my mind is you. And me. Together. We'll figure out the other stuff."

Okay, that sounded a lot more mature, but he still didn't want to let Niall out of his sight.

After breakfast, they stopped by Niall's so he could change clothes, then drove to his house. Niall read while he worked on his playbook for the upcoming game. Every so often he'd glance up, and Niall would catch his eye. After the third or fourth time, Niall set his book in his lap.

"What is it?"

How to explain when it almost didn't make sense to him? "Nothing, I guess. And that's what's nice. Being here with you and doing nothing somehow means more than all the parties and clubs. I guess I understand now what my mother used to say. Home is where you go to rest your heart."

"That's beautiful. And yeah. It's nice to know you're here, even if we're not doing something together."

They shared a smile.

A car door slammed, and voices punctuated the stillness. Keller chuckled. "Buckle up and prepare to meet the whirlwinds."

"I raised a little boy. I can handle it."

Keller had the door open before Elijah could knock. "How was the day?"

Elijah had a sleepy Kennedy in his arms while Deirdre held Marli, who lay conked out on her shoulder. "Down for the count. I told DeeDee we need to do this more often."

Laughing, Keller waved them inside. "Bring them upstairs, and they can sleep in my old room. The bed is against the wall, so it'll be safe for the little one."

Deirdre kissed his cheek. "We'll be right back."

"I know you will," he murmured, closing the door behind them and joining a slightly pale Niall, who stood by the sofa. "You look like you're ready to puke. What's wrong?" He rubbed his shoulders, but Niall stiffened and pulled away.

"I've never met anyone's best friend…as their boyfriend. I don't know what to do."

"You could kiss me. It'll make you feel better."

Grumpy-faced, Niall smoothed his hair and fidgeted with the top button of his polo. "Very funny."

He wasn't trying to be, but he'd figured it might break the tension. "You're worrying for nothing. I think Elijah's figured it out, and Deirdre's been after me for years to meet someone."

"We both have." Elijah's deep voice had both him and Niall jumping. A big grin beamed from his face. "And yeah, I did figure it out. Nice to see you again, Niall."

"You too, Elijah." Seemed that Niall had forgotten to be nervous and was smiling and shaking hands. "Did you have luck with the apple-picking? Best time of the year up here."

Deirdre joined them. "Let's just say it's a good thing I make a mean cobbler and that the girls love applesauce. Hi, I'm Deirdre. You're Niall? Elijah told me he had such a nice time at your house for the victory party."

Keller chuckled as Deirdre slipped an arm through Niall's. "Man doesn't stand a chance," he murmured to Elijah, who stood beside him.

"Him or you?" Elijah asked with that same shit-eating grin. Keller scowled, but Elijah only snickered. "Don't give me that look. I told you right away you had it bad for him."

No sense in denying it. "Yeah. He's a nice guy."

"Hey, you don't have to sell him to me. I could see he

was the real deal that first night. I bet you never discuss football." Elijah elbowed him. "Or do much talking at all."

He grew hot. "Shut up. There's more to this than sex. I could get that anywhere, anytime. Niall's more than that. He's my friend. We just have stuff to work out."

As he and Elijah spoke, he kept an eye on Niall, who was happily chatting with Deirdre about children's books and the school districts upstate.

"You'll be okay. I can see he means a lot to you. You fell as fast for him as I did for Deirdre."

"Elijah," Deirdre called out, "Niall says that a lot of people from the city are getting second homes up here. I think we should look into it. It would be nice for the girls to get out of the city and have space to run."

Keller sat next to Niall on the couch, while Elijah took the more comfortable recliner facing them.

"I'm listening." Elijah nodded, glancing around the living room. "A nice house with some land. Maybe a pool and outdoor kitchen for grilling in the summertime. Better than the Hamptons. That's not my scene."

"Where I live has houses like that. You should take a drive around and look. And a little farther north, just outside of Overlook, they have nice places with lots of land that aren't in subdivisions." Niall already had his phone out and was scrolling. "See?" He handed the phone to Deirdre, who nodded.

"Sounds good to me," Deirdre agreed. "I loved seeing the kids running through the orchards and breathing the fresh air. Now that Ms. Roberta's passed, we can have the whole family up here for the holidays." Eyes shining, she clasped her hands. "Imagine Thanksgiving and Christmas in the country."

"Baby, I'm all for it. And we get to be neighbors here with my man."

"And his man," Deirdre was quick to add. "Can I just

say, I couldn't have wished for a better person for you to be with. I can see Niall is the real deal."

He rested a hand on the back of Niall's neck. "I know."

"I think I'm pretty lucky too," Niall stated in that quiet way he had. "I wasn't willing to give him a chance at first, but he's persistent."

"When I want something, I don't like getting told no."

Deirdre's brow puckered. "Why would you say no to Keller? He's a great guy."

"Thanks for the cheering squad, but we've worked it out." He winked. "Obviously." His fingers played with the hair curled at Niall's collar.

Niall raised his eyes to the ceiling, muttering, "God help me," and glared in his direction before smoothing out his face and turning to Deirdre. "We had some history—nothing critical, but I was stubbornly holding on to the past instead of letting it go."

"Which you did, eventually."

"He chased me until I let him catch me." Niall's smile was smug, and both Elijah and Deirdre hooted while Keller pouted.

"Everyone's a comedian."

"Except you." Niall snickered.

"Oh, damn." Elijah clapped. "He's got your number."

"Okay, okay. Who's hungry? We can get the diner to send over burgers, or there's a pretty decent Asian place in town."

"Burgers sound good." Elijah looked to Deirdre. "What do you say, honey?"

"Make that burger a grilled chicken sandwich and those fries sweet potato ones, and I'm all for it." She patted Elijah's cheek. "You know your doctor said to cut out the red meat."

"Yeah, yeah. I know." Elijah sighed. "How's the team doing?"

"I can't tell you what a thrill it is to work with them. They're a great group of kids."

"Mommy," a voice from upstairs cried, and Deirdre took off like a shot, calling over her shoulder, "Order the kids something from the children's menu, but no hot dogs."

"Yes, dear," Elijah grumbled. "You'd think I don't know what my kids like."

Keller handed him his phone. "Tell me what you want."

They gathered at the front door for good-byes, and Keller said, "It was great having the whole family here."

Deirdre finished putting on the children's jackets, and with a smile of regret, zipped up her own. "I wish we could stay. I truly love it here. Niall, you have my number and email. I'll be contacting your friend Dara."

"She'll help you. She lives right down the road from me, and she and her husband are two of my closest friends."

"Do they know about you two?" She looked to Keller, who shook his head.

"No one does. It's up to Niall to decide when to tell people. I'm following his lead."

"But you haven't come out either. Aren't you concerned? Or you don't care anymore?"

"No. Like I told Niall, I'm ready to live my life on my terms. If someone doesn't like it and decides they're no longer my fan, that's fine. But I'll be damned if I let them drive me away from coaching those kids. I *will* put up a fight about that."

Niall faced him with a worried expression. "Do you think they'll do that? *Can* they?"

He shrugged. "No idea. I'm sure the haters would love to if they had the chance."

"Mommy, I wanna go." Kennedy tugged at Deirdre's

jacket.

Elijah scooped her up. "Yeah, baby girl. We're going. Mommy'll take you to the car while Daddy says good-bye." He handed her to Deirdre, and Keller found himself hugged. "You take care of yourself, and if you need me, just give a holler."

"I will. Good to see you."

Elijah surprised Niall by hugging him as well, and then Keller watched as they drove down the street and disappeared. He closed the door. Niall stood rubbing his arms and laughing.

"Ow. He's strong."

"He is. Let me." He rubbed Niall's back. "Feel good?" he murmured in Niall's ear. "I can rub something else and make it feel good too."

"You have a one-track mind, don't you?" Niall responded, his breath catching in his throat. "As tempting an offer as that is, I have to go home too. It's getting late, and David will be home soon."

Keller took Niall by the shoulders so they faced each other. "You know this isn't only about sex, right? I don't want you to think that's the case."

Niall met his eyes with steely determination in those blue-green depths. "I wouldn't be here if I thought that. At first I thought you were a player, but the more I get to know you, the more I see that's not the truth and it was an unfair label."

Keller wrapped his arms around Niall. "You can call me a player. I don't mind. As long as you know that the only game is the one where you're the prize for winning." He put his lips to Niall's ear. "And I don't plan on losing."

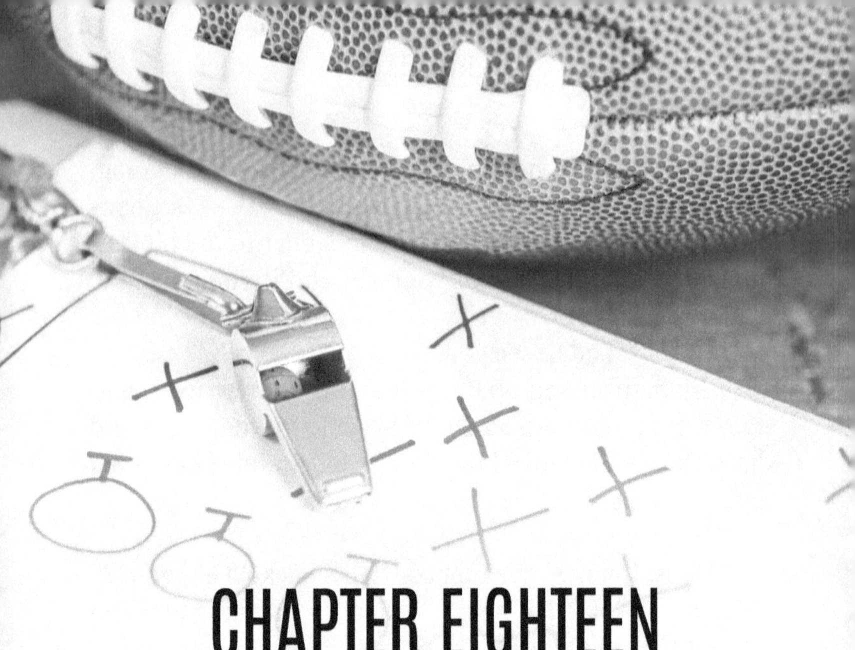

CHAPTER EIGHTEEN

Two weeks passed, and the Tigers continued their impressive winning streak. Keller was the darling of the town, and everywhere Niall went, people were talking about the team taking the state championship. Along with running the library, Niall had been subbing for several English teachers who'd been sick with the flu that had made its perennial appearance. The end of every day found him exhausted to the point of falling into bed at night before the ten o'clock news, with barely enough energy to brush his teeth.

Keller had gone to New York to film some endorsements, and they'd spent the previous weekend FaceTiming.

"I wish you could be here with me. I have this whole hotel suite and no one to share it with."

"Another time. I hope you're having fun at least."

"Meh." Keller made a face. "It's no fun being in the

city alone. I wish you were here with me.”

“Me too.” His heart pounded. “I miss you.”

“I’ll see you Friday night after the game. We’re staying in.” His eyes twinkled, and Niall couldn’t remember the last time he’d been so happy.

But that Friday after the game he could barely keep his eyes open, and it hurt to swallow. He told David he wasn’t feeling well, and went home and fell asleep on the couch, never hearing Keller’s multiple calls and texts. Saturday morning he awoke feeling sniffly and headachy. Alarmed that he’d be so sick he’d miss school and the extra money from the classes he was scheduled to sub, he sent David to the drugstore to stock up on Vitamin C and cold medicines. When he wasn’t sleeping, he drank orange juice and the soup David heated up for him. Most of the time he slept. By Sunday night, he felt human again. David was in his bedroom FaceTiming with Renee, so he called Keller.

“Hi. I’m sorry I didn’t get back to you. It wasn’t deliberate. I wasn’t feeling well, and David stayed home to look after me.”

“I heard at practice. David mentioned to some of the guys that’s why he wasn’t hanging out over the weekend. Why didn’t you let me know you were sick?” Keller demanded, and Niall smiled at the outrage in his voice. “I was going crazy not knowing what was happening when you didn’t answer my calls or texts.”

“I was asleep most of the time. And what could you have done? Come over and fed me chicken soup? David was with me, and I feel much better now.”

“I could’ve dressed up in a cute nurse’s outfit, and we could’ve played doctor.”

“I hardly think you’d want to wipe my runny nose,” he teased.

“No, but I could’ve given you an oral…exam.”

Niall busted out laughing. “God, that was the worst. I

think I'm feeling sick, but this time from all the bad jokes."

"How about this week? Can we get together?"

"I can't," he said with regret. "I'm subbing AP English and Mrs. Schechter's literature classes. Too much work. I'm exhausted."

"Dammit," Keller swore. "But after the game on Friday, you're mine."

He tingled with awareness. "I'll be waiting. David won't be home. You can stay the night."

That Friday night the Tigers won again, and David was staying at Chris's house. Nervous, Niall paced the foyer, and when he heard the sound of a car engine, he opened the garage door. Keller entered and crushed his lips over Niall's, the door slamming closed as they clung to each other as if trying to make up for their separation for the past three weeks with a single, hungry kiss.

Ten minutes later they were naked and in his bed, Keller moving slowly over him, wringing more pleasure from his body than Niall could've imagined existed. "I missed you." He withdrew and thrust deep. Over and over. Niall moaned. "So damn much."

"Me too," he choked out, and picked up Keller's rhythm so they rocked together. The world fell away, and it was only the two of them and the glide of their bodies. Skin to skin. His cock lay trapped between them, and the delicious friction proved too much to bear. He came, feeling not broken into pieces but put together, finally whole. A few seconds later, Keller drove into him hard, and the condom filled with heat as Keller's dick throbbed.

"I'm never going away again," Keller mumbled. "And

I'm not sure I can move."

Niall kissed his shoulder. "I'm okay with that."

Keller nuzzled him for a moment before leaving him to clean up, then lay beside him. "Does David go away every weekend?" His fingertips drifted over Niall's chest, and Niall had never known such contentment.

"Usually, yes. Sometimes they all come here, but I know most of the parents feel sorry for me being a single parent so they don't mind hosting. But only during football season. Some people would say he should be home and studying, but I want him to have that wonderful high school experience I never had. And David knows he has to keep his grades up and get all his homework done. As long as he continues to do well, he can go. The minute I see them slip, he'll stay home."

"Makes sense. And at least you know where he is. When I was his age and we won, we'd all go to the lake, get drunk, and hope the cops didn't bust us." His face a mask of memories, he stared into space. "I never had the chance to hang out all weekend like a lot of the other kids because I had to help my mom, so I crammed as much as I could into that one night of freedom."

Niall gazed up at his somber profile. "How did you get alcohol?"

Keller shrugged. "One of the kids' older brothers got it for us. I don't remember who." His fingers played in Niall's soft chest hair. "On one of those nights I lost my virginity to Louisa Baker."

"I remember her. Blond, big blue eyes. She was, uh, very friendly with guys, from what I heard."

"She was wild and took me into the woods. She had a very talented mouth. I closed my eyes, and at some point, it didn't matter that it was a woman. We did the deed, and then she left me. I remember sitting there, wondering if it would always be like that. Having to pretend. Having to hide."

"Hey." Niall touched his face. "I'm not pretending how I feel when I'm with you."

"Me neither." Keller held him tight, and they kissed.

On Sunday, they decided to do some exploring up by the Finger Lakes. They visited a couple of antique stores he and Angie used to frequent, plus a few farm stands and another orchard. Keller bought another pie, and Niall decided he could use some more apples and vegetables for the house. They walked between the apple trees, fingertips brushing, sharing heated glances and small smiles. Occasionally, Keller would pull him behind a tree and steal a kiss. Around four thirty, he pulled into the spot next to Keller's car in his garage and cut the engine.

Keller toyed with his hand. "I wish I could do this in public. You deserve it. I can't even give you a good-bye kiss when we're alone in the car, can I?"

More than anything, Niall wished for that as well. But there were way too many hurdles in their way. "Maybe soon."

"Do you think about it? Coming out? Or telling David about us?"

"More than ever lately," Niall admitted. "I don't want you to think I'm leading you on."

"I don't. At all. Whenever you're ready. Until then, I can wait," Keller reassured him. "I'll see you during the week."

A final squeeze of his hand, and Keller left. Niall watched him drive off, and sat, making no move to go into the house.

What should he do?

He deserved to be happy—everyone did. Opening himself up to Keller allowed him to imagine a world he'd never bothered to take ownership of. A world of possibilities. Keller made him think…hope…dream of life again.

How could that be wrong?

But was the time right to reconcile those feelings? Could David handle knowing his father was dating his coach? Was he ready to explain it to his friends?

You're being ridiculous. Stop working yourself up into a frenzy.

But even though their time together had been short, it had shown him a life he'd yearned to be a part of. One he should be free to enjoy.

Niall sighed and exited the car. He showered and changed and was reading when the kitchen door opened.

"Dad? Are you home?"

"Yep. In the living room."

David appeared in the hallway. "Hi."

"Hi, yourself. How was the weekend?"

"Great. Got all my work done and even some stuff on papers due next month for History and English." He flung himself on the couch. "What about you?"

"I had a nice weekend too. Got some reading in. Went up to the Finger Lakes, did some antiquing and more apple-picking—they're in the fridge, if you want."

"Thanks, but Renee's mom has a ton. I'm all appled out." He chewed on his lip. "Uh, so, who'd you go apple-picking with?"

His heart slammed. "Are you asking me if I went with a date?"

David shrugged. "I mean, come on. You told me you went with friends, but I know Chris's parents were home all weekend. So…yeah. Did you go with a date?"

He refused to lie. "Yes. I went with a date. We had a great time."

"Are you gonna see him again?"

He nodded. "Are you okay with that? Because eventually,

I am going to make it public."

David thought for a moment, and Niall could see his mind working. "Yeah, I know. I meant what I said earlier. I know it took me a while, but I'm behind you, a hundred percent. If you're happy, that's the only thing that matters. I know we don't spend as much time together, not like we used to…"

"I'm okay with that," he rushed to reassure David. "I want you to have friends and get to do everything in high school I never had the chance to. As long as you're doing your work and getting good grades, which I know you are."

"Yeah, and I'm gonna be going to college soon. I don't want you home alone."

Overcome, he blinked back tears. "Thanks, David."

"Tell me about him. Is it serious?" David settled into the couch, and Niall wondered exactly how much he was ready to say.

"It could be. I mean, it's on its way to becoming…" He faltered, and David, who was quick, grinned.

"How long have you been seeing this guy?"

"For a while," he admitted sheepishly. "A couple of months. I didn't want to say anything in case it didn't work out."

"But it has. Obviously. Cool." He hopped up. "I'm gonna shower. Are we having pizza for dinner?"

Niall had thought David would've already eaten, and he wasn't all that hungry, but he'd chew nails to sit at the table with his son.

"You bet. I'll order it now, so it'll be ready when you're done showering."

"Thanks, Dad. You're the best."

Niall watched David tear up the stairs, thinking how lucky he was and how life couldn't get much better.

The week passed, and their schedules prevented them from seeing each other during school hours. Late-night texting helped some with the loneliness, but the truth was, Niall missed Keller and his teasing humor.

Can we meet tomorrow? Keller texted him at midnight. *Just to say hi.*

Niall smiled. Who knew big, tough Keller Williams was really a pussycat?

How about the teachers' lounge at one for lunch?

He received a thumbs-up and a grinning emoji.

Of course, the best laid plans always fell through, and instead of sitting with Keller in the teachers' lounge, eating his turkey sandwich, he'd been held up by a state-wide school-librarians conference call. He'd shot off a quick apology text to Keller, which was why he was so surprised, when he finished the call and was eating his sad little sandwich alone, to get a FaceTime request from him.

"Hi. Where are you?" Niall squinted at the phone. "It looks familiar."

"It should. I'm sitting in my car. I have about fifteen minutes before the kids come for practice." He drank from his Gatorade bottle, and Niall made a face.

"I could never understand how you can drink that stuff."

Keller's brows waggled. "You taste a thousand times better, but I haven't had the opportunity."

His face flamed. "Shh."

"What? I'm in my car. All alone and by myself and you're in your office." Turning serious, Keller leaned in closer to the phone. "I hate this separation."

Warmth settled in his chest. "I do too."

"I can still see you after the game?"

"Yeah. And I'm picking David up after practice tonight, so I'll get to see you then too."

"Not the same, but it'll have to do. I'd better go and get ready."

The phone went dark, and he touched the screen, as if he could still feel Keller's vibrant presence through his fingertips.

That evening he sat in the stands, waiting for David. Doing so made for a long day, but he didn't care—in addition to watching his son play, he could also stare as much and as long as he wanted at Keller without feeling self-conscious or concerned that it seemed out of the ordinary.

The kids lined up, and Keller ran back and forth along the sidelines. Niall was impressed. They were focused and determined as if this were a real game and not merely practice, but Niall knew their toughest competition was Friday night and that Keller had worked relentlessly to make sure they were at the top of their game.

"Kids are looking good, don't you think?" Dara sat next to him, and without taking his eyes off Keller—because damn, the man looked as good from behind as he did from the front—Niall agreed.

"They are. Every throw Shane's made has been spot on, and they're in sync, even with all the new plays Keller's taught them."

"I know. It's like he's been coaching for years." Dara put away her sunglasses as twilight had begun to descend. "By the way, I got a call from Keller's friend, Deirdre? Thanks for recommending me. She seems very sweet."

"She is. And her daughters are adorable." He froze, realizing he'd disclosed more information than he'd meant to, and Dara picked up on it right away.

"Oh, you've met them? When did that happen? I assumed you talked to her husband at the party and he filled her in."

Terrible liar that he was, he grasped for an explanation.

"I saw them in town a few weekends ago. She and her husband were visiting Keller after they went apple-picking. She mentioned loving the area, so I told her about all the city people getting homes up here, and of course I recommended you."

From her puckered brow, Niall could tell she was trying to figure out the logistics, but Bobby Contard saved his ass by acting the fool as usual.

"Come on, Shane. Don't be a goddamn wuss," Bobby yelled.

The offensive coach was at Shane's side, touching his arm, and Niall's eyes narrowed as he could see Shane was in some type of discomfort.

"He needs to shut up and leave the kids alone," Niall muttered under his breath.

Shane glanced up at the stands and shook his head at something the coach said. He windmilled his arms a few times and grabbed his biceps. The coach walked him off the field, and the second-string quarterback ran out to play.

"Play through it, you ain't no pansy. Get back out there, Shane. What the hell is going on here?" Bobby called out, and Keller, who'd been in a huddle with the players, left them and stalked over to where Bobby sat.

"That's enough. I told you already I'd toss you out if you started this again. Keep quiet."

But Bobby remained unconcerned. "Kid's got to toughen up. Be a real man."

Keller's frown deepened. "What's that supposed to mean?"

Bobby snorted. "You goin' soft now that you ain't in the pros no more? C'mon, Keller. You know how it goes."

A dangerous light gleamed in Keller's eyes, and Niall held his breath. Keller didn't suffer fools, and Bobby was an idiot. "No, I guess I don't. Why don't you tell me all about being a real man?"

"You been hanging around too much with the PC groupies?" His gaze cut to Niall, and he smirked. "All this kumbaya crap. Football is about winning. Hitting first before you get hit. Playing through the pain."

"You don't know jack about anything if you say that. Football is about being a team. No one player is more important than anyone else. That's why they have backup quarterbacks. Yeah, it's about winning, but as a cohesive unit."

"Shane is gonna play no matter what."

"You don't decide that. I do. And if his arm hurts, he *will* sit this game out."

Bobby rose from his seat. "The fuck he will, Keller. Shane told me there are gonna be scouts from colleges watching. He needs to show them how he can throw."

"Get out. Get off the field right now." Keller pointed. "No one curses and undermines my authority. Leave."

"Fuck you. You can't make me."

Niall hated that he was right. There was no security at practices to toss out unruly parents. The daytime school guards went home at the end of classes.

"I'm warning you. Sit there and be quiet, or I'll have you banned from the actual games. And that I do have the power to make happen." Keller glanced up at him and Dara, sitting wide-eyed. "I'm sorry you had to hear all that."

"It's okay, don't worry about it," Niall reassured him, and Keller gave them both a quick nod and left to rejoin the kids and start the drill over.

Bobby snorted. "Aw, whassamatta, Harper? Your ears too delicate? Like the rest of you?"

Normally he'd ignore Bobby's taunting, but anger made him reckless. "You don't need to run your mouth and act like an animal. Dara doesn't need to hear your crap."

"Don't pay attention to him, Niall." Dara put a hand on his arm.

"That's right, Harper, listen to her," Bobby sneered. "You're used to being bossed around by women. We all know who wore the pants when you were married. Hey," he barked, "I know a few toilets that your face would look good in." He snickered to himself.

Trembling with a combination of anger and humiliation, Niall sat facing forward but kept silent. The rest of practice passed without incident, and afterward he walked Dara to her car.

Dara stood to chat for a moment. "I'm going to speak to Deirdre Randolph tomorrow. I'll tell her you said hi."

"Please do. I hope you find them something."

Dara's eyes sparkled. "With the budget she gave me, I have little doubt."

Chris came running up. "David'll be out in a sec, Mr. Harper. I'm starving, Mom."

"I knew you would be. I have dinner all prepped. Dad's late tonight with a delivery, so let's go. See you at the game, Niall."

"Yes, you will."

He waited as the other parents who'd come to pick up their kids filed by. Bobby Contard walked by with Shane, who gave him a tentative wave, which he returned. He watched them drive away and wondered about what really went on in that house.

"Hey, Dad. Everything okay?" David stood in front of him.

"Yeah, of course. Ready to go?"

Keller walked up to them. "He played well today. Made some nice catches."

David lit up from the praise. "Thanks, Coach. We're all psyched for tomorrow night."

Keller stood there, and the physical pull toward him was undeniable. Niall could hardly concentrate on what David was saying. All he could remember was their weekend together and how waking up with Keller next to him was the definition of perfection.

"Big game, right? The Bedlington Rangers were the number one team last year. The state champs."

"We're gonna win. I know it."

Keller grinned. "That's the attitude. A positive mindset is half the battle."

"And I've got your favorite meal—meatballs and spaghetti all ready for you."

"That sounds a lot better than my microwave dinner." Keller smiled. "Enjoy." He walked to his car, a few spots away.

Before Niall knew what he was doing, the words fell out of his mouth. "There's plenty if you want to join us."

David chimed in, "Yeah, Coach. My dad got the recipe from my grandma. They're better than Casa Napoli."

That was the old-school restaurant in town that had been around since he was a kid. It was David's birthday treat to go there every year, where he'd order their chicken parmigiana dinner and devour it all.

Keller's eyes twinkled. "I dunno. Casa Napoli is pretty awesome. Are you sure?"

Their gazes locked, and Niall understood they'd be under the microscope with David sitting there, but the thought of Keller going home and heating up a frozen meal hurt his heart.

"Yeah," he said softly. "Join us, please."

It was a wonderful dinner, and Keller kept them laughing with tales of his and other football players' mishaps on the field. The meatballs were pronounced a success, and Keller helped them clean up afterward.

"I can make coffee if you want. David, you finish your homework?"

"I have some math problems, but only a few. I'll finish them, and can I FaceTime with Renee after?"

"Just make sure everything's done. And bedtime's at eleven."

"I know, I know. See you later." He ran up the stairs, leaving them alone.

"Coffee?" He stood by the counter. "Do you drink it so late at night?"

"I can have coffee anytime." Keller washed his hands and dried them. "But first…" He took Niall's face between his hands and kissed him. "Sitting across from you all night has been torture."

Niall's heart thundered. "I know. But we can't get carried away, not with David in the house."

"Make the coffee, and let's sit outside. It's dark enough, and I just want to be alone with you for a little while."

Niall couldn't deny it was what he wanted as well. "Okay."

They carried their mugs to the deck and sat on the couch. When they'd bought the house, he'd fought against having outdoor furniture, but he'd never been so glad as he was now to have given in. Sitting in the cool air, with Keller's arm around him, was pure bliss.

"This is very nice back here. I see why you'd never want to move." Keller set his coffee on the rattan table and Niall did the same. "When I was a kid, I used to ride my bike up and down these streets, and pretend that one day I'd have enough money to live here." His chuckle rumbled in the quiet. "And now I do, yet here I am. Back where I started."

"We can run from who we are, but we can't escape." Niall recalled all the years spent alone, thinking he'd always be an outsider, never fitting in.

"I'm not looking to escape." Keller faced him, a gentle smile brightening his face. "In fact, I think I'm right where I belong."

"I think so too."

With Keller's hand on his cheek, their lips met in a hot, hungry kiss. Keller's tongue pushed into his mouth, and he sucked on it, moaning softly.

"Niall, *Niall*," Keller's rough growl had him fighting for control.

"I want you too. But I can't…not yet."

Breathing heavily, Keller pulled away but rested their foreheads together. "I should go because I can't be near you without wanting to touch you." Instead of following through on what he said, Keller kissed him again, and damn if he didn't cling to those broad shoulders.

"I wish you could stay."

"Maybe this weekend? Tomorrow and Saturday?"

"I'll see what David has planned and let you know."

They collected their coffee mugs and left the deck. Keller took Niall's and put them in the sink, and then Niall walked him to the door.

"Thanks for the dinner invite. I'll see you at the game. Tell David I said good-bye."

Niall cast a glance up the stairs. "He's FaceTiming with his girlfriend, which means I won't see him until morning." They stared at each other. "Night."

"Bye."

He waited at the door, watching Keller drive away. When he turned around, David was behind him, and he jumped. "Jesus, you scared me. I thought you'd be busy with Renee." He walked into the kitchen, and David followed.

"I was, but she had to go."

"Oh. Well, that was fun tonight."

"Dad?"

"Yeah?" He rinsed out the cups in the sink and started

drying them.

"Are you and Coach Keller…is he the man you've been seeing?"

The cup in his hand crashed onto the tile floor, and he kneeled to pick up the broken pieces and throw them into the trash. He pulled out the broom to sweep up, but even after he'd finished, his hands still trembled. "Wh-what makes you say that?"

Oh, shit. Oh, God. What the hell am I supposed to say?

David swung into a chair at the kitchen island. "I finished my math homework and wanted to get a drink before I got on the computer with Renee, so I came downstairs. I heard voices on the deck." He blinked rapidly, and bright-red spots bloomed on his cheeks. "I wasn't snooping or eavesdropping, I swear. I saw you through the window. You were…kissing."

For a brief second, he closed his eyes to gather his strength. He opened them to find David gazing at him with no judgment, merely curiosity.

"If I tell you something, you have to promise it will remain between us. No talking to your friends or Renee about it, okay? I'm serious now."

His face solemn, David nodded, and Niall took a seat next to him. "Yes. Keller is the man I've been seeing."

David's jaw dropped. "Wow. I didn't know he was gay."

"Me neither until…" He shrugged. "Well, whatever. It doesn't matter. But he is. And he hasn't come out, so you have to keep this to yourself. It's important."

"Yeah, of course. I get it."

"Tell me what you're thinking. Are you okay with Keller and me seeing each other?"

He appreciated that David took his time to answer. "Yeah. I mean it might be a little weird at first, but he's a really cool guy. And if you like him, that's what matters, right?"

Joy over David's easy acceptance rushed through him.

Overcome, Niall struggled to keep his composure. "Thank you," he whispered. "You have no idea how much this means to me."

"Dad, hey, it's okay. I mean, at first, when you told me you were gay, I was freaked out, but I thought about it, and it shouldn't matter who you love, right? As long as you're happy. That's what you and Mom always said. It wouldn't be right if it was okay for everyone else but not when it comes to you. I'd be a hypocrite."

He pressed the heels of his hands to his eyes before answering. "I only care what you think. No one else."

"Well, me and Coach Keller." David grinned.

"Wise guy. Go get some sleep. You have a big night ahead of you tomorrow."

To his astonishment, David hugged him. "Night, Dad."

"Night."

He sat at the island for a few minutes, then picked up the phone and texted Keller.

David knows.

His phone rang immediately. "What do you mean, he knows?" Keller demanded. "How? What—"

"Shh, it's okay. He saw us. Out on the deck."

"Shit," Keller cursed. "I'm sorry. I know you wanted to keep it to yourself. I didn't mean—"

"Stop. It's fine. We talked, and I'm so proud of him. He's growing up to be exactly the type of person I'd hoped."

"With a father like you, I'm not surprised."

"Trust me, I've screwed up plenty." He gazed off into space. "I'm lucky."

"David's the lucky one. You've sacrificed so much to protect him."

"I'd do it all again. I would. I'd do anything for him."

"I know. But now you're free. You can finally be who you are."

Niall had to ask. "Obviously, I told David not to tell

anyone, but you have to still be worried."

Keller made a dismissive sound. "You can tell anyone you want. I've already won." His voice dropped. "I told you before, you were the prize worth waiting for."

"What do I have to do with it?" Puzzled, he stared at the phone. "I'm—"

"Everything. You are everything."

Niall trembled at the magnitude of those simple words. "Keller, I—"

Keller interrupted him. "I gotta get to bed. It's a big night tomorrow, you know? See you at the game."

The phone went dark, and Niall sat thinking.

The score was 20-17, the Bedlington Rangers in the lead. It was late in the fourth quarter, and Overlook had the ball. Keller paced along the sidelines, and Niall hadn't been able to take his eyes off him all night. He was in complete control of the team and never lost his cool, even when the referees made several bad calls that cost the Tigers precious yards.

"I heard from Chris that several college scouts are here tonight." Michael handed him his soda and bag of popcorn. They'd come extra early and scored field-level, front-row seats.

"Yeah. That's what David said too. Glad to see they're not nervous about it. Win or lose, they're holding their own against the best team in the state, and that has to count for something." He chomped on a few handfuls of popcorn.

"Keller Williams has been a good influence." Michael drank from his water bottle.

"He's a great coach. David really likes him. He's brought a sense of teamwork to them. Plus, I'm sure the scouts are here because of him."

Dara, who'd been unusually quiet for most of the night, fiddled with the strap of her handbag. "I met with Deirdre today. You never mentioned you all had dinner together, just that you saw them."

He licked his lips. "Uh, yeah, I guess I forgot."

"You did?" Dara's meticulous brows shot up. "You made a big impression on her."

"You had dinner with Keller Williams and Elijah Randolph? Damn, Niall." Michael looked suitably impressed. "That's the big leagues. How did you and Coach Williams get so friendly?"

Could he tell them? They were his best friends, people he could trust—couldn't he? It should be all right. He hoped.

"Keller and I…we're dating."

Michael and Dara glanced at each other, and Dara put a hand on Niall's arm. "When you divorced, I told Michael I wasn't surprised. You and Angie were best friends, I could see, but I never felt the spark between you. It makes sense now."

Michael was more direct. "Keller Williams is gay? I never saw that coming, but I guess he had to hide it when he was a player." He shrugged. "Good for you both. He seems like a great guy."

"He really is."

And just like that, his lifelong secret was out, and the world didn't stop spinning on its axis.

The whistle sounded, and the team lined up.

"Don't fuck up, Shane," Bobby yelled. "Throw the ball. Show them your arm."

"I wish he would shut the hell up," Niall muttered.

They ran the ball, and Van sprinted across the field like a demon, eluding the tackles. Niall, Michael, and Dara rose to their feet, cheering as Van scored. The team swarmed him, and Niall searched for Keller on the sidelines and found him shaking his fists in the air and screaming along with the rest of the Tigers' fans in the crowd. Keller looked up, and somehow their eyes met. Niall grinned and raised both fists in the air.

"Damn, Niall. Go you," Michael razzed him.

The extra point made, Keller had the defense guarding the opposing side like white on rice. No matter how hard the Rangers tried to push past the line of scrimmage, they were thwarted. With a failed third down and the Rangers too far for a field goal attempt, they had to kick the ball. The Tigers ended up on their own thirty-five yard line. Keller called a time-out.

Niall said, "He's gonna run out the clock, right? No way is he going to risk Shane throwing an interception with the score so close." Watching David take instruction from the offensive coach and Keller, Niall shoved some popcorn into his mouth.

"That's what I'm thinking," Michael answered. "What a game."

Offense took the field, and then Niall heard it. "Throw the ball, Shane! For fuck's sake. Throw the goddamn ball!"

Shane handed the ball off to David, who ran wide to the outside. The clock ticked to twenty seconds.

"Throw the fucking ball, you dumbass," Bobby screamed.

"They need to get him out of here." Niall glared behind him.

"What're you lookin' at, wimp?" Bobby sneered.

"Shut up, Bobby. Leave the kids alone. Keller's the coach, not you."

"He's gotten weak. He's a pussy." Bobby stood up. "Throw the ball, Shane. Fuck the coach! He's an asshole."

Two burly security guards approached Bobby.

"Sir, you're going to have to come with us," one of them stated. "Let's go."

"My son is the quarterback. You ain't throwing me out."

"You're disrupting the game. Either you come with us, or we'll call the sheriff's office."

Grumbling and cursing under his breath, Bobby left with them, and Niall was able to enjoy the final few minutes and cheer himself hoarse when the Tigers upset the state champions with a 24-20 score.

"Awesome game." Michael high-fived him.

"Amazing."

Michael put a hand on his shoulder and gave it a quick squeeze. "Thank you for sharing your news with us, Niall. I know it couldn't have been easy all these years, but I hope everything will work out now."

"Thank you. It really means a lot to have your support."

Dara hugged him. "I'm glad you're dating someone you care about."

Niall's attention was drawn to the field, where the teams had shaken hands and the kids were excitedly headed to the locker room to change. To his surprise, Keller didn't leave with them but jogged over to where he stood. His heart pounded as Keller drew near, and he left Michael and Dara in their seats to meet him at the fence.

"Congratulations, Keller."

A grin that sent a wicked thrill through him curved Keller's lips. "I came to collect the winner's prize."

And before he could make a move, Keller grasped him around the neck and took his mouth in a kiss that curled his toes, rivaling any Fourth of July fireworks.

CHAPTER NINETEEN

Keller knew it would be a scene, but he didn't give a damn. All that mattered was Niall's soft mouth under his. In the background, the clicking of cameras and the excited gasps and chatter of people faded the longer he kissed Niall. And he wanted to keep kissing Niall forever.

"What…why?" Niall breathed, holding him close.

"Because." He smiled into Niall's eyes. "I don't want to hide anymore. Now that David knows, this seemed like the perfect time and place."

Microphones were shoved in his face, with the reporters shouting rapid-fire questions.

"Keller, are you gay? Is this your boyfriend?"

"Keller, how long have you two been dating?"

"Keller, did the Vegas Players' organization know?"

"Keller, are you concerned that parents won't want a gay man coaching their children?"

"Keller!"

"Keller!"

His head spun from the barrage of voices. His arm around Niall's shoulder, Keller faced the crowd of local reporters, who'd come for a high school football game and got the sports story of the year. Behind them he saw parents, students from Overlook, as well as Bedlington townspeople, all holding their phones up, videoing.

"All right, everyone. I'm only going to say this once, and then that'll be it." His arm tightened on Niall, needing him by his side more than he'd anticipated. "Yes, I'm gay. I've always known, but being out in professional sports wasn't in the realm of possibility when I was active. Or even now. Why? I kiss my boyfriend after a huge win, and it's going to be a national story. Any other coach who'd kiss his wife or girlfriend under these same circumstances would barely get noticed. So this is on you, folks, for making it impossible for people in the queer community to be our true selves because you're just so damn interested in what we've got going on. Some of you asked if the Vegas Players knew. They didn't. Why not?" He spread his arm wide. "Look at you all. You're like vultures, trying to get this story for a high school football game. The Players' organization and my teammates didn't need the distraction every time we took the field."

He paused for a moment, and Niall rubbed his back. For once the reporters were quiet, as was the crowd gathered. "I've never been happier than I have been coaching these kids. Am I concerned that Overlook High won't want me coaching anymore? I shouldn't have to be. I'm there to teach these kids football. That's it. I've committed no crime and done nothing wrong. All I want is to be who I am. No one should have to hide who they love. And for the people who want to know if this is my boyfriend..." He paused and gazed at Niall with a tender smile. "Yeah. But I'm not talking about my relationship with him." He set his jaw and stared directly into the news cameras filming him. "My personal life is off-limits, and I expect you to respect that. He didn't sign up to be in the limelight, so I hope you'll give him the privacy he deserves. I'll take questions about the game, but not about anything else."

"But Keller, your fans deserve to know," a sports reporter from one of the local news stations said.

He stepped away from Niall. "Yeah? And why's that?"

"Because you're a public figure. People look up to you—kids *and* adults."

"First of all, I'm not a public figure. I'm a retired NFL player who's now a high school football coach. Second, where is it written that because I ran faster than other people and caught a ball for a living, you're entitled to the details of my personal life? What right do you have to know? I am no different than the man who stepped out on this field three hours ago. If your perception of me has changed because I've come out, I suggest you look in the mirror, or better yet, in your heart, and ask why. Because I see that as your problem, not mine. Thank you and good night."

"That was an incredible speech. Well done," Niall murmured. "I'm sure it won't be the last time you'll be giving it either."

"You're most likely right." He grimaced and dipped his head. "Let's get out of here." He hesitated. "Can I…is it okay if I come over?"

"Of course." Niall's smile was sweet. "There's no need to hide any longer." Peering over his shoulder, Niall's eyes widened and he tipped his head. "You might want to turn around."

He did, and saw the entire team standing behind him, his coaches included. Taken aback, he ducked his head, hating this had to be done in public. "So, uh, how much of that did you hear?"

"All of it," Leon stated, his grizzled face determined.

"And we support you one hundred percent, right, team?" Hank faced the kids, who began to clap.

"Coach, Coach, Coach! We are Tigers! Hear us roar!"

Hearing he had the support from these kids he'd known for less than three months meant the world to him. Tears streaked down his face, and he searched for and met Van's eyes. The teenager smiled and gave him a thumbs-up, then resumed clapping. David separated himself from the crowd and came up to him and Niall.

"I'm not going with the guys to celebrate, Dad. I want to be home with you."

For the first time, Keller wished he had a child, because if he had, he'd want them to grow up to have a heart like David. Niall hugged him.

"No. This is the biggest win of your season. I want you to be with your friends and go to the party. I'll be all right."

David cut his gaze to Keller. "Are you going to be with my dad?"

"Is it okay with you if I am?" A funny feeling danced in his chest. More than anyone else, he wanted—needed—David's approval. Niall had said he was okay with their relationship, but Keller wanted that reassurance straight from David.

"Well, yeah. I mean, it's Friday night." He squared his shoulders. "I just want my dad to be happy again."

"Me too, kiddo."

The rest of the team crowded around him, Van the first to speak. "Man, I gotta say I did not expect this, but thanks, Coach. It gives me hope that if I'm good enough, I can go pro one day and not have to worry."

"I hope so, but I think we'll always have to be careful. You were a big inspiration for me."

Van's dark eyes grew huge. "Me?"

"Yeah." Keller rubbed his chin, hyperaware that the

crowd still watched them with avid eyes. "There you were, proud of who you are, no regrets. I thought if a kid could do it, I sure as hell had no reason not to. So thank you."

"Wow, uh, yeah, well, it was a different time, I guess, when you were growing up. And it's not like there's been a rush of players to come out while in the pros. There's still a long way to go. But maybe I could be that one."

Keller patted him on the shoulder. "I'm thinking if anyone can, it's you."

The team all lined up to shake his hand, and it took Keller a moment to recover after they'd gone to the showers, leaving him with Hank and Leon. Hank held out a hand to him.

"I hate that you had to do it, but you gotta know you just made it easier for a whole lotta people in the game."

"Maybe, I don't know. I still didn't have the guts to do it when I was active."

"It's never too late." Leon patted him on the shoulder. "You were a great player, and you're a damn fine coach. The kids are playing the best I've ever seen in all the years I've worked here. They respect you, and I do as well. I'm proud to work by your side."

"Thanks. It means the world to have your support."

"Always."

And then it was only him and Niall, who'd stood by in the stands, patiently waiting. At a distance, a few reporters hovered, but he ignored them.

"So I guess I'm coming to yours tonight?" Keller turned away from the cameras, unwilling to have them intrude on his conversation.

"I'd like that." Niall's eyes shone, his face beaming bright. "I can even lend you a toothbrush."

To Niall's surprise, but not his, reporters had already camped out on Niall's street. Flashbulbs popped as they pulled into the garage and shut the door. Even inside the house they could hear the commotion from the press.

"Well…" He sighed. "That's that." His phone buzzed over and over. It had started while he drove to Niall's, but he'd ignored it. Seeing Elijah's name among all the calls, he was about to call him, when a FaceTime request from Elijah popped up.

"I gather you've heard?"

"Yeah. Proud of you, man."

"Thanks. But I didn't do anything special, like find a cure for a disease. All I did was kiss my boyfriend in public. It shouldn't be something I have to defend." With a grunt he sat on the couch. Niall had left him to go to the kitchen, but returned with two glasses of wine. He took one, mouthing, *Thank you* to him.

"You know what I mean. You think there'll be any fallout?"

"Fallout? Like from the job? I hope not." He frowned into the golden liquid he swirled. "I'd like to think they're more concerned with my ability to coach. I'll rest on my record."

"You want us to come up tomorrow? Just say the word."

"For moral support?" Lucky man he was, to have friends who'd drop anything to be there for him. Beside him, Niall sat quietly, looking at his phone, frowning. "Nah. I'll be with Niall."

"Good. Keep the people you love close. It's what my mama always said."

"No one knew better than Ms. Roberta. Give DeeDee

a hug.”

"I will. Talk to you tomorrow." He set his phone on the coffee table. "What's wrong?"

"I don't really go on social media, but years ago, Angie set up a family Instagram account to post pictures of David's football games and stuff like that. I'm now getting all this hate mail. Some are bitching I turned you gay, others say I'm not good-looking enough to be your type. And there are the pictures." His brows rose. "And I'm being inundated with texts and emails from television and radio stations and newspapers. Look."

Niall offered his phone, and Keller winced at the stream of texts—some polite, some tactless and grasping, and a few, as expected, hateful ones citing God, the devil, and eternal hellfire. The dick pics weren't surprising. It was why he rarely went on social media himself.

"Are you upset? I probably should've said something to you first, but—"

"No," Niall burst out, harsher than Keller had ever heard him speak before. "Your life is for you to live." His eyes warmed. "For once you're going to do things the way you want, not how someone else wants you to."

Keller pulled Niall close. "The only thing I want is you. Every day, more and more."

Niall's cheek creased against his in a smile. "Seems we want the same things. Because all I want is you too."

"You have me. All of me." He took Niall's hand and put it over his rapidly beating heart. "Feel how fast it's beating?" Niall nodded. "It's trying to make up for all the time without you."

Their lips met, and they pulled off their clothes and lay naked on the couch. Keller licked the tip of Niall's shaft, grasped him at the root, and took him to the back of his throat. Groans and harsh cries rose in the air.

"*Mmm*, good, so good," Niall gasped, his hips rolling,

but Keller had bigger plans.

"Shh. Let me do this."

He redoubled his efforts on Niall's cock, pulling off for a moment to slip two fingers into his mouth to wet them, and continued to suck and lick Niall, running his tongue along the thick vein while flirting along the rim of his hole. Loving how Niall wriggled and squirmed as he played with him, Keller slid both fingers inside and pumped his hand.

"Oh, oh fuck," Niall yelped and panted. He humped Keller's hand, trying to get more of Keller in him. "Keller, please."

"*Mmm*. Beg me." He pushed another finger in and watched Niall stretch wide to take him. "You're so hungry for me. Don't worry, I know what you want." He withdrew, and Niall wailed, but when he kissed the recently vacated hole, the protests turned to pleading.

"Keller, please. Please. I need you."

"I need you too. But not here. In a bed so we can go nice and slow."

Hand in hand, they ascended the stairs to Niall's bedroom. Niall slipped his arms around his waist, and Keller forgot everything except how well their bodies fit together and how he'd never wanted anyone else more.

"Niall, I want you so much."

"You have me. All of me. Everything. I want everything from you." Niall kissed his neck, his chest, and teased his nipples. "It's like a dream to be here with you in my bed and not have to be afraid." Eyes glittering and face flushed, Niall reached into his nightstand and grabbed the lube. Loving this fierce and lusty Niall, Keller let him take the lead. He lay pliant as Niall's long fingers slicked up his cock, and then Niall kissed his balls, poked his tongue into his belly button, and tickled the slit of Keller's dick. Keller twisted the sheets in his hands.

"Baby, please."

Niall moaned. "Say that again."

He smiled into Niall's eyes. "Baby. I want you so much, it's killing me. I need to be in you."

"Take me. Fuck me."

Hearing those words from Niall's gasping lips, Keller couldn't stop to think about anything else. He rolled Niall under him and pushed a knee in between his thighs. The head of his lubed cock nudged into Niall, and the heat and tight fit almost caused him to lose it before they even started. Niall tilted his hips, and he slid inside, thrusting deep, the wildness that had been building all night bursting free.

"You're everything, Niall. My everything."

"*Keller…*" Niall thrashed on the pillow. "I need you."

"You've got me, baby." He bent Niall almost in half, holding him tight, the sweat on their skin mingling, and captured his mouth in a searing kiss. "You've got me."

Niall grew stiff in his arms, and his trapped dick throbbed, caught between his and Keller's stomachs, spurting sticky release. It was such a turn-on to hold his twitching body, and knowing he'd given Niall pleasure, Keller thrust into Niall hard and held him tight as his climax overpowered him.

They lay together in the aftermath, trying to catch their breaths. Keller slipped out of Niall, and wetness dripped down his leg. "I guess we got a little carried away."

"You guess?" Niall chuckled. "And only a little? I may never walk again."

"Did I hurt you?" Worried, Keller rubbed their cheeks together. "I keep forgetting you haven't been with anyone else."

"No." Niall stretched and rubbed a foot over his. "I don't think you could hurt me."

"Um, there's something else. We need to talk about the fact that we didn't use protection." Keller ran his nose along Niall's cheek. "I've never had that happen, where I've forgotten everything except being in the moment. Seems every time I touch you, I lose my mind. Which isn't an excuse. I'm sorry for not thinking. But just so you know, I haven't been with anyone in a long time and had a full physical when I was hired."

Was he babbling? The last thing he wanted was for Niall to sense any regret over their lovemaking. So many emotions were playing through him at that moment, he almost didn't know what was going to come out of his mouth next.

"Shh. It's okay. Fact is, I didn't even think of it." Niall's lips rested on the corner of his mouth. "I wanted you so much, I couldn't think of anything else but getting you inside me."

Late-night confessions with a lover were unheard of for him. Keller loved hearing what he knew was heartfelt because Niall didn't speak simply to fill the silence.

Still holding him, Niall rolled onto his side and met his eyes. "All those years of going through the motions of sex left me wondering what losing myself to real passion would be like." He touched Keller's cheek. "And now I know. Feeling you in me completely…fully? It was beyond anything I ever imagined. I loved it."

"I love you," Keller said, then stared openmouthed at Niall, who froze in his arms. "I—"

"It's okay." Niall disengaged slowly from him, his face becoming strained. "I know you didn't mean it." Now, instead of legs tangled in between his and soft lips kissing him, there was space between them.

Keller didn't like that.

"Why are you so sure? How do you know what I'm feeling?"

"I don't, but we barely know each other." Wide-eyed, Niall pressed up against the headboard.

"That's where you're wrong. I know you." Keller slid close. "You're loyal and have a huge heart. You'll do anything for your family and friends. You believe in doing the right thing and stand by your convictions." Keller braced his hands over Niall's head, caging him between his arms. "You're an incredible lover, so passionate, someone who twists me inside out. I go to sleep wanting you next to me and wake up sad if you're not. I can't stop thinking about you. All. Day. Long."

"Keller…" Niall breathed. "This can't be happening."

"Why?"

"Because…it's me." Niall's matter-of-factness broke Keller's heart. Did he still have no idea how special he was?

"Yeah, I know. And that's exactly why. Because it's you. Niall. *My* Niall. Who else could it be?"

"But—"

"Shh." Keller's mouth settled over Niall's. "No buts. No what-ifs. You kiss like you're giving me a piece of your heart. Your soul." He brushed their lips together. "And I accept. I want it all. If you'll give it to me."

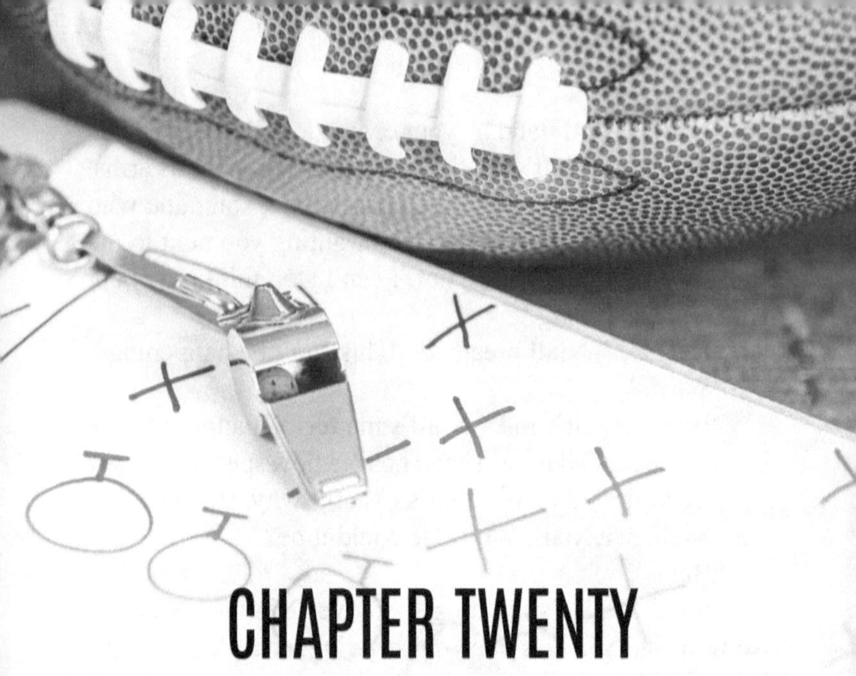

CHAPTER TWENTY

He couldn't lie.

And yet as desperately in love with Keller as he was, he refrained from flinging his arms around him. The teenage boy who lived inside him refused to let him go.

"When I married Angie, I tried to be the best husband I could, even though the love I felt for her wasn't all that passion and fire people talk about. As the years passed, I figured I'd never know, but I reconciled myself to the fact that I had the family I'd always wanted. I thought it would be enough, but it wasn't. And even after the divorce, the fear of coming out, of rejection and humiliation, kept me from possibilities."

"You deserve so much more." Keller nudged his cheek. "It's time to live."

"Everyone deserves to own their truth."

"I agree. Maybe me going public will help others who've

been hiding and give them the strength to take that step."

He gazed into Keller's eyes and saw an open heart calling to his. "You are so much more than I ever dreamed."

"And I never dreamed I'd be lucky enough to find someone like you." Keller's lips curved upward. "I don't need bright lights when I can share the darkness with you and feel safe. There's no more wishing when I know reality."

"I don't want to let you go." Niall ran a hand over Keller's biceps.

"Then don't." Keller kissed him, and the last of Niall's inhibitions floated away.

"I love you, Keller. Your corny jokes and smiles come from your heart, where it counts. You always make me feel like I'm the most important person in the room."

"You are the most important person in my world. There isn't anything I wouldn't do for you. You just have to trust that it's all going to work out."

It wasn't as simple as Keller would like to think, but with warm lips on his, Niall could allow himself to believe.

"I hope you're right."

Late Saturday morning, Niall left a sleeping Keller to go downstairs and make coffee but became sidetracked by noises outside. He peered through the curtain and his jaw dropped. No less than ten news trucks were parked haphazardly outside the house, blocking the road, and several reporters were standing on his lawn, talking into cameras.

"The fuck they're going to do this to him." Niall fumed and was about to stomp upstairs to get dressed so he could tell them to get the hell out, when his phone rang. Seeing Angie's name pop up, he sighed, figuring he'd need to speak to her at some point, so he might as well do it now.

"Hey, how are you?"

"How am *I*?" Her voice rose with amusement. "I'm fine. How the hell are *you*? I can't believe the stories I'm reading." Her tone dropped. "Are you really having an affair with Keller Williams?"

Annoyed at her choice of words, he snapped at her. "You're making it sound tawdry and illicit, and it's anything but."

"I'm sorry. I just feel so left out all of a sudden. We used to talk about everything, and now your whole life is upside down and I'm as clueless as the newspaper reporter. You're still my best friend, Niall."

Her words hurt, but they were true. Angie had always stood by him. She deserved more than what she read in the papers. He pushed a hand through his hair. "I'm sorry. It's more than an affair. We've been seeing each other for a while. Last night he said he loved me." Her sharp indrawn breath whooshed in his ear.

"Niall, that's wonderful."

"I know we're close, Ang, but I needed time to figure things out for myself."

"I get it, and I'm thrilled for you. David is okay with it all, I'm assuming?"

"He's been terrific. And yes, he knew before last night. It wasn't a surprise to him—Keller would never do that. We talked about it, and even though it was an uncomfortable conversation for me, he's growing up. He has a girlfriend, and sooner or later he's going to become sexually active. I want him to know he can trust me and come to me with any and all questions. I'm always going to tell him the truth."

He needed coffee, and as he talked to Angie he brewed a pot. When it was done, he poured himself a cup and sat at the kitchen island.

He sipped the hot hazelnut coffee and heard more car

doors slamming and the hum of voices.

"No offense, but right now I have news trucks and reporters outside, and I have to decide how to handle it. I can't have the neighborhood disrupted like this."

One thing Angie was good at was taking control of a situation. "Well, if you want, I can act as your spokesperson and send out a statement to the press that you're not giving interviews, and since there's a minor involved, they need to stop invading our family's privacy. If Keller wants to give his own statement, that's up to him."

"I don't know what Keller wants to do. I just came downstairs to this mess. I'm sure he's used to handling them."

"Handling what? Is that coffee?"

He glanced over his shoulder to see Keller bare-chested, standing in the entrance to the kitchen, wearing only his briefs. His messy hair, morning stubble, and sleepy bedroom eyes made Niall's heart tumble, and he spoke into the phone. "I gotta go. I'll talk to you later."

"Wait, do you want me to contact the press for you?"

"Yeah, sure. Thanks, Angie." He set the phone on the counter. "Hi."

"Hi." Keller kissed him. "*Mmm*, hazelnut."

Laughing, Niall pointed to the cabinet next to the sink. "Get a mug and pour yourself some. We have to talk."

Keller peered at him sharply but did as Niall requested, and when he had his coffee, he sat. "About? And who were you talking to?"

"Angie, but that's not the issue. There's a horde of news trucks and reporters camped outside. We need to figure out how to handle them."

Instead of springing into motion like he'd expected, Keller merely smiled at him. "I like hearing that."

"What?" He searched through what he'd said. "That there are people waiting for you outside?"

Keller cupped his jaw. "Nah. I can handle the press." He kissed him again, his mouth lingering and tasting sweet. "I like hearing you say *we*. Like we're in this together."

"Aren't we?" He gazed steadily at Keller. "That's what love is supposed to be."

Keller's crooked grin had his heart pounding double speed. "Yeah. I guess having someone by my side is the part I'll have to learn."

Niall kissed his cheek. "Happy to help."

They dressed quickly, and Niall trailed behind Keller as they returned downstairs. "What're you going to say?"

Keller lifted a shoulder. "I dunno. Depends on what they ask."

He put a hand on Keller's arm to hold him off from opening the door. "Please keep David out of this."

"Of course." Solemn-faced, Keller nodded. "Don't worry." He opened the door and stepped outside. The crowd rushed toward him, shouting questions. Niall remained in the background. Keller raised his arms.

"Please. I'm here simply to make a statement. I won't be taking any questions, so I suggest you listen carefully." He glanced over his shoulder and winked at Niall.

Keller was enjoying this. Niall wanted to laugh but pressed his lips together and listened.

"What I stated yesterday after the Overlook Tigers beat the Bedlington Rangers hasn't changed. I'm gay. I was gay when I played professional football for the Vegas Players. I was gay when we won the Super Bowl. I chose not to discuss my sexuality because I didn't feel it had any bearing on my ability as a player. Just like I don't think who I love matters to my ability to coach. I decided to come out because I'm in a loving relationship with a man who doesn't deserve to be hidden."

"How did you meet, Keller? You coach his son, don't you?" a voice in the crowd shouted, and Niall's jaw hardened.

If Keller wouldn't shut it down, he would.

He needn't have worried. Keller folded his arms. "My kids listen to directions better than you adults. No questions means no questions. He's a private person. He didn't sign up for this, and just because we're together doesn't mean you get free access to his life or his house. And it goes without saying that you keep away from his son and every other kid on the team because if you start stalking or harassing them for gossip, trust me, you will not be happy. If I see any pictures of the kids in the press other than an article about how great the team is, you'll have a lawsuit faster than you take your next breath. That's all I plan to say about this. I'm hoping you'll give us privacy and leave us alone the same way you leave other couples alone to enjoy their weekend."

"Aw, come on, Keller. Your fans deserve—"

"My fans deserve my football life. No one *deserves* my private life except the people I choose to let in. Now I see the sheriffs have arrived to make sure you all follow the town parking rules, so I suggest you listen to them so you won't get ticketed and towed. Have a good one. Oh, and one more thing." He paused, and the crowd of reporters went silent. "Queer people are here to stay. We aren't asking for your permission to live, because we don't need to. You can try and vote our human rights out of existence, but we won't go quietly. I was gay ten years ago when you all loved me as a Super Bowl champion. I was gay when you thought I was a player, on and off the field. Nothing's different from the man I was then, to the man I am today, except that I'm lucky to have found someone to love who loves me back."

He strode over to Niall. "Let's get inside."

Niall's phone rang as soon as they closed and locked the door. "Hey, David."

"Are you all right?"

"Yeah, we're okay. How are you? Any issues?"

"A few. It's okay."

He didn't exactly like the sound of that. "Where are you now?"

"Having breakfast at Brenden's."

"Do you want me to come get you?"

"Will…will Coach be with you?"

His gaze cut to Keller, who shrugged. "Do you want him to be?"

"Can you come alone? I just think it'll be better right now."

"Sure."

"I'm almost done, so you can come when you want."

"I'll be there in fifteen minutes." He hung up and put the phone into his pocket. "David wants to come home. He doesn't sound right."

"I heard. Go get him. I'll wait here."

Niall nodded and hesitated, gave him a quick kiss on the cheek, and hurried off to the garage. The crowd had mostly dispersed by the time he pulled out of the driveway, and he noticed that the town had left a sheriff's car parked out front. He slowed while passing them.

"Sorry about all this. I appreciate your helping out."

"No problem, Niall." Deputy Taylor Lundquist tipped his hat. They'd also gone to high school together, and he'd married Maisie, a girl in their class who worked in one of the hair salons in town. "Abel and I will make sure they keep away and don't cause problems. Just keep your doors locked."

His brow furrowed. "I always do, but why?"

Abel's lips thinned. "Because these people will stop at nothing to get what they want, and you and Keller Williams are the biggest news around here in years."

He could feel the heat radiating off his face. "People need a life," he mumbled, and the two deputies nodded.

"We're not going anywhere."

On the road to Brenden's, Niall's anxiety grew. Was

David all right? He'd always looked forward to spending the weekend with his friends and hadn't ever come home early, unless he was sick. He turned the corner and saw David waiting outside with his backpack. Niall was convinced something was wrong.

"Hi. Hop in."

"Thanks." David buckled his seat belt but stared out the window instead of talking. Niall decided to push him.

"How was the party last night? You all must've been stoked."

"It was fine. We had pizza."

"Good old pizza. I don't know what I'd do without it." Niall's laugh sounded forced to his own ears, and David didn't acknowledge him. Instead of driving home, he drove to the park, pulled into the lot, and cut the engine. "What's wrong? Tell me."

Eyes shiny, David blinked. "It's Renee. She said she can't see me anymore because…" Red spots burned on his cheeks. "Uh, because of you and Coach. Her parents say it's wrong, and they don't want her hanging out with me anymore and 'being exposed to that lifestyle.'" He sniffled. "It's not fair, Dad."

His protective instincts roared to the surface, and Niall wanted to drive over to Renee's house and tell her parents exactly what he thought of their small, bigoted minds. But he took a deep breath as he struggled with his shockingly violent thoughts, closed his eyes for a moment, and unclenched.

"I know it's not. I'm sorry my personal life is hurting you."

"It's so stupid. Renee thinks so too."

"So she doesn't agree with them?" Niall was happy to hear that at least.

"No, of course not. One of her closest friends, Leslie, is bi. Renee thinks her parents are being stupid, but they told her they'll pull her off the cheerleading squad if we continue to date." David rubbed his eyes. "Coach is a great guy. Her dad was his biggest fan before…before he found out."

"I'm really sorry you have to become involved in this. Our personal lives shouldn't mean anything. All these players are always getting arrested for domestic violence, gun or drug charges, and that's okay with them?" He fumed. "It's bigotry, plain and simple."

"I know. That's what she tried to tell them. I mean, Shane's dad hits him, and they don't have a problem with that?"

A chill ran down his spine. "What're you talking about? Bobby Contard hits Shane? Why didn't you ever say anything?"

Looking uncomfortable, David shifted in his seat. "A bunch of us thought it might be happening, but we didn't want to say anything. Yesterday, though, Shane came to the party with a black eye. He said it was from the game, but Van told us he saw Shane and his father arguing in front of Shane's house when they came home, and Mr. Contard punched Shane. He was mad that Shane didn't throw the winning touchdown."

"My God." Niall hoped he wouldn't be sick. "Why—what was Van doing at Shane's house? Wasn't he at the party?"

David couldn't meet his eyes. "Can we go home now?"

"Sure." Niall started up the car, and in less than ten minutes, he was in the garage. "Let me make sure the door is closed first. There was a big crowd outside this morning."

"So, uh, Coach is still here?" David's gaze flicked to the door and returned to him.

"Yeah. Is that all right?"

"Yeah. Sure. I said it was, yesterday."

That was then and this is now, Niall wanted to say, but remained silent.

Once inside, David kicked off his sneakers and pushed

them under the bench in the mudroom. "You don't have to worry. I'm still okay with you and Coach being together."

He had wondered if David would have a change of heart now that it was out in the open and in the press, so it was a relief to hear him say it out loud.

"I'm glad. Because I really care about him."

Keller walked out from the kitchen. "Hi. Everything okay?" His eyes and voice were wary.

"Yeah, Coach. Just got some stuff to work out."

"We can practice in the backyard later on, if you'd like."

For the first time, a smile lit David's face. "Yeah? That'd be cool. Maybe Chris could come over too? Would that be okay, Dad?"

"Of course."

" 'Kay. I have to finish my math homework and start a history paper that's due at the end of the month."

"Better get cracking." He tipped his head, and David hefted his backpack onto his shoulder and ran upstairs.

Niall waited to hear David's door close before walking to Keller, who opened his arms and hugged him. He rested his head on Keller's shoulder and closed his eyes.

"His girlfriend broke up with him."

"Let's go outside."

With Keller's arm still holding him close, they walked outside, where, to his surprise, Keller had set out a bottle of Chardonnay and two glasses, along with some cheese and crackers. His blue eyes sparkled.

"DeeDee taught me how to make a cheese platter. I know it's a little early, but—"

"It's all good." He sighed, sinking onto the sofa, and poured some wine into his glass but didn't drink. "I wish I could say the same for the kids."

"What's wrong?" Keller sat beside him. "Your eyes… it's something big. I can tell."

"Renee had to break up with David because her parents

don't approve of our relationship. David's upset, but I'm hoping maybe they can eventually work it out. But that's not what's upsetting me. It's Shane." With no taste for the wine he'd poured a moment earlier, Niall put it aside.

In the middle of cutting some cheese, Keller set the small knife on the board and left it sitting. "What happened?"

"Did Shane get hit in the face during the game last night?"

Keller thought for a second. "No. Why?" His eyes narrowed.

"Because he showed up to the party with a black eye."

"That bastard," Keller cursed. "It's Bobby. I knew he was hurting that kid, and I let it happen. I should've followed up with the police instead of just making that one report."

"Of course you didn't let anything happen. This isn't your fault. You went to the cops and reported your suspicions. You asked Shane, and he always had an excuse." His reassurance was met with more cursing.

"Until now. How's he going to explain the black eye?" Keller jumped to his feet and paced. "Son of a bitch is going to ruin that boy. I can't let it keep happening."

And before he could say anything, Keller walked away and into the house.

Niall scrambled after him. "Wait, where are you going?"

CHAPTER TWENTY-ONE

"Keller, what are you hoping to accomplish by confronting Bobby?" Niall chased after him to the garage and opened the car door. "You can't just barge into his house and hurl accusations."

Keller gripped the wheel, then rested his forehead between his hands. "I'm afraid for Shane. I think he's got problems. Big problems."

Niall placed a hand on Keller's shoulder. "What could be worse?"

Anguished, Keller met Niall's horrified gaze. "At the beginning of the season, I saw bruising on his back, which Shane explained away as having received when he and his father were throwing a ball around in the yard and he hit a tree. I didn't believe it, so I went to the police and reported it, but they said they found nothing out of the ordinary, and Mary, his wife, said nothing was wrong. If what I suspect is true…" He made a fist and pounded the steering wheel. "I think things are escalating. I have to find out what's happening." He started the car. "You don't have to come with me."

Niall glared. "Seriously? You think I'm going to let you go there alone? Bobby is a loose cannon. Who knows what he's capable of?"

"Okay. Let's go."

"I'll text David to let him know we're leaving."

Keller took off. Luckily, the reporters had abandoned their stakeout for the day, but he had no doubts they'd return.

"Why do you think Shane has big problems? What could be bigger than being used as a punching bag by your father?"

Keller's jaw worked hard as he drove out of the Estates and onto the main road to town. He didn't want to reveal the confidential information he'd been entrusted with, but Niall wouldn't judge him for speaking. He hoped.

"It has to do with those late-night phone calls from the kids."

"Like the one you got the first time you came over."

"Yeah. I know that might seem unusual, but coaches and players have a unique relationship. Plus, if my father had lived, I just know he and I would've been close, and a lot of kids don't have that kind of relationship with their families." He navigated through the winding roads leading into the main area of town. Bobby hadn't moved far since graduating from high school, and lived a few blocks away from the home he grew up in. The houses were built close to the road and in a less desirable part of town, as it bordered the train tracks. Keller recalled playing chicken on those tracks when they were young, dumb, and thought nothing in the world would ever change from those long summer nights spent under the stars.

"I remember how you spoke to the boy who called you. You were patient and kind. Sometimes simply having another ear is all that's needed."

"I want them to know they have a safe space with me."

"You're a very caring person. I've learned that about you, so it doesn't surprise me." Niall laid a hand over his on the steering wheel. "I'd never repeat what you tell me, but if you don't feel comfortable, I understand."

It was a fine line between what he was told and what he believed to be hidden in the whispered words. If, in fact, it was Shane who'd called him, and if what Keller suspected the young man was alluding to was true, the issues ran deeper than football, and Keller wasn't sure he was equipped to handle it alone.

"Since school began, I've received several phone calls from students, and I think I've been able to help them by simply listening as they worked out their problems. I'm never judgmental and mainly give the reassurance that they have an ear and a shoulder." He shot a glance to Niall, whose smile was one of encouragement.

"Kids need that," Niall agreed. "Sometimes an outside person has the clarity to see the truth. If you're too close, it's hard to separate yourself. Your outlook is clouded by what you want."

"Exactly." Keller stopped at the red light. A train horn split the quiet, and he waited. "The kid who called told me he kissed another boy and is questioning his sexuality. But he's called me before, and I picked up the insinuation that there are problems at home."

"And you think it's Shane who called and maybe Bobby found out?"

The light turned green, and without answering, he gunned the Porsche's engine and took off. He found Shane's street and parked a few houses away from Shane's.

"Should I come with you? Would it look weird?" Niall seemed to be struggling.

"I kissed you in front of an entire stadium filled with

parents and kids, not to mention the local press. I think the time for weird has passed."

With Niall at his heels, he walked to the small, two-story house. The steps sagged, and the roof needed repairs. Someone had made an attempt to brighten the yard by planting impatiens, but it did little to distract from the peeling paint and taped-up screens in the windows.

"I swear. The guy works at Home Depot. Why the hell can't he fix his own house?" Prepared to knock, Keller's attention was drawn by shouting from behind the house, and he took off to the backyard.

"What the hell is going on?"

Bobby had Shane pinned to the tree, his meaty fist cocked. Seeing red, Keller sprinted and jumped Bobby.

"Get the fuck offa me, you little bitch." Bobby twisted, but Keller caught him around his neck. His arm hurt, but not as much as it would if he stood by and did nothing. He was already damaged. It was his job to make sure Shane was protected.

"Touch him, and you'll wish you never woke up this morning." He shoved him facedown, and chest heaving, took in Shane's disheveled appearance.

"Did he hurt you? Tell me the truth."

"N-no. He was chasing me and I fell, but he didn't hit me." Shane gulped and swallowed a sob. "You came before he could."

"You bastard," Bobby spat. "Shane was fine until you started coaching. Now I have to find him kissing some queer? What the hell did you do to these kids?"

"You ignorant ass." Keller's eyes bore daggers into Bobby's sneering mug. "No one is turned gay by someone else." Giving Bobby his back, he faced Shane. "What happened? Can you tell me?"

Shane dropped his gaze to the ground. "Last night, I came home after the party. I told Van to meet me here."

"That little qu—" Bobby started to rave.

"Shut up," Keller snarled. "You were with Van?" Shane nodded. "How'd you get the black eye?"

"He fell," Bobby answered for Shane.

"Into your fist?" Keller sneered.

"He's acting like a little punk. He shoulda thrown the ball and shown those scouts."

"Are you for real?" The lack of remorse from Bobby was stunning. "You abused your son because he was following what I told him to do? I'm the coach. I decide how the kids play."

A cunning glint lit Bobby's brown eyes. "Yeah? Let's see for how long."

Keller took a step toward him. "What's that supposed to mean?"

"I don't gotta explain nothing to you. Now get off my property."

Ignoring him, Keller asked Shane, "Are you okay? Do you feel safe if I leave?"

Shane nodded. "Uh, yeah. I'm fine. I gotta go to work. I got a job delivering pizza. Thanks, Coach." He took off running, leaving him with Bobby.

It broke his heart that Shane was too afraid to stand up to his father. Keller knew he had no reason to stay any longer, and spying Niall hovering on the periphery, he trekked past Bobby.

"That's right. Get outta here," Bobby said mockingly, apparently having found his courage. "Go back to your girlfriend." The snide remark almost caused him to turn around and smack it off Bobby's lips, but Niall shook his head as he drew near.

"Don't. It's not worth it."

"Yeah, listen to your *girlfriend*."

His hands curled into fists. "I can't let him talk about you like that."

Niall's smile was surprisingly light. "You think I give one goddamn what someone like that thinks of me? He's a nothing. You, on the other hand, are everything, and if you hit him, you'll be the one to get arrested. Let's get out of here."

They approached the car, and Keller had a hard time controlling his shaking hands to pull the keys from his pocket. When he finally managed to dig them out, Niall plucked them from his fingers.

"Let me drive. You're too rattled."

They climbed in. "And you're not?" Niall started the car while Keller continued to fume. "He insulted you twice."

"And I said I don't care what some idiot Neanderthal says or thinks. And at least you stopped him from assaulting Shane." Niall stopped at the intersection for a red light. "Now that we know for a fact Bobby hit him, we can make a report to the police and let child services get involved."

He rubbed his face. "What a fucking mess. I never knew Bobby was the violent type until I saw what he did to Shane."

Niall coughed. "He's always been a no-good son of a bitch. Bobby's one of the people who used to shove my face in the toilet and trip me in the cafeteria."

Shame burned through him. "And there I was having dinner with him and Mary when you were on your date. No wonder you hated me." He stared out of the window.

The Porsche bounced over a few potholes. "I didn't hate you." Niall frowned. "That's a strong word. Call me mistrustful of your actions. Initially. Then I saw the allure."

Through his misery, Keller felt the brush of Niall's hand. "Allure, huh? Tell me more."

"Silly." Niall turned worried eyes on him. "Seriously. You sure you're okay? I don't want you to reinjure your arm, just for me."

"I'd walk through fire for you."

Niall squeezed his hand. "Let me make you feel better."

Twenty minutes later Niall lay spread out naked on Keller's bed, body bathed in sweat, face flushed as Keller slid in and out of him.

"Oh God, Keller, oh, oh."

Fiercely concentrating on giving Niall as much pleasure as he could, Keller pulled Niall's hips to his and thrust hard and deep as Niall vigorously worked his dick. Niall's thighs tensed, and Keller, sensing his impending climax, bent over him, crushing their lips together in a kiss. Warm stickiness spread between their bodies, and he couldn't help the absolute joy spreading through him. Hearing the soft moans of pleasure breaking free from Niall unraveled him, and he came, pulsing hot and heavy inside Niall.

"I love you," he whispered. "I wish it could've always been you."

"Always starts now." Niall nudged his cheek with his nose. "But first I need to shower." He chuckled. "Afterward we can go to my place, and you can hang out with David and Chris."

He rolled off Niall and watched as he left to go to the bathroom. That tight-muscled ass called to him, and he smiled to himself hearing the shower come on. Keller swung his legs over the side of the bed and rose to his feet, ready to join Niall, when his phone buzzed.

"Hello?"

"Keller, this is Dan. Dan Brockman."

"Hi, how are you?" Convinced the principal was calling to congratulate him on the win, he settled down, ready to receive the praise.

"I'm well. We need to talk."

"Sure. Wasn't that a great game? The kids are on fire."

"Keller, we've had a few phone calls."

"Phone calls?" His heart, only a moment ago dancing in his chest, slowed to a quiet murmur. "About? And from whom?"

A sigh echoed in his ear. "You know this isn't anything personal."

Actually, Keller had no clue, but he refrained from being a wise-ass and kept silent.

"But," Dan bumbled along, "after what happened at the game…you know, you, uh, kissing Niall Harper, uh, a few of the parents of the boys on the team, as well as parents of other students in the school, came to me, expressing their concerns."

Anger buzzed through him. "Concerns about what? Or let me guess," he said with enough sarcasm there could be no doubt he saw through the bullshit. "They think I'm going to corrupt their boys? That's it, right?"

"Among other things, yes."

"What other things?" His stomach sank. "Is it about Niall? That we're involved?"

"We don't advocate teachers getting personally involved."

Niall walked out with a towel draped around his waist. He raised his brows, but Keller was too upset to respond.

"I can't believe you're dragging Niall into this."

Niall froze in place, pale as the towel covering him.

"Let's talk on Monday. My office at nine."

"Fine."

The conversation ended, and then it was his turn to huff out a sigh. "That was Dan. Seems some parents were offended by what happened Friday night…our kiss."

Niall joined him on the bed. "I figured it wasn't the win. What did he say?"

"They think I'm going to corrupt their boys. And he mentioned you and that the school frowns on teachers dating.”

“You’re not a teacher, and I only substitute.” Niall brushed his wet hair off his face. “That’s bullshit.”

“I want to know why it’s okay for Contard to pound on his son and no one says a word. If he touches his kid, ten to one he’s laid hands on Mary. Meanwhile, the self-appointed God Squad is busy worrying about who’s in my bed.”

Niall took his hand and laced their fingers together. “Maybe you should ask him.”

“I haven’t been called to the principal’s office since I got caught cutting class freshman year,” Keller joked, facing Dan. There was no return smile, and Keller clasped his hands in his lap. The rest of the weekend had proved to be a bit tense, and over Niall and David’s protests, he decided to spend Saturday night and Sunday at home. Keller wanted them to have some father-son time together and also draw the press’s attention away from them, plus he needed to concentrate on the game for the upcoming Friday night. He and Niall FaceTimed well into the night, but it was a poor substitute for holding him and waking up seeing his face on the pillow next to him.

“Okay. Let’s get into this, Dan.”

“Look, Keller. You’ve done a great job with the kids, but—”

“But none of that matters now because of my sexuality?” His lips thinned. “Be careful, now. You might want to think twice if you’re planning on firing me. Last I heard, it was illegal.”

Dan frowned. “I don’t like threats.”

“And I don’t like bigots,” he shot back. “Have any of the kids claimed I’ve done something wrong?”

"No, but some parents have concerns."

He folded his arms and quirked a brow. "Such as?"

Here Dan reddened. "They're worried about their children being exposed to sexual practices they don't believe in."

"You're kidding me. What the hell do they think is going on? I'm here to coach football, nothing more."

"Are you sure?"

There was something in Dan's tone that set off warning bells. "Meaning what?"

"Some of the boys told their parents you gave them your personal cell number and said they could call you anytime, day or night." Dan's stare was filled with innuendos that both angered and sickened Keller.

"And? I'm not seeing a problem."

"Coach Weaver never did that."

Stunned by how much Dan's words cut him to the heart, Keller grew frustrated and waved a hand in the air, then made a fist. "Coach Weaver was seventy-five when he retired and didn't even own a cell phone. I want the kids to know they can trust me. If they have problems they can't talk to anyone about, they can call me."

With a lift of his brows, Dan pursed his lips, and there was little doubt what he was thinking. Keller lost it.

"No, Dan. Are you fucking crazy? You think…Jesus, that's ridiculous." God, he couldn't even voice out loud what Dan was insinuating.

"When you made your statement to the press, after the game, you said you've never been happier since you started coaching at Overlook."

He drew in a deep breath and released it quietly.

I will not lose my shit. I will not lose my shit.

But damn, he was close.

"It's true. Once I met Niall, I've never been happier. Not even playing in the Super Bowl."

"Well." Dan cleared his throat. "The school board has called an emergency meeting, Wednesday night. They want to talk to you."

"We've got practice. We're in a race for the state championship, in case you all forgot."

"Be there, Keller. It's not a request." The phone rang, and Dan tipped his head. "That's all. I need to take this." Gone was the friendly camaraderie from the start of the term.

Keller left without a word, storming through the hallway in a daze, unseeing and not returning the students' greetings with his usual cheery smile. He slammed into the locker room, startling the kids getting ready for PE, and didn't stop until he reached the football field. Standing on the grass, feeling the wind blowing in his face and the sun warming his shoulders, he began to run. By the time he slowed down, his legs were sore and sweat poured off him.

Leon stood by the entrance to the gym. "What's wrong? You looked like the devil himself was chasing you."

"Close enough."

He explained, also filling Leon in on the scene with Bobby and Shane on Saturday. Leon's eyes grew hot with anger. When Keller came to the part about parents being upset over the kids having his phone number, Leon became outraged.

"Are they fucking kidding me? They're trying to accuse you of what?"

"You know what," he responded, too sick to his stomach to say it. "All I wanted was to help the kids because I remember how hard it was for me at that age. Meanwhile, Bobby Contard can give his son a black eye, but that's okay? Make it make sense, Leon."

"It doesn't. But you best believe, when Wednesday night comes around, you're not gonna be alone."

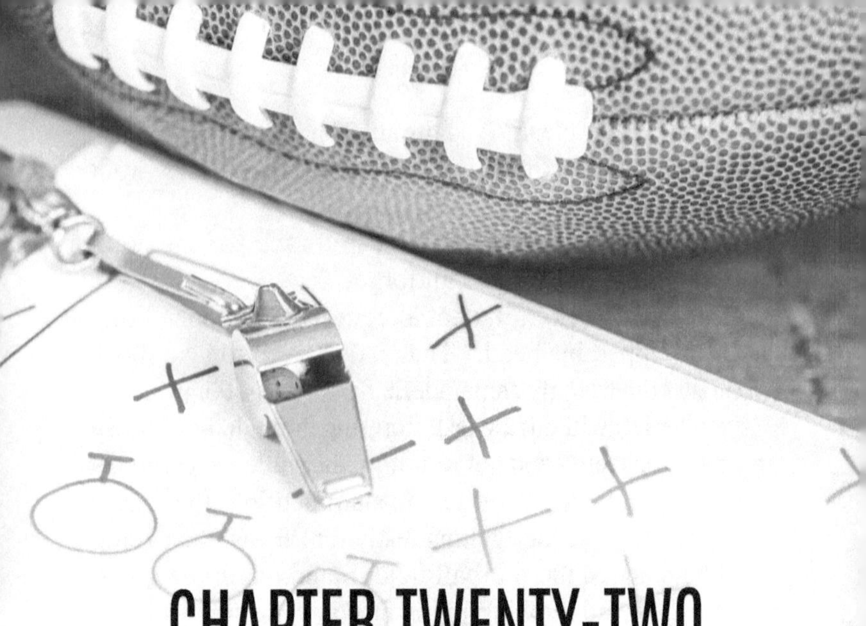

CHAPTER TWENTY-TWO

"I'm sorry, Dan, what?"

Niall narrowed his eyes at the principal, who barely granted him attention from the papers on his desk.

"It's nothing personal, you know that. We've been searching for a permanent English teacher since Susan Forest left. Now we found one. So you won't need to substitute teach any longer."

"Nothing personal, of course. But just like that? All of a sudden?" he mused. "How come you never mentioned you were interviewing?"

That drew the principal's attention. "Because, Niall, I don't owe you an explanation for what I do as the principal."

"Fine." He rose to his feet. "I'll see myself out."

"Just one question. When did this thing with Keller Williams start?"

Anger bubbled through him. He strode to the door and

opened it but stopped before exiting. "Like you said, Dan, I don't owe you an explanation for what I do."

Back in his office, he wanted to text Keller to hear about his meeting, but it was monthly inventory and book-ordering day, and there was precious little downtime. At lunch, he sent Keller a text telling him about his conversation with Dan, but only received a return text that read: *He's a bastard. Talk later.* Knowing the stress Keller was under, he didn't want to press him. It could wait until dinner.

"A school-board meeting? What the fuck, Keller?" Niall fumed in his seat at the kitchen island. David was at a study session for an upcoming test, so Keller had picked up sushi for the two of them. The initial rush of press had subsided, as they'd found some other poor soul to sink their teeth into. Once or twice a day, a reporter would call, and he'd taken to not answering any calls from numbers he didn't recognize.

"Yeah. I can't believe some parents are complaining that I gave the kids my phone number as a way to get close to them. In a creepy way." Usually Keller ate with gusto, but that night he toyed with his rolls, eventually tossing aside the chopsticks. "Why are they so afraid? The kids are doing well, and we're on our way to a state championship. What do they want? Blood? They can't have everything. My life, my heart, those are mine."

Niall took his hand. "They're mine too. And my heart is yours. Which is why we'll see this through together."

"No, no. This is my battle, not yours."

"That's bullshit." Niall slapped his chopsticks on the kitchen island. "Yours, mine…it's *our* problem to face. The good and the bad." He glared at Keller. "I'm going to the hearing with you. And I'm not asking. I'm telling you."

Keller slung an arm around his neck and planted a kiss on his cheek. "I like it when you get bossy." The curve of Keller's lips pressed into his cheek. "It's hot. And I can't think of anyone else I'd rather have at my side."

He couldn't stop smiling. "You're a silly man, but I love you."

They finished their sushi just as the front door opened. "Dad? You home?"

"In here."

David didn't seem surprised to see Keller there. "Hi."

"Hi. Get lots of studying done?"

"Yeah, I think we're ready." He shifted on his feet. "Uh, some of the kids said their parents told them Coach might be fired?" Niall froze, and his eyes darted to Keller, who looked unfazed. "That's not true, right?"

"Not if I can help it." He sighed. "I'll have to wait and see."

Keller went to the sink, both hands full with the remnants of their sushi dinner, and David followed. "They gotta be crazy. You're the best coach ever. We're gonna win state championship." His voice cracked, and Niall hurt for his son. To be so young and have to see your dreams about to be dashed to pieces at your feet was hard. "Why? Why do they wanna fire you?"

"It's complicated." Keller separated the trash from the recycling, then leaned against the counter. He met Niall's eyes, and David picked up on their unspoken signals. He should've known better than to try and hide anything from his son.

"Because you're dating my dad? They want to fire you for that?"

Keller shrugged. "Among other things. When parents found out I gave you kids my phone number, some of them didn't like it."

"But that's not fair. I know kids could tell you stuff they couldn't tell their parents. You helped us." He ducked his head. "Even me."

A frisson of surprise rolled through Niall. "You called Keller?" Why hadn't Keller ever said anything? A quick glance to Keller showed his focus was on David, his face completely neutral.

David pulled out the seat next to him and sat, head bowed, gaze planted firmly on the floor. "Yeah. It was when you first told me…you know…that you're gay." His eyes rose to meet Niall's. "I'm sorry. I was just so confused. I needed to talk to someone. I know you said Mom knew, but I didn't want to talk to her."

"It's okay. You didn't do anything wrong."

"I never told Coach who I was or what you said to me. I just said my father told me something really personal and I didn't know how to handle it."

"Because you were upset?" All his life Niall had fought to make sure David had the childhood he didn't, and he'd thought he'd succeeded. To think he'd called Keller because he was so lost was like a blow to his stomach. Keller remained silent.

"It's hard to explain. No, I wasn't upset. But I was. If that makes any sense. I thought you never loved Mom, but I know that's not true. I just…" His voice dropped to a whisper. "I was ashamed of myself because my first thought was that I wished you weren't because I didn't want to be different from my friends." He swiped at his eyes. "And I hated myself for it because you're such a great dad. I didn't mean it."

"I know." His heart squeezed. "I love you, David. Believe me when I tell you I struggled for a long time about telling you, for that very reason. Sometimes I wonder if I even made the right choice if it caused you pain."

"No." David responded vehemently. "You can't live

your life for me. And after talking to Coach and thinking about it, it doesn't matter. I said that before, and I meant it."

"I'm glad I could help you, David. I didn't know it was you, but after Niall and I became closer, I figured it out."

"And you never said anything to me?"

Keller frowned. "No. Why would I?"

Was he kidding? "Because he's my son."

"The purpose of giving my number to the kids was so they knew they could talk to me in complete anonymity. I'm there to listen, not judge. To offer an ear and the occasional suggestion. I don't ask for their names. I want them to feel safe. Who they are doesn't matter."

"Oh." Now he felt foolish. "I'm sorry."

"Yeah, Dad. I don't know if I would've felt comfortable talking to Coach if he knew it was me, but because he never asked for my name, I could tell him stuff without it feeling weird."

"That makes perfect sense. I'm glad you had someone to talk to. Kids have so much pressure heaped on them these days. They need to know there are safe spaces where they can be free to speak without judgment."

"That's why it bugs me so much. For them to accuse me of using my relationship with the kids…" Keller's face darkened with anger. "I'll be damned if I let them get away with it."

"Hopefully once you speak at the school-board meeting, they'll understand."

"Meeting?" David searched Keller's face, then his. "What're you talking about? What meeting?"

"The school board is holding an emergency meeting on Wednesday to discuss Keller's situation," he explained, which as he spoke caused the anger to boil up inside him.

"Situation? What situation?"

Niall raised his brows, and David's jaw dropped in disbelief. "But that's not fair. So what if you two are dating? Lots of teachers have." He blinked and turned red. "Last week we saw Mrs. Wright kissing Mr. Grainger in the parking lot after practice, and they're both married to other people. Why isn't that a problem?"

"Because people get a stick up their—" Keller began, and Niall jumped in.

"They're hypocrites, is what Keller was going to say."

"Sorry." Keller hung his head, and David laughed.

"Come on, Dad. I'm almost sixteen, not six."

"Yeah, Niall." Keller's eyes twinkled, and Niall rolled his eyes.

"Well, someone has to be the adult here."

"But it's gonna be fine, right? They're not gonna fire Coach?"

The lighthearted atmosphere faded. "I don't know."

David's eyes narrowed. "They can't. You'll see." He got to his feet. "I'd better go shower."

"See you later. By the way, anything new with Renee? Have you spoken to her at all?"

David shrugged. "Yeah. She was at the study session for chemistry. She's really mad at her parents and isn't talking to them."

"That's sad."

"It's not only about you and Coach. It's her best friend too. Her parents said Leslie can't come over anymore to study after school when they're not home because she's bisexual. I mean, they're so stupid. Just 'cause Leslie's bi doesn't mean she's interested in every girl. Why do people have to be so dumb?"

"When you figure it out, let me know." Keller's lips pressed thin, his eyes wary and sad.

Shaking his head, David walked away, his steps heavy on the stairs. Niall left his seat to put his arms around Keller and rested his head on his shoulder.

"It's going to be all right. It has to be."

Keller rubbed his back. "I guess we'll have to wait and see."

Marty strolled into the library. "Well, look at that. I go away for a few days and miss the story of the year." Niall hated the gleam of gossip in his eyes.

"What do you mean?" Pretending innocence, Niall continued entering the new books in the computer inventory system.

"You're going to sit there and pretend? Niall. I saw the kiss. They've replayed it on every news show all weekend long. And Keller's statement outside your house? C'mon."

"Okay, so you know everything."

But Marty was relentless and joined him behind the desk. "Are you kidding? You're getting nailed by Keller Williams, and you think I'm not gonna have something to say?" He leered. "How is he? I bet he's got a dick like a fucking elephant."

"Shut up," he hissed. Face burning, Niall glared. "I'm working. And you should be too."

"I've got a free period." Supremely unconcerned, Marty snorted. "And you? I totally missed *that*. I just thought you were the quiet type—you know, one of those guys who lets his wife run the show." Marty's assessing gaze raked him up and down. "If I had known, I would've made a move years ago. You must be wild to satisfy a guy like that. I heard he's an animal in bed."

Niall's stomach turned sour. "Cut it out. I'm not a damn piece of meat."

"I bet you like Keller's meat." His brows waggled. "Come on. Throw me a bone. So to speak." He snickered.

Disgusted, Niall pointed his finger in Marty's face. "You better hope they don't try and do to you what they're doing to Keller. You're not immune."

Marty's grin faded. "What're you talking about?"

"You didn't hear they've called an emergency school-board meeting tonight about Keller?"

Evidently not, because he turned pale. "Because he's gay?"

"That and a few other things. So better lie low if you don't want them coming for you." He stormed away to his office and slammed the door shut. His phone buzzed, and when Angie's name popped up, he groaned and set it on the desk, unanswered. The last thing he wanted at the moment was to deal with her. Of course, never one to be ignored, Angie called him again. And again. The fourth time, he grabbed the phone.

"What do you want?"

"What happened to the mild-mannered librarian I married?" she joked, but he was in no mood.

"That was as big a farce as me pretending to be straight all those years," he snapped, and immediately felt remorse. "I'm sorry. You don't deserve my bad temper. You just caught me at a lousy time."

"The reporters still harassing you? I can make another call if you want."

"No, it's not that." He explained the situation, and brisk and efficient as usual, she had an answer.

"That's ridiculous and discriminatory. We have a very good lawyer here who's licensed to practice in New York and specializes in employment discrimination. I can have him start legal action."

This was Angie's forte. She was the problem-solving type, and it had always been easy to allow her to run with it.

"It's not up to me. It's Keller's decision. And he's got people of his own, I'm sure. He and I will deal with it."

"How is David handling it?" She sounded more curious, and Niall wondered how much she knew.

"He seems okay. Has he said anything to you?"

She took her time answering. "After you told him, he called me and we had a talk. He was never upset or angry with you. Confused and uncertain, more like it. Plus, I think he wanted reassurance that we still cared about each other."

"I told him I loved you but not the way either of us deserved."

"And now we're both happy. You and Keller must be serious if he's willing to risk it all—a job he loves and the goodwill of fans."

"I know it might look fast, but I care about him so much. I've never felt so alive before him."

"It's not fast. When you know, you know. You're not kids. I've got to go, Niall. Give David a kiss for me and take care of yourself. You deserve it."

"I didn't upset you, did I? By what I said?"

She laughed. "Not at all. Both of us have what we want now. I'll talk to you soon."

There was something odd about Angie's tone, but at the *ding* of a text, and seeing it was from Keller, it slipped from his mind.

I'll see you at the meeting. Just have some things to take care of.

Why so cryptic? He frowned, then realized he was being foolish. *Keller knows what he's doing. He's faced bigger audiences than a school board.*

But a niggle of doubt spun around in his mind.

What was Keller up to?

CHAPTER TWENTY-THREE

Keller opened the door to furious knocking. Elijah's big frame filled the space, but there was no usual smile to greet him.

"What the *hell* are they thinking?" He stormed in, followed by a man in his early forties, who remained silent but unfazed by Elijah's rant. His sleek salt-and-pepper hair gleamed in the overhead light, and cool green eyes assessed him.

"You know what." He turned to the man. "Hi, I'm Keller, and I have no idea who you are."

"Logan Silver. I'm Elijah's attorney, and he thought it would be a good idea for me to tag along and see what's going on up here in this adorable little hamlet." He grinned. "We *are* still in New York? I don't think I've ever been so far upstate."

Elijah snorted. "Logan's never been off the island of Manhattan."

"Untrue," Logan protested with a twinkle. "I grew up in Brooklyn."

"And when did you leave—for college?" Elijah asked. "Or did you have to get outta town quick because you ran through all the available men and women?"

"I'm sorry, is this a recitation of my life story?" Logan murmured, clearly uncomfortable. "I thought you brought me here to help."

"Help who, me?" Keller raised his brows in surprise. "For what? I'm sorry. Come in and sit down, please."

Elijah and Logan sat next to each other on the couch, and he took his mother's recliner. Logan again gave him the full force of a calculating gaze.

"Elijah told me of your problems with the school board. I handle many people in the sports and entertainment industry, and I've been with Elijah for years."

"Logan negotiated my contracts with the network, and he's also Remi Angel's lawyer. You know, the singer?"

"Yeah, of course." Keller's brows shot up, and pain throbbed in his chest. "My mom loved his music. She was a huge fan. I took her to his show in Vegas one year. But still, what does this have to do with me?"

Logan steepled his fingers beneath his chin. "You're going in front of the school board, which, it sounds like, has an agenda. One that involves erasing you, despite the fact that you're coaching a team that is undefeated this year and just beat last year's state champs. You were their golden boy and could do no wrong in their eyes until you kissed your boyfriend in front of the entire stadium." His lip curled. "Then all that good somehow vanished, and you're now a bad influence because you personally extended yourself—as coaches often do—to helping kids with issues they may have off the field."

"I'm sure once I explain it to them, they'll see I was only trying to be helpful."

Logan's brows shot high, and a corner of his mouth lifted in a sardonic grin. "You're kidding." He appealed to Elijah. "Tell me he's kidding. He's an ex-football player. He can't be that naïve."

"You are, right?" Elijah asked, obviously confused. "I know you're smarter than that."

Keller was aware how foolish he might sound, but he held on to the hope that people would judge him on his work ethic and not his sexuality. "This is all about a few uptight parents, who are in the minority. I'm sure of it. They know what a great job I'm doing."

"Clearly all this fresh air has addled your brain. It can happen to anyone. Well, almost anyone, because I know people suck." As he spoke, Logan took notes on his phone. "I've seen this happen to other clients. Prepare yourself for a fight, is all I'm saying."

"Do you really think so?"

"Yeah." Logan fixed him with a stare that revealed he'd seen a side of humanity many hadn't and probably wouldn't want to. "You're a decent guy, Keller. I can tell. Most people are shit. They only care about themselves and how they can personally benefit. But I think you care about those kids."

"I do," he insisted. "I don't know how it was for you growing up, but while my mother knew and accepted that I was gay, I didn't feel I could tell anyone else." His smile was wry. "Overlook is a far cry from New York City, in case you didn't know."

"I gathered," Logan drawled, not even trying to hide his sarcasm. "I had the complete acceptance of my family, including a mother who wanted nothing more than to have me marry her good friend's son."

"Not a match?" He grinned.

"Remi's a great guy, but we'll never be anything more than friends. And he's married now and living his happy ever after."

"Which you have no desire to do?"

The amused glint in Logan's sharp eyes faded. "This isn't about me." He turned brisk. "Back to you and the reason I spent half my day on the thruway—Elijah thinks you need representation."

"Representation? For what?"

Logan rolled his eyes. "In case they fire you, or for whatever bullshit they plan on drumming up."

Keller wasn't happy with what Logan was thinking. "I can't believe they'd be stupid enough to do that."

"I can," Logan responded grimly. "People can be very, very stupid."

"Then I guess I'll have to be smarter."

The school-board meeting room was filled to overflowing when Keller arrived with Elijah and Logan. He spied Niall in the front row, along with a sprinkling of teachers. He wondered if they were friend or foe.

"Hey." He smiled at Niall and kissed his cheek. "Thanks for saving the seats. This is Logan, Elijah's lawyer."

They shook hands and sat, Keller on one side of Niall, Elijah on the other, with Logan next to Elijah.

"Did you see the protestors outside?" Niall asked with a grim face. There was a small group of five, standing outside the building, holding signs calling out homosexuality as a sin. He'd walked right past them, without saying a word, even as they shouted at him.

"Yeah. I ignored them."

A little disappointed that none of the kids from the team had shown, he was at least happy to see Leon and Hank in the audience. The school-board members filed in and sat at the dais, and the crowd's noise lowered to a murmur. Keller recognized several members of the board, including Edna from the diner and Roy, the car salesperson he'd worked with to get Niall the deal on his BMW.

A burly man with a ring of impossibly-black hair surrounding a shiny bald spot banged the gavel on the table. "Good evening, everyone. I'm Johnny Snow, president of the Overlook school board, and we're here tonight to discuss the continued employment of Keller Williams as football coach of the Overlook Tigers. Many of you have seen last Friday's game of our high school team, where Mr. Williams was seen kissing his male companion. The objective of this meeting is to determine the suitability of Coach Williams to continue to work with young boys."

"For what reason?" someone in the audience called out. "Team's doing great. They're undefeated. Coach Williams is doing what he's been hired to do."

"Please be quiet," Johnny answered. "We will give members of the public a chance to speak. We want to hear from both sides. In the interest of disclosure, we're going to state the complaints received from school parents. First, Coach Williams was seen in a compromising position with a male companion at one of his football games, in full view of young, impressionable children. Second, he requested that the children on the team call him at all hours of the night to reveal their innermost personal feelings and thoughts. Coach Keller instructed the students not to tell their parents about these conversations. A teacher or coach telling a child to keep secrets from their parents is very troubling."

His anger rising with each word Johnny Snow spoke, Keller balled his hands into fists in his lap, his face growing hot. "That is not what I said," he growled and half rose to his feet.

Niall tugged at his arm. "Don't let them get to you," he murmured in his ear when he settled back in his seat.

Logan leaned over. "Keep it together, Keller. They'd love to see you lose your temper and give them more of an excuse."

"Yeah, fine." He might not like Logan's advice, but he understood it and listened. "This is such bullshit."

Elijah nodded. "We know, but look at the line of people waiting to speak at the microphone. They'll set the board straight."

First up was Leon. "I worked under Coach Weaver for over thirty years and had the honor of coaching Keller as he moved up the ranks at Overlook High School. He was a star on the field, and his time playing in the pros was no different. Keller has helped with charities to pay for kids who can't afford to go to summer camp, and worked with disabled youth and adults. Keller is one of the best high school coaches I've seen or worked with. He cares about the kids and their emotional health on and off the field, as well as their physical ability to play football."

"All pretty words, Leon, but giving them his phone number to call at night is a little too personal for me." Keller recognized the school-board member as Chase Summer's father. Chase was one of the tackles on the team and a quiet kid.

Leon said, "Coaches and their teams have a special bond. There's nothing unusual in Keller talking to the kids. You probably don't understand, never having played on a team before, am I right, Mark?"

The man flushed. "No, but I don't like some strange man talking to my son late at night. Especially a gay guy."

"Why?" someone called out. "What're you afraid of?"

"Why does he want to hear about their personal lives? That's not normal," a woman yelled. "And I don't want a gay man looking at my son in the locker room."

"Yeah. These kids don't need to be exposed to unnatural practices." In the audience, finger punctuating the air, Gene

McGowan stood up, and Keller wanted to laugh in his face. This from a man who was divorced twice, both times for cheating with women barely out of college.

"Gene, sit down." Johnny rapped the gavel on the table. "We have people standing in line to speak. Wait your turn and show them respect. Bobby Contard is next."

Tension swirled in his stomach, and as if sensing his unease, Niall took his hand, but he barely felt it. He sat prepared to listen.

Bobby hitched up the jeans that couldn't fit over his sagging belly. "Keller Williams has been messing with our kids' heads since the day he came. Shane was never in no trouble and always listened to me, no questions asked. But now? He keeps saying, Coach says this or Coach says that, and it's the opposite of what I'm saying. No one tells me how to raise my kid. And I sure as hell don't need no gay guy talking to Shane late at night, putting all these weird thoughts into his brain. That's what they do—confuse the kids, and then they brainwash them to become one of them. They ain't gonna do that to my boy. He's gonna be a man's man, like his father."

The ignorance was staggering, even for someone as simple and foolish as Bobby. Problem was, when Keller turned to scan the audience, he saw a large number of people nodding in agreement.

Elijah squeezed his arm. "Don't let the fools get to you. I'm sure there'll be plenty of people to support you."

But one person after the next stepped up to the microphone to bash his character by way of his sexuality.

"Our children shouldn't be exposed to this."

"My son is very impressionable."

"Why does he want to talk to our children at night?"

"It's a sin."

His spirits sank lower than he'd imagined possible. Only his mother's death had left him feeling worse about himself.

Not even Niall's hand in his alleviated the impending sense of doom, and Elijah and Logan wore matching grim faces. Had he truly messed up so bad, trying to give the team a safe space?

Niall leaned in close. "Michael's speaking next. He'll stand up for you."

"I'm Dr. Michael Hitchcock. My son, Chris, plays on the Tigers. My wife and I couldn't be more thrilled that someone like Coach Keller cares enough about our kids' mental well-being, as well as their physical, to make sure they have someone to speak with. Mental-health issues, left untreated, can cause teens to make bad decisions. Chris has told us he's called Coach to talk about things on his mind, and we welcome it. Parents are often the last to know when there are problems, oftentimes with terrible consequences, and if Coach can guide a student to get the help they need, or simply lend an ear for a child to talk out their problems with, I'm all for it. Why do you assume he's only interested in talking about sex? Maybe it isn't Coach who has the problem, but all of you." He glanced around the room, his sharp gaze touching everyone seated, and Keller took note of quite a few red faces and people shifting in their seats.

"Looks like someone hit a nerve," Niall murmured, and Keller could've cheered Michael on.

Michael continued. "Coach Keller was hired to bring Overlook a state championship, and it looks like he's accomplishing that. Don't let petty biases keep our kids from reaching their goal."

"It ain't petty," Bobby Contard yelled. "He's trying to turn my son into one of him."

"Homosexuality is evil," a woman shouted from the far corner.

"Leave our children alone," a man in a black suit yelled. "We don't need his kind up here."

People began to talk over one another, and the voices

turned loud and ugly. Keller saw several deputies by the doors. Obviously, they had an inkling how heated this school-board hearing could get and wanted to be prepared.

Johnny rapped on the table. "Order. Order, please. The board has heard enough. Thank you for your time and—"

"Excuse me, but we have something to say."

Niall's hand dropped his as they both focused their attention on the rear of the room. The entire football team had assembled, and David, with Van, Chris, and Shane at his side, walked up to the microphone.

"Did you know this was going to happen?" he hissed to Niall, who sat wide-eyed.

Niall continued to stare at the kids "No. I swear."

David pointed the mic downward. "My name is David Harper, and I play on the Overlook Tigers. When my dad told me he was gay, it didn't change my feelings for him. How could it? He's my dad, the same person he was when he woke up that morning, only now he gets to live his life the way he should be able to, like everyone else. Coach Keller is a great coach—he explains all the plays and tells us what we did right and where we need to work harder. We all know there's no way we'd ever be in the running for the state championship if he wasn't leading us. Please don't fire him." He stepped aside, and Van stood in front of the mic.

"My name is Van Childs, and I'm gay. I was gay before Coach Keller came to Overlook. Coach Keller is a role model for me because he makes me believe I can be whoever I want, and that no matter what people might say, it's up to me to achieve my dreams. I control my destiny. Coach let me love myself."

Keller wiped his blurry eyes. "God, these kids are so brave and amazing."

David took the microphone again. "The team took a vote this afternoon. If you decide that Coach Keller can't be our coach anymore, we're not going to play any more games and we'll forfeit the rest of the season. We don't want to play if Coach isn't on the field with us."

Shocked gasps rose through the crowd.

"No, you have to play!"

"This is crazy. They can't forfeit the season, can they?"

"If the kids like the coach so much, he can't be doing anything wrong, can he? Maybe this was a bad idea."

"I thought it sounded like a witch hunt. My nephew loves Coach Keller, says he's tough but fair."

Stunned, Keller got to his feet as the buzz of angry voices rose in the room. "No, kids. I can't let you do that. You're on your way to becoming state champions. Forfeiting the season may mean you'll never have another chance. You can lose scholarship chances…just no. Please don't do it."

"Sorry, Coach, but we can't let them treat you like this." Shane met his eyes. "If they fire you, I don't wanna play football."

"You goddamn fool." Bobby had wormed his way through the crowd and grabbed Shane. "You'll play no matter what. You hear me?"

Shane pushed Bobby off. "No. I won't. Not anymore." Seeing Shane stand up to his father made Keller want to cheer. "Coach helped me see myself. I'm not gonna let you hurt me anymore. Or Mom."

Bitterness swirled in Keller's stomach. It was as he'd suspected. And yet people were busy pointing fingers and calling *him* a deviant.

"You shut your goddamn mouth." Face flushed an ugly red, Bobby stuck his face into Shane's, and Keller wondered if Bobby was going to hit him in front of all these witnesses. A beautiful thing happened next. The entire team surrounded Shane, facing down Bobby.

"Coach told us we're a family and we should always have each other's backs," David said. "We're not gonna let you bully Shane anymore."

Bobby glared at them, then turned around and marched out. Shane brushed at his eyes, and Keller watched as each of the kids gave Shane a friendly punch on the shoulder or a fist bump. Van was the last.

"Good job, dude. Proud of ya."

Shane's smile was faint, but his shoulders straightened imperceptibly, and Keller hoped this would mark a new beginning in Shane's life.

He and Niall took their seats again.

"I'm so proud of David. He's so much braver than I was at that age."

Johnny Snow, who'd remained silent throughout, now rapped the gavel. "Order, please. The school board thanks you all for coming tonight, and we are now closing the meeting. We'll take a vote on the subject matter and let you all know our decision."

"When?" Michael Hitchcock called out. "Why should Keller have to wait to find out if he still has a job? I say make the vote public and let the taxpayers see how the votes are cast."

"That's right. As a gay man who's a teacher at this school, I want to know. I have that right."

He and Niall both turned around to see Marty Daniels standing in the audience. Marty caught his eye and nodded.

"At first I resented Keller for coming up here and making more money than those of us who've been teaching for years. But I can see he cares about the kids. And then I found out he's not taking a salary, but instead, is donating the money he's paid to a group to help keep queer kids off the streets. Who could be angry about that? What kind of lesson are you teaching the kids if you fire him? And what does it say about the kind of people you are? Not to mention, you'll get your asses sued big-time for discrimination, which will cost the town a hell of a lot of money. Think about that."

A loud chorus of applause rose from the audience.

"Wow," Niall said. "That was some speech Marty gave. And every word was true. I'm so proud of you."

Elijah patted his shoulder. "I didn't know you were donating your salary. That's a special thing. You done good, man. Your mother and mine are smiling down at you."

His lips trembling, Keller didn't know whether to laugh or cry. "I'm so overwhelmed right now, I don't know what to say."

"Now there's a first." Niall laced their fingers together.

CHAPTER TWENTY-FOUR

After the board voted seven to two in favor of Keller keeping his job, Niall could visibly see the weight of worry roll off his shoulders and the happy-go-lucky man he'd fallen for reappear. Especially in their lovemaking. Keller told him Dan Brockman had tried to apologize, but he wasn't having it.

"I told him to keep his distance from me. Sucks for him because I was planning to get tickets for a bunch of teachers, including him, to the Super Bowl this year. Now his name fell off the list."

Niall cackled. "Evil. I love it."

That Friday morning, he was awakened at daybreak by Keller's warm lips teasing a wet path down his neck. He hummed with contentment, which turned into a purr of desire as that delicious mouth covered the head of his cock and sucked. Niall gasped, trembling on the precipice of pleasure so intense that when Keller's rough hands stroked his balls and licked along the throbbing length of his shaft, Niall came hard, and needed to stuff the edge of the pillow into his mouth to prevent his screams from waking David.

"Are you still alive?" murmured Keller, his wicked fingers teasing his rim.

"Can't be. This has to be heaven. Nothing could be this perfect." Niall sighed, his breath catching on a groan of pleasure-pain as Keller inched inside him. He wrapped his arms around Keller's neck, and they rocked together in harmony, until Keller pushed in deep and came, filling him with warmth.

"This right here. This is perfect. *You* are perfect," Keller rasped, his mouth finding Niall's for a tender kiss. "And nothing could be more perfect than waking up with you next to me."

Niall rubbed his cheek on Keller's. "All I want is to be yours."

Keller's smile curved against his own. "When I think of home, it's here. With you."

Keller had begun staying over on the weekends, but today was the first time he was there on a weekday school morning. When David joined them in the kitchen, he didn't seem to mind or find it odd to have Keller there for breakfast. Niall decided to play it cool and take it as it came.

"All set for the game tonight?" Keller had finished his bowl of fruit and yogurt and was loading their plates into the dishwasher.

"Yeah. We have a good feeling. Can't believe the season is almost over." David spooned cereal into his mouth.

"It's been a heck of a ride, that's for sure." Keller winked at Niall, and he smiled in return.

"Are you going to move in with us?" David asked in between mouthfuls of Cheerios, looking at Keller, who regarded him thoughtfully.

Niall's heart pounded as his mind spun in different directions. Did Keller want to live together? Was that what he meant during their morning pillow talk? That this was home to him?

"Your father and I haven't talked about it, but what would you think if it did happen?"

David finished his cereal before answering. "It'd be cool. I'd be fine with it." He picked up his bowl and put it in the dishwasher. He faced Keller with a hopeful smile. "Maybe you could teach me how to drive on your Porsche. That'd be really sweet. I'll get my stuff together for school, Dad. Be ready in less than ten minutes."

He walked out, leaving the two of them staring at each other. Niall lowered himself to a chair at the kitchen island. "Wow."

Keller arched a brow. "Wow what?"

"I don't know. That was a lot to handle so early in the morning." Was that a flash of hurt in Keller's eyes? "Do you really want David to learn to drive on your Porsche?" His attempt to lighten the moment with humor fell flat when Keller frowned.

"He can have the damn car for all I care. That's not what I'm talking about, and you know it." Three long strides brought Keller to his side, the brightness in those blue eyes dimmed. Long fingers brushed his cheek. "I thought we were on the same page."

"We are."

"But you don't want to talk about me moving in."

Was he being overly cautious, or was he still clinging to the defeats of his past? Maybe Keller could read his mind because he cupped his cheek.

"What are you worried about?"

"It's only been a few months," Niall answered cautiously.

"You think we're too impetuous? I know I'm looking forward to opening my eyes every morning and seeing you lying next to me, instead of having to read a text on a screen. Are you having second thoughts about us?" Keller asked in a maddeningly calm voice.

"No. I love you."

"Then what's the problem?"

"It's a lot of change in a short period of time."

"And love lasts forever." Keller kissed him hard and left the kitchen. A few minutes later, he heard the garage door open and a car pull out.

That cryptic remark stayed with him all day, and by four thirty, when he was cleaning up his office in preparation for the weekend, he'd decided he and Keller would have a discussion that night. The days were getting shorter, and he flicked on the light to make sure he didn't forget anything.

"Maybe we'll have a fire tonight."

What could be more cozy and romantic than curling up in front of a fire? Since Keller had come into his life, he no longer dreaded the long, lonely expanse of the weekends. It wasn't Keller he doubted. It was himself.

A knock sounded on his door, and before he had a chance to respond, it opened.

"Hi, Niall."

Beautifully dressed from her shoulder-length, shiny black hair to the tips of her gleaming stiletto pumps, Angie walked to him. Her boyfriend, Grant, of the strong jaw and perfect corporate haircut, waited by the door.

"Angie. Why didn't you tell me you were coming?"

"I wasn't sure I'd have all my filings done by close of business and didn't want to say anything to David and have him disappointed." She waved to Grant. "Come on inside."

A sheepish expression on his face, Grant extended his hand, and they shook. "Hi, Niall. Sorry to barge in."

"Oh, don't worry," Angie jumped in to answer. "Niall doesn't mind."

Actually, he didn't appreciate Angie answering for him, but refrained from responding. "Nice to finally meet you in person." He and Grant had only seen each other over the computer when Angie and David FaceTimed. He was an attorney specializing in international finance. Whatever he did, David said he was always flying around the world and often wasn't home for weeks when David would be there over the summer.

"Same. I'm excited to see David play. Sounds like he's really maturing on the field."

"He definitely is. The whole team has blossomed under Keller's coaching."

"I can't wait to meet Keller too." Angie stood by the chair in front of his desk. "David was so happy they kept him as the coach. I spoke to Dara, and she told me the whole team came out to support him."

"They did. It was an incredible moment. Keller was very moved." He hated to ask but needed to know. "Are you two staying with us?"

Angie's dark brows rose. "Yeah, of course, why?"

"Just want to make sure because usually you let me know ahead of time when you're coming."

Angie flushed. "I'm sorry, I've been so swamped lately with things. I didn't think you'd mind, but if it's a problem now, we can get a hotel room."

"No," he protested. "That's silly. It's your house as much as mine."

Her surprise visit brought into sharp focus that once David turned eighteen, Angie no longer had to provide support, including contributing to payments on the house. His stomach sank, knowing he could never afford the upkeep on his own.

"Is Keller living with you now? Is that why you don't want us staying there?"

"I never said I didn't want you there, Ang. And we haven't decided anything definite. When we do, though, David, not you, will be the first person I talk to about it. I'm sure you understand."

He couldn't remember the last time he'd seen Angie confused and unsure. "I guess I never thought of you bringing someone else into the house to live." Her eyes grew shiny. "I figured nothing would ever change between us, but that's silly of me to assume."

Maybe he'd leaned on her too much since the divorce and she'd become too comfortable telling him what to do. But Niall knew that part of his life was over. The secrets of his heart now belonged to Keller and the future they would build together.

"You'll always be my best friend, Angie, but my personal life isn't up for discussion."

She wiped her eyes. "I'm sorry. I don't mean to pry. It'll take me a while to get used to everything. My main concern is David."

"As is mine. I know what I'm doing," Niall insisted.

"Angie, leave him alone," Grant's deep voice rumbled. "We're here to see David play, and I want a chance to meet Keller Williams." His eyes twinkled when they met Niall's, and he winked. "Don't screw it up for me."

Niall understood Grant was attempting to lighten the mood, but he refused to budge on this. All his life he'd given in and allowed other people to make decisions that affected him. Not anymore.

Cheeks flushed, Angie dipped her head. "I'm sorry, Niall. I was wrong to barge in without calling and to talk to you like that. You've always made David your top priority, and I'm sure nothing's changed now that you're with Keller."

Her smile was hesitant.

"All I want is for you to respect that we don't have a say in each other's personal lives, except as it relates to raising David. Do you think that me having my boyfriend over is poor parenting on my part?"

Her eyes widened. "No. Not at all. You're a wonderful father—the best. I know you always put David first, even above your own needs. Maybe that was the issue all along." Her eyes became sad. "I'm so used to you stepping aside for everyone, it's taken me a moment to see you belong at the front of the line." She held out her arms. "Hug?"

He squeezed her tight. "Always. Of course you can stay with us. Whether Keller is going to live there or not, it's always your home."

The morning discussion with Keller seemed foolish. What more could he learn about Keller that would change how much he loved him? The man was kind, unafraid to show his emotions, generous, and loving. He understood Niall's fears, and without being dismissive or controlling, offered solutions to help. Keller didn't want to change him. Keller loved him as is.

He put a hand on her shoulder. "Let's go drop your stuff off at the house, then get good seats for the game."

The two-minute whistle blew. It was the fourth quarter, and the Tigers were continuing their winning ways, leading the Culvertown Bears by a healthy two touchdowns. Niall's gaze concentrated on the two most important men in his life—David on the field and Keller on the sidelines. Shane had been on fire, hitting ninety percent of his throws, and David had rushed for almost one hundred yards. Before they arrived, Niall had sent a brief text to Keller, telling him that Angie and Grant were there and staying over. He pressed his lips together at Keller's response.

Guess I'll have to make sure you don't scream too loudly.

The teams took the field at the forty-yard line. The ball was snapped, and Shane faded behind the line of scrimmage. Van had ducked away from the tackles and was open. Shane's throw was like a special delivery straight to Van's arms, and that incredible speed he'd shown in other games took him all the way to the end zone. The special team made the kick for the extra point, and once again, the Tigers roared to a win.

"Way to go, David," Angie shouted, and David ran right over to her. They hugged, and Niall's world had never felt more complete than when Keller strolled over with that wicked, charming grin. From the corner of his eye, Niall could see the news cameras tracking Keller's moves, but he refused to give in and hide. He joined Keller at the gate.

"Hi. Another great game." He leaned over the fence and gave him a quick kiss on the cheek. "Congratulations."

Keller turned his face away to avoid the cameras catching his words. "You can congratulate me properly later."

"Idiot," he whispered. He was so happy, he didn't understand how his heart wasn't flying out of his chest to join the stars in the sky to shine down on everyone with all the love he felt. "I'm sorry about this morning. I was being silly."

"Yeah, you were. But I forgive you because you're cute and have a great ass."

His eyes popped wide. "Shh."

David brought Angie and Grant over. "Mom, come meet Coach Keller."

Niall introduced them. "Keller, this is Angie and Grant."

Always gracious, Keller listened as Grant relayed highlights of his own glory years playing high school football and how excited he was to meet him. Angie offered her hand.

"I'm glad to finally meet you. David is so happy with you as his coach."

"He's a great kid and a terrific player. And I'm looking forward to getting to know you better this weekend."

"Considering we'll be living together for the next two days, I'd say there's an excellent chance of that happening." Her eyes danced.

David said, "I'm not going to the party tonight. I wanna stay home with you and Mom."

Angie shook her head, sending her gleaming dark hair cascading over her shoulders. "Absolutely not. You go have fun and come home in the morning for breakfast. I'll make pancakes. Then we can spend the day together."

David looked to him. "Is that okay, Dad?"

He nodded. "I think that's a great idea. You get to hang out with your friends, and the adults get to know each other better. See you in the morning."

"Okay, cool. The party's at Harrison Wheeler's."

"All right. He lives in town, right?"

"Yeah, near Shane by the railroad tracks."

Keller frowned. "I know you and your friends have your heads on straight, but be careful. The trains have a way of sneaking up on you, and there aren't any gates."

"Oh God, now you're on my case too?" David laughed. "Of course not. Don't worry. See ya."

"Don't worry?" Keller asked. "Is he kidding? I guess he doesn't think we were ever young and stupid."

Niall snickered. "Young, yes. Stupid?" He cackled. "Not me. I'll give you that crown."

"Wise-ass. I'll meet you back at your house after I finish here."

"Okay."

They returned to the house, and it didn't matter that they'd all eaten their fill of hot dogs and popcorn at the game, he set out the charcuterie and fruit platters he'd had delivered that afternoon for them to nibble on.

Keller let himself in, and with a groan, sank into the space next to him on the couch. Niall had poured them all glasses of wine and gave one to Keller, which he accepted with a hearty sigh of pleasure.

"God, that's good."

"It is, though maybe we should've brought champagne," Angie took a sip and set the glass aside.

"Well, it's still a few games away to see if we have an undefeated season, but I'm hopeful," Keller answered.

"Oh, I wasn't referring to that, but it is another reason to celebrate." She took Grant's hand in hers. "Grant and I are engaged. It just happened last Sunday. We've told our parents, but you're the first people we're sharing the news with outside of immediate family. Because you'll always be part of my family, Niall."

He swiped at his eyes. "I wish you all the happiness. You deserve it." He rose to his feet, as did she, and they hugged. "I'm thrilled. That's so wonderful." He shook Grant's hand. "She's a great woman. Congratulations."

"I appreciate so much the relationship you two have. My ex-wife and I have no children, yet there was way too much animosity between us. Angie always tells me she's so happy you remained friends. And thank you for letting me be a part of David's life." He laughed. "When I told people at the office I was going to meet Keller Williams, suddenly everyone became my friend."

Keller's lips twitched. "Guess even gay, I still got it."

Niall nudged him. "I can attest to that."

"As long as I have you."

Keller poured them all more wine. "This is definitely cause for celebration. To Angie and Grant."

They raised their glasses, and Niall clinked his to Keller's. "To love."

CHAPTER TWENTY-FIVE

Keller was brushing his teeth, getting ready for bed. Niall sat on the bed, staring into space. Keller finished and joined him, nudging his shoulder when Niall didn't greet him with a smile or a kiss.

"What's wrong?"

Niall lifted a shoulder. "I don't know. I have a funny feeling."

Keller wrapped an arm around his shoulders. "Are you upset about Angie's engagement?"

Niall's brows shot up in surprise. "Not at all. I'm happy for her. The two of them are a much better couple than she and I ever were."

"Yeah? How so?"

"The way they interact. She doesn't dominate him the way she did with me. I was never an equal in the relationship, but it was because I was so afraid of being myself, I lived like a shadow. In the shadows."

Keller hugged him. "I'll never let you do that. You're my equal—hell, you're so much better than me, I don't deserve a sweet guy like you."

Niall pulled away, his expression darkening. "Says who? 'Cause I think you're amazing."

"Yeah? I guess I see a different person."

"What do you mean?" Niall stroked his cheek.

"I see a man who should've tried harder to take care of the most precious thing in his life."

"Your mom?" At Keller's nod, Niall placed a gentle hand on his cheek. "Want to know who Keller Williams is to me?"

He kissed Niall's hand. "You're my lover…my partner. You're going to say nice things to make me feel good."

Niall punched him lightly. "That's bullshit. I'll always give it to you straight. You're punishing yourself for leaving your mom here while you played ball and lived the Vegas lifestyle. But she had the choice to live near you and made the decision to stay here. She had a good life, and from everything I've heard, you were a good son. We always think we can do more…do better."

Keller hung his head, studying his bare feet. "I could have. I wanted her to be proud of me. She worked so hard and did it all alone."

Surprising him, Niall forced their eyes to meet. "No. That's where you're wrong. She was never alone. She had you. Everything she did, was out of love for you. Whether it was one mile or a thousand separating the two of you, your mother knew you loved her."

Could Niall be right? "I am so fucking lucky. Thank you for believing me—believing *in* me. The best thing I ever did was barge in on your burger dinner at the diner."

They kissed, and lust burned through Keller.

Niall's phone rang.

"Leave it," he growled.

"*Mmm,*" Niall hummed. "I plan to." But the phone continued to ring. Niall tore his mouth from Keller's to grab his phone. Wide eyes met his. "It's David." Niall hit the screen and put it on speaker. "David, what's wrong?"

"Dad, please. You gotta come. It's Shane's dad. He-he's threatening Shane. Everyone. He's swinging around this broken bottle, and we're scared. We're trapped in the backyard and can't get out 'cause he's blocking the stairs."

Keller said, "I know that house. The train tracks run right past it. They can't get out that way." He was already pulling on his jeans. "Let's go." He shoved his bare feet into sneakers and pulled a sweat shirt over his head, then picked up his phone and dialed 9-1-1. In a calm voice that didn't betray the stark fear running through him, he gave the dispatcher the Wheelers' address.

Niall clutched the phone. "David, just stay away from him. Please. Keller called the police. Where are Harrison's parents?"

"They left to get more soda. They were only going be gone like twenty minutes, and Shane's dad came right after they left. Please, Dad. I'm scared. He won't let us leave and said he'll hurt Shane if we try."

Keller's heart skipped at David's terrified voice. "We're on our way, David."

Niall rushed to get dressed, and they flew out of the room to see Grant exiting the bathroom next to their guest room. His eyes narrowed.

"What's wrong?"

"No time to explain. David's in trouble." They ran down the stairs, but before they reached the main floor, Angie burst out of the guest room. "Did something happen to David? Grant, please go with them."

Keller had no desire to stand there and argue with her that Grant wasn't needed. The three of them raced to the garage, and he jumped into the Porsche.

"Let's go."

He didn't bother to stop for red lights. He didn't care if he got a ticket, and actually hoped he'd attract a police officer so he could bring them along. But of course, when you needed to be stopped, there was no one to be found. Niall sat next to him, white-faced, frozen with terror. Keller gave his leg a brief squeeze.

"We'll be there in less than five."

Thank God Grant sat quietly and wasn't the type to bombard them with questions. When they turned onto the street, Keller gave a sigh of relief at the sight of flashing red lights. He pulled to the side and turned off the engine.

"I've never been so happy to see a cop."

Niall had already opened the door and took off running. Keller and Grant ran after him, but all three of them skidded to a stop at the sheriff's deputy's warning.

"Can't go in there. Sorry."

"But my son is there. He called me and said he was in trouble."

"Niall, over here."

They all searched for the voice in the dark, which turned out to be Deputy Taylor Lundquist, who was beckoning to them. Niall was the first to reach him.

"What's happening?" Keller demanded.

"Not quite sure. The Wheelers said the kids were having a party, nothing bad going on, and they only left them alone for a few minutes. When they got back, they heard lots of screaming from the yard. Seems Bobby Contard is there beating up on Shane. You called as well?"

"Yes, David was scared and let us know. He said Bobby's got a broken bottle and is threatening the kids."

"Let me go in there and try to talk to him," Keller asked.

"No way. You'll be putting yourself in danger."

"As opposed to the kids who are frightened out of their minds? C'mon, Taylor. You know what kind of a guy Bobby is. Let me try.”

“I can’t, Keller. It’s too much of a risk. I’ll keep you posted.”

His radio crackled to life, and Taylor walked away, speaking into it.

“Fuck this. I’m gonna go by the tracks and get into the yard that way.” Giving Niall no chance to respond, he kissed him hard and ran, slipping in between houses farther up the street to escape detection by the police.

As a kid, he’d spent many nights hanging out by the tracks—it was a place where he and other gay kids could hide in the dark and discover their sexuality. He picked his way along the railroad line, the leaves crunching under his feet. Trees rustled up ahead, and the air held the acrid smell of woodsmoke from fireplaces. A chilly breeze blew, and he shivered in his sweat shirt. He spotted backyard lights and knew it was the Wheelers’ place.

Tall hedges surrounded the perimeter of the yard, hiding the trains, but Keller spied a small broken section where the light streamed through, and he squeezed past the branches scratching at his face. He could hear Bobby ranting.

“You stupid son of a bitch. I didn’t raise you to be a fairy.”

Keller peeked in and saw Bobby with one arm around Shane’s neck, the bottle in the other hand. He might be older and soft in the gut, but he was strong. And Shane, poor kid, was so used to bending to his father’s will, he didn’t fight him.

“Leave him alone, Mr. Contard. Let him go,” Van yelled. “We weren’t doing anything wrong.”

“You shut up.” Bobby waved the bottle dangerously close to Shane’s face, and a girl screamed. “I saw you. I watched you—both of you. It was disgusting.” He jerked his arm around Shane’s neck. Keller could see Shane already bore the brunt of Bobby’s fist and had a split lip.

"Ow, Dad, you're hurting me."

"I'm gonna do worse than that if I ever see you kiss a boy again. You hear me?" Shane didn't answer, and Bobby tightened his grip and shouted, "I said do you hear me?" He smacked Shane in the head with the bottle, and the boy cried out.

"Fuck this." Unwilling and unable to stand by any longer and wait until Shane or someone else got hurt, Keller burst through the bushes.

"Let him go, Bobby."

He walked toward the two, and Bobby's lip curled in a sneer.

"If it ain't the head fairy himself." His face flushed with anger, and he shifted position so the bottle's jagged edges pointed at him. "You stay away from my boy. Stop putting all these sick thoughts in his head."

"I said let Shane go." There was only one way to get through to Bobby, and that was through football. "If you hurt him, he won't be able to play, and I'll have to put him on the injured list. You want him to miss the state championship?"

Uncertain, Bobby glanced at Shane and pushed him away. Shane stumbled, and breathing heavily, stood beside Van.

"He's gonna play no matter what."

"You'll do anything to relive your glory years, won't you? Even risk your son's life or threaten other people?"

"I was good, dammit. I coulda gone pro, like you. Motherfuckers expelled me."

"You have to go to classes, Bobby. It's not all about football. But Shane knows that. He's going to do well."

"Goddamn right he will. I made him. I showed him how to throw his first football. It was me who went to all the games. I never missed one."

"I'm sure you didn't. That's why he cares about you so much, he wants to please you. But he needs to make his own choices."

"He'll do what I damn well tell him to do," Bobby yelled, swaying on his feet. "He knows better than to hang around with that freak. You'd better leave him alone. He's not gay. Stop making him think he's one of you." He swung the broken bottle in front of Shane's and Van's faces, and they jumped away.

"Don't you move."

Keller's stomach bottomed out, and the kids screamed.

A voice came over a loudspeaker. "Bobby, what's going on? Is Keller Williams with you?"

"I'm here," he shouted. "Stay away." He put his hands in the air. "Look, I'm not gonna hurt you, Bobby. Just put the bottle down, and we'll talk. Shane's a great quarterback, and he's going to play."

"Goddamn right he is. He's gonna get a scholarship and go pro. He's gonna make it. I couldn't, but he's gonna do it." Waving the bottle, Bobby continued ranting.

Keller glanced over his shoulder and saw the kids huddled in the corner. He motioned to them to run. They all escaped through the hole in the bushes from where he came, except for Shane and Van. Keller jerked his head for them to follow their classmates, but they stayed put. He had to talk to Bobby until he could be subdued.

"Sure he is. Shane's a great player. The scouts are talking about him."

"Yeah?" Bobby stopped. "This little pussy needs to leave him alone, and I know how to stop him." He charged at Van with the broken bottle.

On instinct, Keller threw himself at Bobby, knocking him to the ground before he had a chance to get near Van. Pain shot through his weakened arm, but even at less than full-strength, he was able to subdue Bobby with a punch to the jaw and a second to the nose, which knocked his drunk ass out. Shane and Van ran into the house, and minutes later, the backyard was swarming with police. They helped him up, and Taylor pointed a finger at him.

"I thought we told you to stay away."

He shrugged and rubbed his arm. "I don't take direction well anymore. I'm better at giving it."

Taylor didn't find his joke funny. "He could've slashed you, Keller. What the hell is wrong with you?"

Keller watched as a sniveling Bobby was handcuffed and taken away. "I couldn't let him hurt the kids."

Niall rushed up to him with Grant a few steps behind on the phone. "Are you okay? Why didn't you let the deputies deal with it? You could've been cut or worse." Without waiting for an answer, Niall grabbed him and pulled him tight. "You're all right. If anything had happened to you... *God*, you're such a jerk."

"I love it when you whisper those love words in my ear. Tell me more," he murmured, soaking in Niall's warmth. Weariness overcame him now that the adrenaline rush was fading. His arm throbbed and burned. He shivered a bit. "Where's David?"

"Inside the house. I've seen him. Angie's driving over to pick him up. The deputies are talking to him and the other kids, and then we'll take him home. You're shaking." Niall pulled away and ran his hands over him. When he passed over the upper part of his arm, Keller failed to hold back a grimace. "What's wrong? Did he hurt your arm?"

"No. I did it to myself when I punched him."

"Maybe you should see a doctor," Grant suggested. "At least let the medics check you out."

About to protest, another twinge of pain zinged through his arm, and he nodded. "All right. Let's go."

Niall slipped an arm around his waist. "Lean on me."

"That's one benefit of all this. I get to hold you close."

"So annoying," Niall muttered, but his lips twitched, and Keller smiled happily.

Out on the street, he took in the massive number of sheriff's cars, news trucks, and parents waiting.

"Dad, Coach." A visibly shaken David ran up to them, followed by the rest of the kids. "Are you all right?"

"Coach, are you okay?" Shane asked, and Keller's heart lurched at the sight of his battered, cut face.

"I should be asking you. You should see a doctor."

"I'm all right."

"I told him he needs to see a doctor," Van jumped in. "You should go to the hospital for an X-ray or something. I mean, you got smacked in the head with a bottle." Worried brown eyes met his. "Don't you think so, Coach?"

"I do. Van's right, Shane. How about we take a ride together? You and I will go. I need to get my arm looked at."

Shane grimaced. "You got hurt. Dammit. It's all my fault."

Again, it broke his heart to know Shane believed he held any responsibility for what his father did. "Absolutely not. You are not responsible for your father's failures or his lost hopes and dreams."

Shane hung his head. "He always said I wasn't as good as he was at this age and that's why he drove me hard. To toughen me up." Keller didn't miss Van shifting closer and placing a hand on the small of Shane's back. Comforting him with both silence and strength. Damn, he admired these kids. "When he saw me 'n Van tonight, he said he was gonna make a man outta me, no matter what."

Keller took Shane by the shoulders. "You are a man. So much more of a man than your father ever was. Don't let him put those negative thoughts in your head." Something struck him. "Where's your mother?" For the first time he noticed that unlike all the other kids whose parents had rushed over when they'd heard the news, Mary was nowhere to be seen.

"She's visiting my aunt in Pittsburgh. She left the other day. My aunt Sharon had a stroke, and my mom went to help my uncle out for a little while."

"I think you should call her and tell her what happened and that I'm going to take you to the hospital to get checked out. After you finish, come get me. We'll figure out where you can live until your mom comes home."

"He can stay at my house," Van declared. "My mom'll be fine with it."

"Okay, Coach." Shane rubbed his eyes. "I don't know if you figured it out, but I was calling you. I knew I liked Van but didn't know what to do about it because of my father. You helped me." With Van at his side, he walked away to sit on the porch steps and took out his phone.

Maybe he was good for something other than football. Because hearing Shane say those words meant everything to him. In his head, he heard his mother's voice.

"You have so much more to offer than simply catching a ball. One day you'll find your purpose, and you'll know."

"What was that about?" Niall slipped an arm around his waist, and the trembling bits of himself settled. He smiled at this man who somehow managed to make him whole again, who'd found him when he thought he'd be lost forever.

"Just Shane finally coming to terms with who he is and what he wants."

"That's very important. I'm sure you helped him."

"When I took this job, I never imagined I'd become so involved or invested in these kids. I always thought my best years were behind me, but now I see the future, and it's so bright. I don't need to be a player to win the game."

Niall kissed him. "I think we both won."

EPILOGUE

One year later

"Come on, guys, let's do this. We have the chance to repeat the state championship with two undefeated seasons in a row. Never been done before. We're only ahead by a field goal. They can catch us if we make one mistake. Keep the ball tucked in. Superglue that sucker to your hands if you catch it. Don't turn over the ball."

Keller clapped his hands and gave each player a fist bump as they chanted, "We are Tigers! Hear us roar!" then ran onto the field to the thunderous cheering of the hometown crowd.

Shane took his position behind the line of scrimmage. Bobby had been found guilty on a host of charges that would see him doing a minimum of ten years in prison, and Shane had blossomed. He'd proved to be a leader on the field, his grades were good, and he and Van were an out-and-proud couple. He'd been actively recruited by several colleges, and if all continued this way, he'd have his choice of where to attend school on that coveted football scholarship. He'd confided in Keller that he hadn't seen his father since the arrest and didn't plan to. His mother was in the process of getting a divorce.

Shane took the snap and handed it off to David, who ran wide toward the sideline. David had great instincts, and Keller watched with satisfaction as he made the first down, gaining twenty yards. David's cheering section in the stands was full—aside from Niall, Angie and Grant had come, along with their two-month-old baby, Emily. Angie had been pregnant when she and Grant got married, and she'd taken a leave of absence from her job.

Elijah, DeeDee, and the girls were also there. Keller loved that they'd bought a house not far from Niall's, deciding that a permanent move would be best for them, now that DeeDee was having another baby. They wanted their children to grow up in a small town, and DeeDee had fallen in love with Overlook.

"Let's go Tigers!" Elijah shouted from the stands, and Keller grinned. He had no doubt, now that they knew the baby was a boy, that Elijah would have his son in the Peewee league as soon as possible.

"Okay, let's go, let's go." Keller ran along the sidelines, searching for any faults he could see and finding none.

With six minutes left in the fourth quarter, there was still plenty of football to be played, and Keller would feel a lot better if they could add to the measly three-point lead and get more than a touchdown ahead.

"Hut, hut." Shane took the snap, but this time the defense broke through and he had to scramble. He was at his own thirty-five yard line, and the pressure was on.

"Don't throw, don't throw," Keller yelled as Shane was

surrounded. He let himself be sacked, and while they lost most of the yards gained from the previous play, they didn't turn over the ball. The kids knew to drag their feet, letting the clock tick away.

"Second and thirteen, Keller. You gonna have him throw, right?" Leon asked.

"If he can, yeah."

The team stood in a quick huddle and took their places. At the snap, Shane faked a handoff to Brenden, then threw a pass to Van, who caught the ball, tucked it into his chest, and sprinted downfield.

"That was beautiful," Leon crowed with glee.

"Look at him go." Keller whooped as Van crossed midfield before he was tackled. The team surrounded him, and Keller watched with satisfaction as he and Shane hugged.

"First and ten for Overlook," the loudspeaker boomed, and the crowd erupted. Keller glanced at the clock and saw there were just over two minutes left. The team came to the sidelines and waited for him to speak.

"Okay. Let's not be heroes. We're gonna run it unless, Shane, you see a clear path to throw. No threading the needle, no moves to look cool. If we get in trouble, all we need to do is get close enough for a field goal."

"Got it, Coach." Shane nodded. "Let do this, guys. Bring it home."

The team cheered and ran onto the field, and Keller could feel their energy. The clock ticked away, and Shane took the ball and handed it off to Chris, who pushed forward for a two-yard gain.

"They're gonna hold tough and come at us with everything they got," Hank warned. "The team should know that. Lakeside has always been one of our toughest competitors."

"Yeah, but we have something they don't. The chance to go undefeated two years in a row. The kids are hungry for it." Keller whistled and urged them on. "Good job, keep going. David, tighten up to the left. Shane, call it out." He touched his nose, signaling a running play.

Shane nodded. "Blue 72. Blue 72. Hut. Hut." The center snapped the ball, and Shane took a few steps back. Keller watched with approval as everyone did their job and Shane made the handoff to David, who ran for a little over four yards. They hustled to line up, and this time he scratched his chin, indicating he wanted Shane to throw if he could.

And Shane delivered to Chris for a thirty-yard pass. There were fifty-five seconds left on the clock, but in football that was a very long time. Games were made and hearts broken in the final moments.

"Hold the line, hold the line," he yelled.

"White 80, white 80, hut, hut," Shane called out and took the snap beautifully. He handed the ball to Van, who slipped through two tackles like warm butter and sprinted down the field, the crowd screaming with his every step. The buzzer sounded, ending the game as he crossed the line for a touchdown.

Keller, Leon, and Hank hugged each other as the band played the victory song and the cheerleaders performed their hearts out.

"You did it, Keller. Amazing. Two years undefeated and a chance to repeat the state championship." Leon's face creased in a thousand wrinkles. "Extra special for me, since this is my last year. I'm retiring after the season ends."

Shit. Not what he wanted to hear.

"Why? Not that you don't deserve the rest, but is everything okay?"

"Yeah. I'd like to spend more time with my family now that the grandkids are getting bigger. And I'm tired, Keller. Much as I love the game and working with you, it's hard to keep the intensity. I'm ready for the next generation to take over."

"It's been an honor working with you, Leon."

"Same here, Keller."

He watched as the team continued to celebrate, lifting Van on their shoulders.

"We did it, Coach." Shane rushed up to him, no longer a boy but not yet a man, his face bright and his eyes alive with excitement.

"You sure did. I'm so proud of all of you. You deserve it."

"You made us believe we could," Van said, his eyes gleaming. "It's like the pros. So…"

A torrent of ice-cold liquid poured over his head. "Jesus Christ," he yelled and spun around to see the team behind him, holding a barrel of Gatorade. Hank and Leon were holding their sides laughing.

"All right, very funny." He tried to frown but failed miserably and sputtered in laughter as well. "I can't be mad 'cause we did it to our coach when we won the Super Bowl. State championship, here we come again." He peeled the shirt away from his chest. "I'm gonna go shower. Then it's time to celebrate."

It didn't take him long to clean up, and the stadium was still full when he returned to the field. Niall and the rest of the crew were waiting, and Niall got to him first with a kiss and a hug. "This is awesome. Two years undefeated. What a record."

"They're a great group. I'm gonna miss them when they graduate, but we have some great prospects coming up."

"Look at you!" Elijah slapped him on the back. "Coach of the year. I gotta tell you, I wish I'd gotten to the job first. Man, this is a blast."

He thought fast. "Do it. Leon is retiring. Come coach for me."

Elijah's jaw dropped. "You serious?"

"Never more."

DeeDee, holding Marli, broke out in a huge smile. "Oh my God, Elijah, say yes. No more traveling to the city and staying away for days at a time. You could be home with us. We could really build roots here."

"All right, then. The boss has spoken." He ran a hand over his short hair. "If they want me, you got me."

"They will. Trust me."

"Together again, brother."

They hugged, and Keller slipped an arm over Niall's shoulders. "Party's at our house, right?" He'd moved in over the summer while David was with Angie and Grant, but still kept his mother's place. He didn't think he'd ever have the heart to sell it.

Niall beamed. "Yeah. I love hearing you call it our house."

"I love you."

"I love you too."

The skies lit up with a blast of fireworks, and they all stood to watch. Across the field, Keller noticed David holding hands with Renee, and he nudged Niall.

"I thought her parents told her she couldn't see David because of us."

"I didn't know they were seeing each other again. He's coming over with her, so we'll ask."

When David and Renee were close enough, Niall said, "Fantastic game, David. You made some amazing catches. And it's great to see you, Renee. It's been a while."

"I told my parents if they planned on following the Bible, as they insisted, then they needed to do everything by the book." She laughed. "So to speak. Which they weren't."

"She's gonna make a great lawyer, don't you think?" David gave her an adoring look.

"What did they say?"

"They were still not thrilled, so I told them if that's the case, I was going to go live with my older brother and his family. My father had a son with his first wife when he was eighteen. He got her pregnant, and they married after they graduated from high school, but they divorced a few years after my half brother, Robert, was born. I asked my dad why that was okay but it's not for two men or two women to want to be together when they really do love each other. Like you and Coach Keller."

"Renee, David is right," Niall nodded with approval. "You're going to make a hell of a lawyer."

With the fireworks show over, the stadium emptied out. Keller took Niall's hand.

"Come with me, I forgot something."

"Sure." Niall caught Angie's attention. "Can you let people into the house if I'm not there in time? I just have to go with Keller for a sec. He forgot something."

"Yeah, sure."

Hand in hand, they walked across the field to the sidelines, but instead of stopping, Keller tugged Niall. "This way."

"But—"

"Shh." He silenced Niall with a kiss. "Just follow me."

He led Niall around the stands until they stood beneath them. The night was clear and star-filled, with a cool breeze, indicating winter wasn't too far off. He cupped Niall's face between his palms and kissed him, loving how Niall melted into his touch.

"When I used to play, after the games, I'd sometimes slip away for a little while and sit here, wishing I could kiss a boyfriend under the bleachers."

"And now you can." Niall brushed their lips together. "You can kiss me anywhere you want. But I love that you brought me here. Want to know why?"

"Mm," Keller kissed his lips and cheeks. "Tell me."

"Because I would also sit in these stands, watching you be the superstar you were, wishing I could be your boyfriend and that you'd want to kiss me, but knowing it would always be a dream. That a player like you would never go for a guy like me. And now here we are, twenty years later, making wishes come true."

"How about this wish?" Keller reached into his pocket and pulled out a ring. "This was my father's. Marry me? I love you so much."

"I love you too." Niall reached out and touched the ring with reverence. "I can't believe this is happening. In my wildest dreams, I never thought I'd be here with you."

Keller slid the ring onto his finger. "Sometimes it just takes time to make dreams a reality and for wishes to come true."

I hope you enjoyed Keller and Niall's story. I love small town romances and plan on more in the future. I also plan on writing a story for Logan Silver, Elijah and Keller's attorney. You met him in In a New York Minute and his story will definitely be one you won't want to miss! Keep up to date and never miss a release by subscribing to my newsletter and join my reader group, Felice Stevens' Breakfast Club for sneak peeks, teasers and bonus extras!

FELICE STEVENS writes romance because what is better than people falling in love? Her favorite part of a romance novel is that first kiss…sigh. She loves creating stories of hopes and dreams and happily ever afters. Her stories are character-driven, rich with the sights, sounds and flavors of New York City and filled with men who are sometimes deeply flawed but always real.

Felice writes gay romance because she believes that everyone deserves a happily ever after. Having traveled all over the world, she can safely say that the universal language that unites people is love. Felice has written in a variety of sub-genres, including contemporary, paranormal, and she has a mystery series as well. You can find all her book listed on her website.

Felice is a two-time Lambda Literary Award nominee and the Lambda award-winner in Gay Romance for her book, *The Ghost and Charlie Muir*.

BOOKBUB
https://www.bookbub.com/profile/felice-stevens

NEWSLETTER
https://tinyurl.com/y85e69ab

READER GROUP
https://www.facebook.com/groups/FelicesBreakfastClub/

FACEBOOK AUTHOR PAGE
https://www.facebook.com/felicestevensauthor/

INSTAGRAM
https://www.instagram.com/felicestevens

GOODREADS
https://www.goodreads.com/author/show/8432880.Felice_
Stevens

WEBSITE
felicestevens.com

PAYHIP STORE
https://payhip.com/FeliceStevensAuthor

9 798889 490159